CRIME CLASSICS

My Brother's Killer

Also in the Crime Classics series:

MY FRIEND MR CAMPION AND OTHER MYSTERIES
Margery Allingham

BLUEPRINT FOR MURDER
Roger Bax

DEATH WALKS IN EASTREPPS
Francis Beeding

TRIAL AND ERROR
Anthony Berkeley

THE PYTHON PROJECT
THE WHIP HAND
Victor Canning

BAT OUT OF HELL
THE TYLER MYSTERY
THE WORLD OF TIM FRAZER
Francis Durbridge

ALL THE LONELY PEOPLE
Martin Edwards

THE CASE OF THE CROOKED CANDLE
Eric Stanley Gardner

NO TEARS FOR HILDA
Andrew Garve

BEFORE THE FACT
Francis Iles

THROUGH A GLASS, DARKLY
Helen McCloy

WHO SAW HER DIE?
Patricia Moyes

CLOSE UP ON DEATH
Maureen O'Brien

SOME MUST WATCH
Ethel Lina White

CRIME CLASSICS

My Brother's Killer

JUDGED BEST DETECTIVE NOVEL BY AGATHA CHRISTIE

D. M. DEVINE

ABOUT THE AUTHOR

A hugely underrated and unjustly neglected writer, D.M. Devine (1920–1980) combined his day job (as Secretary and Registrar of the University of St Andrew's) with his writing career. The 13 crime fiction novels he authored all share his trademarks of good writing and excellent plots, qualities which were prized by the Queen of Crime, Agatha Christie, who remained a fan of Devine's throughout his writing career.

This edition published in the UK by Arcturus Publishing Limited
26/27 Bickels Yard, 151–153 Bermondsey Street, London SE1 3HA

Design and layout copyright © 2012 Arcturus Publishing Limited
Text copyright © The Estate of D. M. Devine, 1961

Cover artwork by Steve Beaumont, coloured by Adam Beaumont
Typesetting by Couper Street Type Co.

AD002461EN

Printed in the UK

CHAPTER 1

I was deep in an armchair, relaxing over the *Guardian* crossword, when the telephone rang. Recognizing from the tone that it was the office extension and not the exchange, I was tempted to let it go unanswered, but thought better of it. One didn't do that sort of thing to Oliver.

So I got up reluctantly and went out to the hall. I must have left a window open somewhere, for the fog had now seeped in and was spreading its tentacles through the house. In the distance I could hear the Trenton foghorn; nearer at hand the rumbling of a bus, interrupted suddenly by a crunching noise, the tinkle of glass and a rush of excited voices.

The telephone continued to ring. I lifted the receiver.

'Simon? Look here, I'm at the office and something rather urgent has turned up. Could you possibly slip along for a few minutes?'

'For God's sake, Oliver, do you realize what time it is? And what sort of night it is? Won't it keep till—'

I broke off, for he wasn't listening. He never did. I could hear a faint murmuring and guessed that he had his hand over the mouthpiece and was talking to someone else in the room.

Presently his voice came back, suave and dominant as ever.

'Well, this really is rather urgent. So if you could just nip across . . .'

I started to reply, but there was a click and the line was dead.

I looked at my watch. Ten-forty-six. This really was going a bit far, even for Oliver. And who in heaven's name was his visitor in the office at this time of night? How typical of Oliver, I thought, to assume without question that I would drop everything and come at his bidding.

I put on my hat and coat and went out. I was halfway down the drive before I remembered to go back and lock the front door. Even now, three months after Linda had left me, I still wasn't used to it, I still had these moments when I forgot I was living in the house alone.

The fog was now thicker than ever. As I groped my way out through the gate a street lamp not ten feet away from me was visible only as a dim yellow glow. Nothing else could be seen at all. The camber of the avenue carried me safely to the junction with City Road and it was here that I almost walked into a bus, which had slewed right across the pavement and was now tightly wedged between a pillar box and the railings. I remembered the crash I had heard a few minutes before. I could dimly discern a huddle of people alongside the bus and I could hear their voices. A sudden spurt of laughter rang out. Evidently no one could be badly hurt. I moved on.

Within five minutes of crossing City Road and turning down towards the river I was utterly lost. Although I knew like the back of my hand the maze of narrow winding streets and lanes that made up this, the old part of Brickfield, the impenetrable blanket of fog blotted out all landmarks. Only the mournful bray of the foghorn from the river gave me a rough guide to direction. I would have turned back, but I was already more than halfway there and it seemed easier to stumble on. I cursed Oliver for his lack of consideration and myself for my folly in coming out. When I finally found my way into Weldon Square the church clock was striking eleven-thirty. I had taken nearly forty minutes to cover a distance that I walked in ten minutes twice a day.

The offices of Barnett, Waterston and Fergusson, Solicitors, occupy the third floor of a four-storeyed, stone-faced Victorian building, solid in construction but with little architectural merit. In my father's day we had sublet a part of our floor to a Jewish loan agent, but Oliver, on becoming senior partner, had declined to renew the lease when it expired. Although we didn't at that time need the extra space and we could ill afford the loss of the rent, Oliver was already planning an expansion of business. So out went the shrewd and rather kindly little Jew and in came the interior decorators.

I peered up to see if Oliver's window was still lit. All was dark. So dense was the fog, however, that it was doubtful whether a light from a third-floor window could have been seen from the street. Anyway, having come so far, I decided to go in. If Oliver hadn't waited for me after summoning me out in this weather I would have something to say to him in the morning.

By day the various floors were served by a lift; at night one climbed the stairs, as I was doing now. The fog had penetrated into the well of the building and although I had switched on the vestibule and stair lights the illumination was hardly more than enough to enable me to mount without stumbling. As I was on the second flight I thought I heard a door close somewhere above me.

'Is that you, Oliver?' I called out.

My voice sounded unnaturally loud and the echo reverberated eerily from the walls. There was no answer. I decided I must have imagined the sound.

When I reached the third floor, all was silent, nor was there any glint of light through the glass entrance to our office. It was while

I was standing there fumbling for my key that I sensed, or imagined I sensed, the presence of someone close by. I swung round and called out, 'Who's there?' But there was nothing; nothing at any rate that could be seen. The lift gates were open and the lift was standing at our floor. The illumination from the wall brackets threw up a confused pattern of dim light and shadow within the lift. The darkest of the shadows, in the far corner, was vaguely human in shape. I started towards the lift and then stopped. This was absurd: I was letting my imagination run away with me. I turned and went back to the office door and put my key in the lock. But the door was unlocked. Oliver must still be here after all, then, or else had forgotten to lock the office when he left.

I pushed open the door and switched on the corridor light. Oliver's room was at the end of the passage. His door was open and I could see that the room was in darkness. I had walked the length of the corridor and had my hand on the switch in Oliver's room when the corridor lights went out. I stopped in my tracks, puzzled and a little apprehensive. A moment later my ears caught a faint high-pitched whining. It was a second or two before I recognized it as the sound of the lift descending. As soon as I did, I raced back along the dark corridor and out on to the landing. The stair lights were still on and I started running down the steps. But I hadn't got far before I heard the creaking of the lift gates below me, followed by the sound of the front door of the building closing. By the time I had reached the ground floor and got out on to the street there was nothing to be seen. I thought I heard the sound of a car disappearing round the corner of the square but I couldn't be sure.

I climbed slowly up the stairs and turned back into the office. I had little doubt about what had caused the light to go out but I left it for a moment. I groped my way along the corridor and tried the switch in Oliver's room. I was not surprised when the light didn't go on.

The first match spluttered and went out. The second stayed lit long enough to show up the room in its customary meticulous tidiness. It was only as the match was burning out that I observed Oliver's hat and coat lying across a chair. The vague apprehension that was stirring in me began to crystallize, because I could not conceive of Oliver going home on a night like this without a coat. I lit a third match and at once saw on the carpet what I had missed before: the tips of the fingers of a hand protruding from behind the desk. I walked round, still carrying the flickering match, and looked down. The hand was Oliver's and Oliver was dead.

The match burned my fingers and went out. I don't know how long I stood there in the darkness paralysed by horror and grief. But at last I was able to control and repress my feelings and to concentrate on what had to be done. The one emotion I couldn't stifle was self-reproach. I had surprised the murderer and I had let him get away. That it was murder I had no doubt; Oliver would never have killed himself.

The first thing I had to do was to restore the lights. The mains and fuses for the whole floor were in a cupboard built into the wall on the landing outside the entrance to the office. As I expected, I found the switch controlling the lighting circuit had been pulled. It occurred to me while I was switching it on again that whoever had done this must have had some familiarity with the building to be able so swiftly to find the electricity mains. It also occurred to me that the police would not thank me for obliterating possible fingerprints on the switch. But the thought came too late.

I went back to Oliver's room and telephoned the police. Then I lit a cigarette and tried to work out what had happened.

Oliver was lying on his right side, his right arm fully extended and his left still clutching at his chest. His left hand was covered in blood and a dark crimson stain had seeped on to the carpet. His head rested against the leg of his chair, which was a couple of feet back from the desk. His legs were in a crumpled heap under the desk. A revolver lay a few inches behind his right hand.

I stood looking down for some time, beginning to feel again the pangs of grief and loss. And anger, too, at this senseless destruction. Oliver had been so vital a person, so full of zest for life. He had his shortcomings, but they were not the shortcomings of an evil or a mean-spirited man.

I turned away at last and began to examine the rest of the room. For the office of a solicitor it was a room of opulence. When my father retired, Oliver had reorganized the accommodation and had arrogated to himself what had formerly been the general office. He had partitioned off a small area as an office for his secretary. The portion that remained, which was spacious by any standards, had been gutted and reconstructed and largely refurnished. The walls were now oak-panelled and a deep-piled green fitted carpet covered the floor. Although the room, like the rest of the office, was centrally heated, an interior grate had been installed and in all but the warmest of weather a coal fire lent colour as well as warmth to the room. The dying embers of a fire were glowing now. Three walls of the room were lined with glass-bound book shelves, in light oak like the panelling.

The only furnishings which betrayed that this was an office and not the library of a private house were Oliver's desk and the safe. The safe was tucked away discreetly enough in a recess near the door.

The desk, however, was a massive steel affair, commanding the centre of the room in aggressive and uncompromising utilitarianism.

It was on the desk that my attention focused now. It held quite a battery of gadgets, some of them useful, others little more than toys which had caught Oliver's fancy at one time or another. The centre-piece was an exquisitely carved antique writing set, complete with quill pens. Beside that was the dictaphone, an instrument which Oliver, with his penchant for working in the evenings, found indispensable. I noticed that it was open and that there was a wax on it at the moment, which suggested that he had been doing some dictation earlier in the evening. He had also cleared his 'in' tray; a number of letters, signed and ready for dispatch, lay in the 'out' tray at the other side of the desk. The furnishings of the desk were completed by the telephone, an Anglepoise lamp, a patent letter-opening device, a silver cigarette box, a table lighter and an ash tray.

The desk was large enough to take all these gadgets and still leave a clear space for working on. There was a file open on the desk and I crossed over to see what Oliver had been engaged on. It was the trunk road dispute in which, by a series of astute legal manoeuvres, Oliver had successfully resisted for more than two years the planning authority's attempt to acquire compulsorily his client's property. It was a case after his own heart.

I looked, too, at Oliver's desk diary. He seemed to have had a full day of engagements: the County Court in the morning, followed by lunch with Fergusson at the Conservative Club. (Why should he be lunching with Fergusson, I wondered?) The afternoon was taken up with a series of appointments with clients whose names I recognized; and for the evening there was one entry, brief and obscure: 'L. 8.30 p.m.'

I stubbed out my cigarette, observing as I did so that there were already five cigarette ends in the ash tray. Three were of the popular brand which Oliver always smoked, while the other two were filter-tipped and on them I thought I could detect traces of lipstick. The cigarette box was open and was half-full of cigarettes.

I sat down and gazed at the desk while I lit another cigarette. A thought was stirring in the back of my mind but would not come to the surface. There was something incongruous about that desk, something missing that ought to be there or something there that ought not to be there. I puzzled over it for a while but at length gave it up.

I saw from my watch that twenty minutes had passed since my call to the police. The fog must be delaying them too. I was beginning to get restless and I was also feeling cold. I got up and started to pace about the room. It was only then that I noticed that the safe door was ajar. I pulled it open and a heap of papers cascaded on to the floor. As I stooped to examine them I heard a car draw up in the street outside. Moments later there was the tramp of heavy footsteps climbing the stairs. The police had arrived.

I had met Inspector Kennedy only once or twice before, although I knew him well by sight and reputation. He had a gaunt, almost cadaverous face, with a long nose and a small, thin-lipped mouth. His eyes were pale blue and watery, as if he suffered from a chronic cold in the head, and he had a curiously disconcerting trick of fixing them unblinkingly on the person he was addressing. When he spoke it was in a voice so soft that one had to strain all the time to hear what he was saying. A trace of a West Country accent was discernible. I was not personally favourably impressed by Kennedy, although he was well thought of in Brickfield.

The inspector listened without comment to my account of events since Oliver's telephone call. Then he asked me to wait in an adjoining room. He would probably, he said, have some questions to ask me after the police had concluded their examination.

I went through the communicating door to Oliver's secretary's room and closed the door behind me. It was like moving into another stratum of society. This was a long narrow cell, with one door leading to the corridor and one to Oliver's room. Filing cabinets ranged one wall. The only other furnishings were a table with a typewriter and a telephone on it and a small typist's chair. A calendar hung from a nail above the filing cabinets; otherwise there was nothing to relieve the bareness of the hospital-yellow distempered walls.

The room, in fact, was totally devoid of character. And yet, as I knew, its occupant was by no means a negative or colourless person. I thought of Joyce Carruthers with some affection. She had come to us two years before, on the recommendation of Fergusson, who had had good reports of her in her previous post in the south. She more than fulfilled our hopes. For the first six months or so she worked for me and she was by far the most competent secretary I had ever had. But, more than that, she was a girl of great personal charm. There had been a time, indeed, when Joyce and I seemed to be drifting towards an engagement. But that had been before I met Linda. And before Oliver had transferred her to be his own secretary.

I was surprised to find how much I could hear, through the thin wooden partition, of what was going on in the adjoining room. Kennedy, unfortunately, did most of the talking, and his voice was so low that only the occasional word or phrase came through. But whenever the sergeant or one of the two constables spoke it was as if he were in the same room with me. I gathered they were taking photographs, and there was a good deal of talk about distances and angles and exposures. At one point the door burst open and Kennedy asked me abruptly if I was sure that no one had come to the building between my telephoning the police and their arrival. It seemed that it was the police surgeon they were awaiting: he should have been here long ago. 'That damned fog,' the inspector muttered as he went out again.

Minutes went by with no sound at all from Oliver's room. Then there was a crash followed by an imprecation from the inspector. It sounded as if something heavy had been knocked over and had fallen on the hearth. Then another long period of silence. I began to get bored. I took out my cigarettes again and lit one. There was no ash tray in Joyce's room and I remembered that she had given up smoking some months before. I was amused to see a chewing gum wrapper in the waste-paper basket. This was her safety valve. I flicked my ash on to the floor and waited.

At last the inspector came in and sat down on the edge of the table.

'We'll want a full statement from you tomorrow, Mr Barnett,' he said. 'It's a bit late tonight and I've no doubt you're tired. But there are just one or two things I would like to ask you now, if you don't mind.'

As he spoke he was fishing in an inside pocket. Eventually his hand emerged with a small glass phial. He removed the cap and prised out a white capsule. His eyes never left my face during this operation.

'Do you know of any reason why your brother should take his own life?'

'Oliver didn't kill himself,' I replied.

'That wasn't my question.'

'Well, the answer is "No".'

There was another delay while he put the capsule in his mouth and swallowed it. Dyspepsia, no doubt, I thought: he looks the type. When he started off again, it was on a new tack.

'This phone call from your brother – what time do you say you got it?'

'About a quarter to eleven. Ten-forty-six, to be precise. I remember looking at my watch.'

'Are you married?'

The unexpectedness of this question took me off my guard and I hesitated momentarily before I answered, 'Yes.'

'Then no doubt your wife will be able to confirm the time of the call?'

It was at this point that I really took a dislike to Kennedy. Something in his manner, civil though it was, convinced me that he already knew about Linda and me. However, I merely said:

'My wife and I are separated.'

He stared at me for a moment but made no comment. Then he went on:

'Did your brother sound excited or nervous when he spoke to you?'

'On the contrary, he sounded exactly as he always did, merely a little impatient. I've had many similar calls from him.'

'You mean he was in the habit of ringing you up at that time of night?'

'Well, that *was* a bit later than usual. But you see, Inspector, when Oliver got immersed in a problem and found he needed a second opinion, he just lifted the phone and summoned you. The time of night and possible inconvenience to the other person just didn't register with Oliver.'

'Your brother was the senior partner in this firm?'

'Yes.'

'But you are a partner?'

'Yes.'

It was obvious that the inspector found my subservience to Oliver difficult to accept; and I couldn't blame him. But I didn't feel called on to give him the explanation. I would have had to tell him that I wanted to make things as easy as possible for Oliver because I was sorry for him; and I would have had to tell him the story of Oliver's life. It would have taken too long and I doubted if the inspector would have believed me anyway. Thinking on these lines reminded me of Marion. She would have to be told.

'I'm sorry to interrupt you, Inspector,' I said, 'but I'm wondering how this is going to be broken to Oliver's wife. She's – well, she's rather a highly strung person and I'm not sure how she'll take it.'

'She knows already,' Kennedy replied. 'I sent a man across soon after we got here. I had hoped to have a talk with her myself tonight. But I gather she is a bit distraught and I think I'll leave her until tomorrow.'

I was appalled. I blamed myself for not thinking of this earlier and insisting on being the one to break the news to Marion. There were ways of dealing with Marion but they would not be known to the police constable. 'A bit distraught' was, I felt sure, an understatement.

'Do you think I could go over and see her now?' I asked.

The inspector looked uncomfortable.

'I would rather you didn't,' he said. 'I understand that Mrs Barnett is resting. Her maid has sent for a doctor.'

Still that unwavering gaze was on my face. I wondered whether there was something behind this, whether he was anxious to have his own interview with Marion before I had had a chance to talk to her. I was glad enough to let the matter drop. The prospect of a session with Marion tonight was not one that appealed to me. I would see her some time tomorrow.

The inspector returned to his questioning.

'Well, then, you got this phone call at ten-forty-six but you didn't reach the office till eleven-thirty. Is that right?'

'A minute or two after, I should have said. The church clock was striking the half-hour when I turned into the far end of the square.'

'Three-quarters of an hour to walk half a mile? It's a long time.'

'It's a foggy night, Inspector. You weren't very prompt in getting here yourself.'

I was finding his manner irritating. He didn't answer, but turned to something else.

'Now, about this mysterious intruder you saw, or imagined you saw, when you arrived at the office—' The inspector broke off as a constable knocked and entered. 'Dr Moodie is here, sir,' he said.

'Well, Mr Barnett,' said Kennedy, 'I don't think I need keep you any longer tonight. You'd better go home and get some sleep. I want to have a long talk with you in the morning.' He turned to the constable: 'If the fog is still thick outside, Faulds, you might drive Mr Barnett home in the police car.'

CHAPTER 2

I awoke at nine o'clock. I must have slept through the alarm. My head felt muzzy as if I had a hangover, but I revived after a shower and a shave and a strong cup of tea. I took my time over my breakfast. I was in no hurry to get back to the office.

It was after ten before I put on my hat and raincoat and went out. The fog had lifted now and a steady drizzle of rain was falling from a leaden sky.

Although I knew what to expect I still got something of a shock when I turned into Weldon Square and saw the police cars drawn up outside the office building and the crowd of people, huddled under umbrellas, on the far side of the street, gazing with vacant concentration at the third-floor windows. As I approached the doorway, cameras clicked and a group of reporters converged on me, clamouring for a story. They were silenced by the emergence from the building at this moment of four policemen bearing a stretcher whose burden was revealed rather than concealed by the white sheet draped over it. There was a buzz of excited comment from across the street, and the stretcher was quickly slid through the open rear doors of a long black van, the doors slammed, and the van moved slowly away.

I took the opportunity, while the attention of the reporters and cameramen was diverted, to slip through the doorway and into the lift.

I found Joyce Carruthers installed in my room pounding at her typewriter. Her table and chair occupied almost the only bit of clear space in the room and I had to squeeze past her to get to my desk.

'The police put me out of my room this morning,' she explained. 'This was the only haven I could find. I hope you don't mind. I thought you might be glad of somebody to keep the wolves from the door – the wolves being the Press.'

'Of course I don't mind. But what was wrong with Waterston's room?'

'He's in.'

'What! Waterston?'

'Yes. He was here at the stroke of nine this morning, not five minutes after I arrived myself. And he hasn't budged from his room since.'

I was so astonished that I wondered for a moment if Joyce was joking. Sir Charles Waterston, Professor of Private International Law at the University, was technically a partner of our firm. It had been a remarkable coup for Oliver, in 1957, to persuade him to join us, for he was right at the top of his profession and could have commanded a partnership almost anywhere. From Oliver's point of view Waterston's main value lay in the prestige he conferred on the firm, although from time to time we did get his help when a difficult question concerning domicile or the like arose. We had not consulted him for some time, however, for he was on bad terms, for different reasons, with both Oliver and myself. His room, which, next to Oliver's, was the most imposing in the building, had stood empty for months; and indeed I had tentatively suggested to Oliver that I might move in there. But Oliver was too jealous of the impression which the gold letters on the door 'Sir Charles Waterston' made on our clients. He was probably right.

That Waterston should have chosen this particular morning to appear at the office was surprising, to put it at its lowest. I was still pondering this when Joyce came in carrying a cup of coffee. I hadn't even noticed her go out.

'Sit down and drink this, Simon,' she said. 'You look like a corpse. (Sorry, I shouldn't have said that.) Anyway, drink it up. And talk to me if you feel like it. I would like to hear just what happened last night. I've got some things to tell you, too, but they'll keep.'

The coffee was strong and sweet. I lit a cigarette and, reluctantly at first, started on my story once more. I told it better than I had to Inspector Kennedy. Little details began to come back to me which had been crowded out the night before.

Joyce was a good listener. She sat motionless and never interrupted. This was one of the qualities I valued in Joyce – her quietness and absence of mannerisms of any kind. She had large blue eyes in startling contrast to her raven-black hair which she wore cut short and kept immaculately groomed. Her features were regular and her mouth, when she smiled (which was often), somehow lop-sided; the whole effect was unusual and attractive. Add to that a figure which, at thirty-three, had made no compromise with the years, an intelligence much above average, and a highly developed sense of humour. An ideal wife for someone, one would have thought. And yet she had never married. I sometimes had the impression that this was not from choice, that there was someone who meant a great deal to her but who, presumably, did not return her feelings.

Joyce asked a few questions when I had finished my account. Unlike me, she seemed to think suicide by no means improbable.

'Your brother was a strange man, you know, Simon. A restless man. And he's been driving himself pretty hard these past few months.'

But she admitted she could not account for the prowler I had surprised on my arrival at the office.

The telephone rang and Joyce answered it.

'Tell him it will be ready in ten minutes,' I heard her say.

'That was the inspector wanting a typed copy of the stuff Oliver left last night,' she said as she put down the receiver. 'You know he dictated some letters on the dictaphone before he – before he – died?' She stumbled a little over the last few words and then hurried on. 'I had practically finished when you came in. Just a minute – I'll let you hear it. You'll be interested in the last part.'

As she spoke she was switching on the dictaphone transcriber, which was lying on her table beside the typewriter. It was a neat little gadget, not much bigger than pocket size.

'I'm sparing you the first ten minutes,' said Joyce, adjusting the control of the instrument. 'It's the usual drivel about Green and his confounded shop.'

Suddenly Oliver's voice came through, clear and resonant. It was a beautiful, rich voice, free of obtrusive accent or affectation. Curiously Oliver, who was vain about his appearance, his clothes, his personality, his wit, had never seemed to realize what a genuine asset he had in his voice. Perhaps that was why it always sounded so natural.

It was eerie to hear that voice now.

'. . . without any statutory authority. Indeed I would suggest that I write immediately to the Planning Authority on your behalf and ask them to specify the clause in the statute under which they purport to be acting. As I pointed out in my letter of . . . Come in! Well, I began to wonder if you weren't coming after all.'

There was no more. Clearly Oliver had switched off the dictaphone at that point.

'What do you make of that?' asked Joyce.

'His visitor was a woman,' I replied without hesitation.

'Yes, he reserved that unctuous tone for the fair sex, didn't he? – or for certain members of it, anyway.'

'I suppose there's no indication of *when* he dictated that?'

'None – no clocks striking, unfortunately.'

We sat in silence for a moment or two, Oliver's voice still ringing in my ears. Then Joyce gave a little gesture as if shaking herself free of her thoughts and said:

'Look, Simon, I really must finish this typing for the inspector. And that reminds me. He wants to see you. He's been taking statements from the whole staff this morning. We were expected to account for every minute of our time from five o'clock yesterday until nine o'clock this morning. As far as I can gather, most of us were groping about in the fog for a sizeable part of that time, which didn't please Kennedy's tidy mind one bit.

'But you're the one he's really after,' she added with a mischievous glint in her eye. 'You are at the top of the list of suspects.'

'Don't I know it?' I muttered as I made for the door.

'She called me back as I was going out.

'I nearly forgot. Mrs Barnett has been on the phone for you twice.'

'Marion?'

'No, your wife.'

'Linda? What did she want?'

'How should I know? I'm not in her confidence,' said Joyce tartly.

'Come off it, Joyce. There's no need for that tone.'

'Sorry, Simon.' She smiled a little wearily. 'But, really, when I hear the eagerness in your voice – Oh! well, forget it. But, speaking of Marion, don't you think you ought to go and see her? You're the only person who might be able to help her. She likes you, you know, Simon.'

'I'll go round as soon as I'm through with Kennedy,' I replied gloomily. 'He wouldn't let me go last night.' I still wasn't looking forward to that interview.

I had to hang about for nearly an hour before Inspector Kennedy was ready for me. He had Fergusson with him when I went along at first and when Fergusson came out I was forestalled by the arrival of the chief constable, Sir John Mowbray, a small portly man in tweed jacket and plus-fours, whose face was familiar to me from newspaper photographs of society events in the county. He was closeted with Kennedy for quite some time before I was called in.

The inspector was seated at Oliver's desk and beside him sat a young constable with note-book and pencil. Sir John Mowbray, hands in jacket-pockets, was leaning against the wall by the fireplace. He was a cheerful little man and seemed almost to be enjoying the proceedings.

Kennedy looked more lugubrious than ever in the morning light, but he made an effort to be pleasant and to put me at my ease. Having motioned me to a chair and told me I could smoke if I wanted, he remarked that my brother's death must have been a great shock to me and offered me his sympathy. I thanked him.

These preliminary civilities over (they had, I suspected, been mainly for the benefit of the chief constable), the inspector went on to say that the police were now taking statements from everyone who might be able to throw light on the circumstances of Oliver's death. He was sure I would co-operate by telling them everything that might be relevant. To begin with, perhaps I would describe once again the events of last night from the time when I got Oliver's call.

This I found a disconcerting experience. At this, my third telling,

I was almost word perfect in my story, and even to my own ears it sounded like a part well rehearsed rather than a statement of the truth. I was distracted, too, by the constable's pencil weaving patterns of shorthand in his notebook and by Kennedy's unwavering gaze – as if he were measuring my neck for the gallows, I felt. I faltered once or twice and once I had to ask to be allowed to correct something I had said. But I got through it well enough and I don't think I left anything material out.

In fact I remembered one point of some significance which had slipped from my mind until then. This was the bus accident the night before at the time of the telephone call from Oliver. I pointed out that they would confirm the time of the call, since presumably there was a record of when the accident happened. Kennedy exchanged a sour glance with the chief constable when I spoke of this, but did not interrupt.

As soon as I had finished, the questions began. Sir John Mowbray seemed to be mainly interested in the security arrangements for the office.

'Do you mean to tell me', he exclaimed, 'that anyone could walk into this building at any time of the night without so much as picking a lock?'

'Into the building, yes,' I replied, 'but it wouldn't do him much good. He would get no farther than the stairs and the landings. The door into our offices is always locked at night and so, I believe, are the doors to the offices on the other floors.'

'Your office door wasn't locked last night from your own account.'

'No, but remember Oliver was inside. He wasn't in the habit of locking himself in. And his murderer had no particular reason – and in any case no time – to lock the door after him.'

'Well, then –' the chief constable was still unmollified – 'what about this lift? Surely it's highly dangerous to leave an open lift in a building that anyone can get into?'

'The lift is locked and padlocked each night when the offices close at five o'clock. But Oliver had a key to it. He worked in the office nearly every evening and he refused to climb three flights of stairs. No one else had a key.'

Inspector Kennedy was clearly not interested in these questions and was fidgeting impatiently. He broke in as soon as he politely could.

'You mentioned, Mr Barnett,' he said, 'that the phone call from your brother was on "the office extension". Does this mean you've got two telephones in your house?'

I explained as succinctly as I could the complex Oliver had had about telephones. Although he used the telephone a great deal, he never could reconcile himself to its limitations. When he wanted to speak to someone it upset him beyond measure to have to wait, even if only for a minute or two. He had always had the exasperating habit of ringing up his partners at their private houses in the evening, which was the time of day when he did much of his work, and he would fret and fume if the number was engaged. This was a comparatively rare occurrence but it did happen occasionally after my marriage that Linda would be using our phone when Oliver tried to get through to me. So eventually he had extensions run from our office private branch exchange to his own house and to Fergusson's and mine. He even thought of providing the same service for the fourth partner, Waterston, who lived in the city, nearly twenty miles away; but the estimated cost of this was too much even for Oliver. As it was, the cost of installing the extensions and the rent we had to pay to the GPO was out of all proportion to the value of the service.

Kennedy took a moment or two to digest this. Then he asked:

'That means, I suppose, that your brother's call last night must have come from the office?'

'It did come from the office – he said so.'

'It's useful to have corroboration,' said the inspector testily.

'Well, I'm afraid I can't corroborate it. The call could have come from any of the office extensions – from my brother's house, for example, or from Fergusson's for that matter. We can get through from any extension to any other extension by simply lifting the phone and dialling the appropriate extension number. But why should Oliver—'

'If you don't mind, Mr Barnett, I'll ask the questions,' Kennedy broke in. 'It is at least certain that the call was not made from an outside line altogether?'

'Yes. Or rather not *absolutely* certain. If our office exchange line were switched through to me, then any incoming call to the office would go straight through to my extension. It's the usual system for night calls. In actual practice the line was always put through to Oliver's house at night except when he was working late at the office. But I suppose that if someone *had*, for some obscure reason, phoned to the office from an outside line, then—'

I was interrupted again. 'You're sure it was your brother who spoke to you?' said the inspector quietly.

Only now did I begin to see the implication of his questions.

'You see,' he went on, 'if your story is correct, your brother was alive at 10.46 p.m. Unfortunately quite some time elapsed before the police surgeon examined the body, so that he couldn't give a precise estimate of the time of death. He puts it between nine-thirty and eleven-thirty. Now suppose Mr Barnett is killed at ten o'clock and the murderer, for the purposes of an alibi, rings you up at a

quarter to eleven, imitating your brother's voice . . . ?' He left the
sentence dangling.

I thought hard about this, but I had no doubt about the answer,
'It was Oliver who spoke to me. To that I would swear.'

The inspector sighed and fell silent. When he spoke again, it
was on a new topic.

'Tell me,' he said. 'Your partner, Sir Charles Waterston – he's
your father-in-law, isn't he?'

'Yes.' Something warned me – the elaborate casualness of the
inspector's tone, an almost imperceptible tensing of the chief
constable – that this was the crucial point of the interview, that the
64,000 dollar question was to follow. Even so the shock when it
came sent a chill down my spine.

'Did you know that your wife was in this office with your brother
last night?'

I could hear the ticking of my watch in the silence that followed.
With a sinking feeling I remembered the entry in Oliver's desk
diary, 'L. 8.30.' At length I said:

'Did Linda – did my wife tell you that?'

'We haven't been able to contact your wife yet. Her father told
us. He drove her here last night. She had an appointment with
your brother at eight-thirty, although, because of the fog, it was
about nine o'clock before they got here.'

'And when did she leave?'

The inspector permitted himself a rare smile. 'That is one of
the things we would like to find out,' he said. 'I just wondered,' he
went on, 'whether you happened to know what your wife's business
with Mr Barnett was?' He gazed closely at me as he spoke.

'No,' I replied. I think that Kennedy noticed the hesitation but
before he could say anything the chief constable spoke. I had almost

forgotten he was there.

'This chap Waterston, is he the man who sent that obnoxious letter to the *Herald* a few weeks ago about the inefficiency of our police forces?'

'The very same,' said Kennedy grimly.

'Well, well, we'd better not slip up on this one, eh, Inspector?' And he sniggered with appreciation. The inspector was not amused.

The tension, however, was now broken. Kennedy did not return to the subject of Linda but asked me ('for the record', as he put it) to give an account of my movements the previous day.

That was easy enough. I had spent the morning at my desk and had driven to the city in the afternoon to discuss with a client the terms of his will. I dined with the client and got back around nine o'clock. I spent an hour or so in a pub and then went home. I had been in the house about half an hour when Oliver phoned.

Beyond asking the name and address of the client and the name of the pub the inspector did not probe further into this statement or ask me to amplify it. He ended with a few questions about Oliver, his character, habits, financial position, interests and friends. I replied briefly because that was what he seemed to want. His main concern was to find out whether I knew of anyone with a grudge against Oliver. When I said 'No', he appeared to lose interest. He told me that all I had said would be transcribed and read over to me and I would be asked to sign it.

The inspector yawned and stood up. The interview was at an end. Before I left, however, there was one point which I wanted to clear up.

'May I ask you, Inspector,' I said, 'whether you still think my brother committed suicide?'

Kennedy frowned, then glanced at the chief constable, who gave a quick nod.

'The possibility has not been excluded,' he said, picking his words with care. 'Your brother's fingerprints are on the revolver. But I think I can tell you that the prints are in such a position that it would have been virtually impossible for him to fire the gun.'

'These were the fingerprints of his right hand, presumably? I remember the revolver was lying beside his right hand.'

'Yes. Why?'

'Well, I think I can remove any lingering doubts you may have. Oliver was left-handed. I'm sorry I didn't remember this last night.'

'Ah, well,' said the inspector, 'that's one matter settled anyway.' He did not seem unduly surprised.

As I left the room I heard the chief constable muttering about the folly of leaving buildings unlocked at night.

CHAPTER 3

I was surprised to find that it was nearly one o'clock. As I passed Fergusson's door he called me in.

Fergusson was almost hidden behind a mass of books and papers piled high on his desk. George MacAndrew, the most junior of our apprentices, was reading to him a passage from a volume of *The Times Law Reports*. With a wave of his hand Fergusson silenced him.

'Interesting, no doubt, but scarcely relevant,' he said. 'I'm still sure there was a case on the point but it certainly wasn't that one.'

He turned to me. 'George and I have been trying to interpret a rather obscure clause in Miss Willis's Trust Deed and Settlement. An ill-drawn document,' he added, shaking his head in disapproval. 'Slovenly draftsmanship.' This, to Fergusson, was a crime as heinous as any on the statute book.

He asked me if I would lunch with him. Surprised though I was, I accepted readily. Fergusson was pretty shrewd and I hoped he might have some ideas about Oliver's murder. George was dismissed and scuttled out with relief patent on his face.

As he put on his coat and hat Fergusson suggested that we go to his club.

'I know you generally lunch at the Chilton, but in the – ah – circumstances I fear we might be too conspicuous there.'

He made no further allusion to Oliver's death as we went down in the lift, nor even when we had almost to force our way through a crowd of newspapermen to get to his car. Instead he started on a long explanation of his difficulties in the administration of the Willis estate. I could not make up my mind whether this indicated callous indifference or whether he was in some way trying to spare my feelings.

The Conservative Club is housed in a large, ungainly building in what was once the fashionable part of the town. It used to be a private house, in the days when one family could afford to employ half a dozen servants. Its neighbours had long since been split into flats or demolished and replaced by semi-detached villas and shops. The Conservative Club was founded some forty years ago and, although constantly threatened with insolvency, had somehow managed to survive. It was the only club, in the proper sense of that term, in Brickfield; indeed the town was scarcely big enough to support even one. In recent years only the excellence of its cuisine had saved it, for it had little else to commend it. The chef was in his own field a genius and it was widely recognized that the best lunches and dinners in the town were to be had there, better by some way than at the otherwise impeccable Station Hotel.

We had a couple of sherries in the bar before lunch. Fergusson was now launched on a rambling account of his holiday in Northern Ireland the previous summer. I knew now that he was labouring under some embarrassment. Although inclined a little to ponderousness and pedantry, he was not normally garrulous and was rarely a bore.

It was only when we had placed our order and the waiter had come with the soup that Fergusson brought his spate of trivial reminiscences to a close. His eyes travelled round the gloomy dining-room and he remarked:

'It's strange to think that twenty-four hours ago it was your brother who was sitting at this table with me.

'I want to tell you about that lunch, Simon,' he continued. 'Oliver said one or two rather puzzling things, and I can't help wondering whether they have any bearing on his subsequent – ah – demise.'

'What puzzles me', I replied, 'is how you came to be lunching with him at all. Your last meal with him was not, if I remember, a resounding success.'

'Oh, that,' said Fergusson, gesturing with his hand as if waving away an irrelevance. 'Did Oliver ever tell you what that quarrel was about? No? Well, perhaps I can come to that later. But first, about yesterday.

'This is what – Friday? Yes, well it must have been Wednesday evening about half-past nine that he rang me at my house and asked me to come round and see him at once. I told him it wasn't convenient. Neither it was. I had invited Dr Peacock round to hear some of my records and I failed to see why I should get up and leave him at Oliver's whim.

'Well, of course, Oliver got into one of his rages and blustered for a bit, but when he saw that I was adamant he calmed down and suggested that we meet some time the following day – that was yesterday. He insisted that the discussion must not take place in the office; hence the luncheon arrangement.'

He broke off at this point and turned his attention to the fish, a nice bit of sole. I studied him as he ate. A strange, remote sort of man he was. He must have been in his late fifties, although it was hard to judge from his craggy, weather-beaten face. A strong face; great beetling eyebrows under a massive forehead; coarse, wiry hair now bleached almost white; and a determined mouth and chin.

Fergusson had joined our firm some three years previously, in the late summer of 1958. He had had a thriving practice in the city but had thrown it up on the death of his wife early in that year. A few months out of harness had convinced him that a life of retirement was not for him. He was by this time living in Brickfield and he approached Oliver, who was known to have ambitions to expand his practice. We were, of course, delighted to offer him a partnership, for he had an established reputation, and we for our part were much in need of someone of his experience. It proved an excellent bargain, for not only was Fergusson a man of unusual intellectual gifts and of great industry, but he brought with him a number of valuable clients from his former practice.

Socially, however, he was less of an asset. There was a reserve about him which none of us ever broke down. He lived a solitary existence in a small house he had bought on the outskirts of the town. A daily woman came in to do some of the housework: otherwise he looked after himself. Apart from a few acquaintances who shared his interest in early classical music he saw no one, so far as I knew, out of office hours. I sometimes had the impression (based on very little, it is true) that he showed rather less indifference to me than to the others in the office, and there had been once or twice when he had seemed to be on the point of confiding to me something of what went on under his mask of polite frigidity. But he always shied off at the last moment. The result was that I knew virtually nothing of the real Fergusson and nothing either of his background and earlier life. It was rumoured that he had lost a son or a daughter as well as his wife, but if that was true we had no evidence of it.

All this was passing through my mind when Fergusson resumed his narrative.

'Well, as I was saying, Oliver and I had lunch here yesterday. He seemed to be in an excited and restless mood and if I hadn't known how temperate he was, I would have suspected he had been drinking. He always was a good talker, as you know, but yesterday there was a touch of hysteria about it. He went racing on from one anecdote to another with scarcely a pause for breath and although it was all rational enough, I'm sure only a small fraction of his mind was on what he was saying.'

Fergusson paused to take a sip of his drink.

'A nice hock this,' he remarked. 'Not too blatant. You should try it. But I see,' he added, eyeing with distaste my pint of Export, 'that in one respect at least you share the plebeian tastes of your brother.'

'I have never liked wine at this time of day,' I replied coldly.

'Ah, well. Anyway, we were nearly halfway through the meal before Oliver broached the subject for which our *tête-à-tête* had presumably been arranged. And even then he did it in a very round-about way. He started by defining his relationship to you, Simon. He seemed to regard himself as defender and protector of the weak. You were just like your father, he said, intelligent and able, but too naïve and defenceless for this modern rat race.'

I smiled sadly. 'Poor Oliver,' I said.

'Yes, indeed, poor Oliver,' echoed Fergusson. 'That's what I said to him. I told him he was much mistaken in his reading of your character. But he was already going on to say that if he had done anything wrong it had been for your sake as much as his own; and that it was morally justified anyway. Don't ask me what this meant: I haven't the least idea. Then he asked me what I thought of your wife.'

'And what did you reply?'

Fergusson gazed at me evenly, 'I said that I scarcely knew her.'

His eyes held mine for a moment and then he turned back to his food.

'In any case,' he went on, 'I don't think Oliver was really interested in my answer to that particular question. I have been thinking a lot about this in the last twenty-four hours and I believe your brother was simply casting about for something to break the ice between us, something that would start me asking questions. He wanted my advice or my help, of that I'm sure. But he couldn't bring himself to say outright what his problem was. Unfortunately I am a difficult person to confide in, as others besides Oliver have found. It may be, too, that he was crediting me with some partial knowledge of what he was hinting at. But I could not help him. It was all meaningless to me.

'He did make one last attempt to get through to me, and this time he came rather nearer to a direct statement. He said (I can remember his exact words): "someone is trying to do something which could wreck not only my life but others' as well." '

'And you simply sat there and ate your lunch.'

'And I simply sat there and ate my lunch – or rather drank my coffee. Yes, I know, Simon, it seems callous, but what could I say? It sounded to me melodramatic and maudlin gibberish. And after all I didn't *know* he was going to be murdered last night.

'Speaking of coffee,' he added, 'let's have it in the lounge.'

The lounge, with its dark woodwork and drab leather armchairs, was even more austere and cheerless than the dining-room. It had the chill atmosphere of a museum – the sort of room where you instinctively lowered your voice.

A waiter brought in our coffee. Fergusson waved away my offer of a cigarette and instead took out a cigar.

'I don't know what the cancer statistics are for cigar smokers,' he remarked as he leisurely removed the band, 'but I should think that two a day won't kill me.'

He looked so smug sitting there that I felt an unreasonable anger. And yet 'smug' wasn't precisely the word: it was simply an aloofness, an indifference to the petty emotions of others frailer than he. How I wished that Oliver had come to me instead of to this iceberg.

We smoked in silence for a few minutes.

'Have you told Inspector Kennedy the story of your conversation with Oliver?' I asked at length.

'The gist of it, yes. He was interested but I doubt if it will help him much. It was all too vague. But I did wonder if you might not be able to throw some light on what Oliver was talking about. Can you?'

I sensed something more than polite interest in Fergusson's voice, despite the casual tone of the question. He really wanted to find out what, if anything, I knew.

'It's as much of a mystery to me as it is to you,' I answered.

He tapped the ash off the end of his cigar. 'A pity,' he said.

Again I had the faintest of impressions of an undercurrent in his tone. Was it merely imagination or was there relief there? I looked closely at him: he was as stolid and impassive as ever. I decided I had imagined it.

He poured out more coffee but showed no inclination to resume the discussion.

I reminded him of the occasion of his quarrel with Oliver the previous winter. The incident had created quite a stir in the office at the time and there had been much speculation about the cause of the breach.

It happened on the evening of the annual office dinner dance. This was in fact a joint function for the staffs of the four offices in our building – an insurance company and a shipping agency on the floors below us and a firm of architects above us, as well as ourselves. It was traditionally held at the Chilton Restaurant in the week before Christmas and it followed much the same pattern every year. The dinner was always an uncomfortable affair with much forced bonhomie; and the dance was usually slow to warm up, too. However, after the necessary courtesy dances between top executives and their secretaries, like gravitated to like; the dance floor became the prerogative of the young, while their elders settled with relief in the bar. By the end of the evening those who had earlier been vowing inwardly that this was the last such function they would ever attend were enthusiastically acclaiming its success.

It was immediately before the dinner on the evening in question that the incident between Oliver and Fergusson occurred. Most of us were crowded into the bar pushing back a drink or two before the coming ordeal. I remember Linda and I were talking to Victor Wallis, a young actuary with the insurance company. We were recalling how it was at the same function a year before that Linda and I had first met. I don't think Wallis was really listening, although he nodded and smiled politely from time to time. His eyes were casting round the room, no doubt in search of Joyce Carruthers, for whom he was known to cherish a hopeless passion. In any case he probably couldn't hear what we were saying. The babel of voices was deafening.

Suddenly, however, there was a crash of glass followed by a shout in what was unmistakably Oliver's voice. The din around us subsided like a radio switched off and Oliver's words rang out with awful clarity:

'You filthy-minded old swine. When I want advice from you I'll ask for it.' And Oliver, with thunder in his face, pushed his way through the crowd and went out.

Fergusson was left standing beside the table that Oliver had kicked over, mopping ineffectually at his trouser leg, on which some gin had been spilt. It was the only time I had seen him thoroughly disconcerted and angry. His lips were white and a nerve was twitching in one eye.

As for the rest of us, we just couldn't cope with the situation. Some sort of pretence was made of ignoring what had happened but it was a miserable failure. Little spurts of conversation broke out and quickly died and it was a relief to all of us when dinner was announced. I slipped out to look for Oliver. I found him in the men's room combing his hair. Apart from a hectic colour in his cheeks he seemed normal, and he made no reference, then or later, to the quarrel. 'Dinner ready?' he remarked, and followed me in. Over dinner he was in his best form as a raconteur, and if the response of his audience to his anecdotes was strained, at least there was an appearance of gaiety at his table and something was salvaged from the evening. Fergusson, I observed, sitting at a table some distance away, was grimly silent throughout the meal and left soon afterwards.

Naturally it was a sensation much talked about, although always in the absence of the principal participants. Neither Fergusson nor Oliver was the kind of person one could ask about such a thing. I had hoped that Oliver might volunteer an explanation to me. When he did not, I knew it would be a waste of breath to ask him.

I was therefore eager to hear what Fergusson now had to say.

He seemed to find it difficult to know how to begin, and indeed was silent for so long that I wondered whether he had heard my question. At length he said, hesitantly:

'I'm not sure, Simon, if I ought to say anything at all. I know that, despite the cavalier treatment you got from Oliver, you had a genuine affection for your brother. I have no wish to destroy your illusions.'

'I have no illusions about Oliver. I know his faults.'

'All of them? I wonder.'

We were the only two left in the lounge now, apart from an elderly man in the corner asleep in a chair. The room had grown darker. The rain was battering on the window beside us and a wind was getting up. It was more like a November day than mid-April.

There was another lengthy pause before Fergusson spoke again. When he did, it was to ask a question.

'What do you know of Oliver's personal life?'

'His personal life?'

'Well—' Fergusson seemed to find it distasteful to be more specific – 'his relations with women?'

'I know he wasn't faithful to his wife, if that's what you mean.'

'Ah! well, that's something. Then perhaps you know that he had a flat in Gribble Street where he conducted his – ah – affairs.'

'That I didn't know. But I'm prepared to believe it.'

'You can take it from me it's true. "Flat" is a misleading description really: it is nothing more than a couple of rooms in a tenement in a dirty back street.'

Gribble Street is in the industrial quarter of Brickfield. It houses the better class of artisan and his family; an unpretentious street, but respectable. To describe it as 'a dirty back street' indicated a lack of objectivity uncharacteristic of Fergusson. I wondered if there was a strain of Puritanism in him.

'You're not shocked by this?' It was almost as if Fergusson had divined my thoughts.

'Not particularly,' I replied. 'There were at least extenuating circumstances. Oliver didn't have a very satisfying home life.'

'You're thinking of Marion? Perhaps so. Anyway, Oliver spent every other weekend there. I had known about it for quite some time, but it was no business of mine.'

I interrupted him here. 'Do you happen to know if it was the same girl every time or a succession of them?'

'I'm coming to that,' he said. 'It would have been all right if he had stuck to professionals, as it were. But it came to my knowledge towards the end of last year that he was having an affair with a woman of a very different sort. It was exactly as if a doctor were misbehaving with a woman patient. The scandal, if it had come out, would have ruined Oliver and would have done great damage to the firm too. I was not greatly concerned about Oliver but I had an interest in the firm. I decided to try to put a stop to it. That's what I spoke to Oliver about on the night of the dance.'

'I gather the woman was one of our clients?'

'I didn't say so, Simon.'

'No, but – well, who was she?' I asked the direct question.

Fergusson looked at his watch. 'Good heavens!' he exclaimed. 'It's half-past two. I really must be getting back.'

He stood up. 'Please don't ask me that, Simon. Oliver kept it pretty dark, I'll say that for him. I doubt if anyone except myself knows of it. And it would be wrong for me to reveal the woman's name, even to you.'

'Why did you tell me the story at all, then?' I asked in some irritation as we moved away from the table.

Fergusson's face broke into a smile. 'Vanity,' he said, 'sheer vanity. Oliver's reaction to my homily, you will remember, was violent and he used some singularly ill-chosen words about me in front of all these people. "A filthy-minded old swine", he called me. These words rankled, and I wanted to convince you at least that they were without justification.'

I wasn't so sure that he had convinced me, but I made no comment. I did, however, ask one more question.

'Why did you choose so public an occasion to open a subject like that with Oliver?'

He smiled again. 'There were reasons, Simon, there were reasons.'

CHAPTER 4

There was silence in the car as we drove back, apart from the purr of the engine and the click of the windscreen wipers. Fergusson showed no inclination to talk and I was busy with my thoughts. In accepting Fergusson's invitation to lunch, I had intended to discuss with him the circumstances of Oliver's death. Fergusson, however, had so manipulated the conversation that that subject had scarcely been touched on and instead I had been treated to two extraordinary stories. Each of them had the ring of truth in it up to a point, and yet I was convinced that Fergusson had, in both stories, been less than frank. What puzzled me most was why Oliver should have gone to him of all people with his mysterious hints of impending disaster. They had never been close, and since the incident at the Chilton they had seen as little of each other as they could, even in their work.

I asked Fergusson to drop me at Oliver's house. I knew I would have to see Marion and the sooner I got it over the better.

The house was tucked away behind a screen of firs which Oliver had planted, partly as a windbreak (the house was right at the top of Church Lane and exposed to the full blast of the north-east wind) but mainly for privacy. The garden was extensive and with its screen of trees created the illusion that you were in the country and not in the heart of an industrial town.

Oliver had chosen the site well. He had also taken great pains over the design of the house, which had been built largely to his specification. It was fortunate perhaps that the architect was one not easily dismayed by unusual demands by his client and had, moreover, sufficient strength of character to resist Oliver's more eccentric and impracticable conceptions. At all events the house when completed was not the monstrosity one had feared but seemed to fit harmoniously enough into its surroundings. The interior was the very essence of comfort, planned to the last detail, and although Marion was apt to grumble from time to time that the house was too big for them I think she would have hated to live anywhere else.

With some trepidation I rang the bell. The door was opened almost at once by the maid. Millie was really something rather more than a maid. She had come from Ireland as a young girl over forty years ago and her first job had been as temporary help to my mother during the later months of her first pregnancy. So handless and ignorant was she that my father nearly dismissed her after the first week. She was a hard worker, however, and almost pathetically eager to learn, and my father relented. My mother took a long time to recover after the birth of Oliver, and Millie stayed on. By the time I arrived she was an accepted part of the household and it was unthinkable that she should leave.

I had known Millie all my life and we had a tolerant respect for each other. But it was on Oliver, the first-born, that she doted. In Millie's eyes he could do no wrong. When my father died in 1955, Oliver was already engaged to Marion and indeed the wedding took place only a month or two later. I moved out to a flat and Oliver and Marion took over my father's house. It was natural that Millie should stay on; and when Oliver moved to his new house three years later Millie went too.

I sometimes wondered what Marion thought of Millie, who did not measure up to the normally accepted standards for a maid.

By this time in her late fifties, she was plain and untidy in appearance and she had never fully mastered the finer points of her
profession – how to receive and introduce visitors, the correct way
of serving at table, and so on. But she was a good worker and above
all she was fiercely loyal. Oliver had chosen Marion as his wife,
and therefore, whatever her private opinion of Marion, she gave
her unstinted service.

Even in the dim light of the hall I could see that Millie's eyes
were red from weeping. She led me into the kitchen and switched
on the light. The blinds were drawn here as they were throughout
the house.

'Mrs Barnett's having a rest in bed,' she said. 'The doctor gave
her a sedative. But I don't think she's asleep and she said as how I
was to take you up if you came.'

I stood awkwardly, still holding my coat and hat. I sensed
that she wanted to say something to me but was waiting for me
to set the ball rolling. But I could think of nothing better than
the banal remark:

'This must have been a great shock to you, Millie.'

'Well, it was and it wasn't, if you see what I mean, sir,' was her
unexpected reply. 'Mr Oliver hadn't been himself these last few
days. He came in one night – Wednesday it was – with a face as
white as death. I knew he was real upset because he poured himself
out a straight whisky and tossed it over at one gulp, and then he
had another right after it. And you know as well as I do, sir, that
he scarcely touched a drop of the stuff as a rule.'

This was, to some extent, corroboration of what Fergusson had
told me.

'Do you happen to know, Millie,' I asked, 'if Oliver phoned Mr

Fergusson shortly after that?'

'Yes, that he did. And terrible angry he was too. He wanted Mr Fergusson to come and see him at once but he wouldn't come seemingly. I couldn't help overhearing,' she added apologetically. 'I was working in the kitchen and I kept the door open. I was that worried about him. He looked like he was going to take a stroke. I couldn't hear much the first time, though. He spoke quieter then.'

'The first time? You mean he phoned somebody else before he spoke to Mr Fergusson?'

'Yes, but I don't know who it was.'

'You must tell this to Inspector Kennedy,' I said.

'I've told him, sir. He was here at eight o'clock this morning. But I wanted you to hear about it because I thought you might know where Mr Oliver had been that night that he got such a fright. I'm certain sure it's got something to do with – with what happened last night.'

'Wednesday? No, I don't. What time was this, by the way?'

'Well, he had dinner here as usual at half-past seven. As soon as it was over, he got the car out and off he went. He wasn't away very long – maybe an hour. I didn't really notice the time when he came in.'

'Anyway, it was roughly between eight and nine that he was out?'

'Yes.'

A thought suddenly struck me.

'Tell me, Millie—' But here I was interrupted by Marion's voice calling from upstairs.

'Millie, is that Simon you've got with you?'

'I'd better go up,' I said. 'Don't bother coming with me.'

I walked slowly up the stairs, wondering what sort of state

Marion would be in and what on earth I was going to say to her. I tapped on her bedroom door and went in. The room was in darkness except for the glow of a cigarette to my left.

'Don't switch on the main light, Simon; it's too harsh. Just a moment.' I heard a faint rustling, the cigarette described an arc and then was steady, there was a click, and the room was bathed in warm light from a table-lamp beside the bed.

My first reaction on seeing Marion was one of relief: she was calm and she was sober. The bed was hard against the wall of the room and Marion was reclining on it, half propped up by pillows. She wore a peach nylon nightdress, with a matching negligee thrown carelessly over her shoulders. Seeing her like this in profile, the youthful lines of her figure accentuated by the flimsy clothing, I could almost believe that she hadn't changed from the beautiful girl Oliver had married six years before.

She turned to face me and the illusion was gone. Those terrible, disfiguring scars running right down the left side of her face made a mockery of her looks. Plastic surgery had toned down some of the worst effects of the smash but the skin was pouchy and discoloured and those scars would be with her for the rest of her life.

Marion stubbed out her cigarette. She saw me glance at the ash-tray, almost overflowing with stubs, and smiled.

'Yes, I've been chain-smoking,' she said in a rapid monotone. 'I have been trying to analyse my emotions. An interesting exercise when your husband has just been murdered. Give me another cigarette, Simon, there's a pet. My packet's finished.'

I gave her a cigarette and took one myself. As I felt for my matches I wondered how I was going to stop this spate of words, which was verging on hysteria.

'Don't you think, Marion,' I began, 'that you ought to rest for a bit and— ?'

'No, no, Simon. Please don't stop me. I must talk to you about this. You see, I was horrified to find that once I got over the initial shock of hearing that Oliver was dead the only thing I could feel was relief. Yes, relief. Don't look so shocked, Simon. At least I'm being honest.'

She paused to take a long pull at her cigarette. There was a wildness about her eyes that I didn't like.

'I know you think I treated him badly in the last couple of years,' she went on. 'So I did. And he was so good to me, so considerate—' she put venom into these words – 'so he was. Yet I hated him, Simon, hated him, loathed him. Oh! it wasn't because of his other women. (You thought I didn't know about that, didn't you?) No, I couldn't blame him for that; after all, I turned him out, didn't I? and he was only human. No, I hated him because he was alive and healthy and unmarked and I was a cripple with a face that people couldn't look at without revulsion. God, how I hated him!' She was sobbing uncontrollably.

I said nothing. What was there to say? I understood Marion better than I understood my own wife. I understood her and pitied her; but I could not help her. Unless, perhaps, it helped her to have someone to pour out her heart to occasionally. The present outburst was not the first I had listened to. Sometimes, as now, it took the form of a vitriolic attack on Oliver as the prime agent of her misfortunes; at other times she would be in a mood of grovelling self-denigration, blaming herself for lack of moral fibre and for blighting Oliver's career; and occasionally she would be so steeped in melancholia that she would drop dark hints about suicide. All these emotions were genuinely felt at the time, but they were shifting, transitory moods which she could not sustain for long. The trouble was that Marion had never come to terms with life since the accident.

It had happened three years ago, not long after they moved into their new house. Up till then their marriage had been, by most standards, a happy one. Marion, the only daughter of a successful local doctor, had emerged unspoilt from a sheltered upbringing. With her striking good looks, her proficiency at games, her wit and good humour, she never lacked for suitors. But she held them off firmly until the right man came along. The right man was Oliver; of that she never had any doubt. They were engaged within a few months of their meeting and married a year later.

They made a splendid partnership. Oliver liked to entertain, partly, I suppose, with an eye to the main chance, for his guests often included business associates who might be useful to him. But he genuinely liked good company and good talk and good food. Marion played her part magnificently. She was an intelligent woman and, with no experience to build on, taught herself to be a first-class cook. She was also, by nature as well as by upbringing, a good hostess, one who never failed to put her guests at their ease. Their dinner-parties became quite celebrated in Brickfield.

I gathered from a few chance remarks that Oliver once let slip that both of them had some regrets that no children had come along. But that seemed to be the only cloud in their sky. And then it happened.

They set off one June morning for a motoring holiday in Europe. Oliver had just bought a new and more powerful car and was eager to try out its paces. They were doing about eighty on a long straight stretch not far north of London when a large furniture van came out of a side road on the left fifty yards ahead and stopped, broadside on, right in Oliver's path. The driver, who was a learner, explained later that his engine had stalled. There still should have been no danger. Oliver braked and swerved but, just as he was about to pass, the van driver in a panic started his engine and moved forward a fatal few inches. The front of the van tore off the whole near-side of Oliver's car. Oliver and the two men in the van were not seriously hurt. Marion was maimed for life.

It was many weeks before she came out of hospital. At first she would see no one. Oliver told us that her face was badly marked and that she would always have a limp but that otherwise she had made a good recovery. He himself seemed on the surface as ebullient and forceful as ever, but I noticed that he was smoking heavily and that he was working longer hours at the office. The dinner-parties were never resumed. But after a time Marion took to inviting along two or three of her own friends, women whom she had known before her marriage but had seen little of since. They played bridge usually. Marion had always liked the game and now became something of an addict.

One evening Oliver rang up and asked if I would go round and make up a bridge four, as one of Marion's friends had let her down at the last moment. I agreed to go as I was intrigued by the prospect of seeing Marion. I was shocked by her appearance; not so much by the actual disfigurement as by the change in the character of her face. It was the face of a discontented, neurotic woman. The bridge was good, however, and I enjoyed the evening. When it was over, Oliver ran the two women home while I stayed and talked to Marion. I asked her why Oliver didn't play. She made some non-committal reply, but her tone made it clear to me that things were very far wrong between them.

That was the first of many such evenings. Bit by bit I pieced together the situation. Marion was, beyond doubt, making Oliver's home life a hell. Even to her friends she constantly criticized her husband, although always in a gentle, long-suffering manner which acquired for her a quite undeserved reputation for having met disaster bravely. In private she treated him with a refined cruelty, nagging him relentlessly, knowing exactly how to cut him in the raw. Oliver for his part showed exemplary restraint, did all he could to make life easier for her, and refused to be provoked by her tirades. In his own way he loved Marion still and I think that, although he was in no way to blame for the accident, he felt an irrational remorse, especially after he began to seek solace elsewhere.

All this I got from Marion herself, who was still sufficiently in touch with reality from time to time to see the truth and confess it to herself and to me. She had for some reason admitted me as a confidant and soon was pressing me to call and see her with more and more frequency. The excuse of bridge was abandoned: she wanted to see me alone. Oliver encouraged and even urged me to visit her. He thought it did Marion good to unburden herself. It was always difficult to refuse Oliver and so the sessions continued, distasteful though they were to me.

During the brief months of my marriage my visits to Marion ceased. It would have been awkward in any case, but Marion made the break easier for me by her antipathy to Linda. We had a violent quarrel on the night when I told Marion I was engaged. She described Linda as a flinty-hearted gold-digger; and what angered me most was that she was in one of her more rational moods that night and that her judgment of Linda could not be lightly shrugged off as the jealous working of a diseased mind.

After Linda left me I was back seeing Marion once or twice a week, again at Oliver's urgent request. Our relationship resumed where it had broken off, but I was saddened to see that she was more neurotic than ever. And she was drinking now, heavily, although not yet as an addict. The only hopeful sign was that Oliver had at last secured for her a doctor – a psychiatrist – whom she found tolerable and with whom she was prepared to co-operate. He had made quite a name for himself in the city and he seemed to take a great interest in her case. He came over to see her every Thursday afternoon and he stayed sometimes for two hours and more. Lord knows what Oliver had to pay him.

The only time I met Dr Fairbairn I had a remarkable conversation with him. I was going up the drive to Oliver's house one evening when he emerged from the front door. He must have stayed for dinner.

'You'll be Simon,' he said without preliminaries. 'I've heard a lot about you. I don't know whether you're doing more harm than good. She's in love with you, you know, or thinks she is. Watch her. She could be dangerous. I've tried to warn her husband, but he won't listen.' And he was off.

These remarks of the doctor came back to me now as I looked at Marion sobbing on the bed. They had indeed been my first thought when I found Oliver's body the previous night. Could Marion have done this? I was convinced that Marion was in love with Oliver, had never ceased to be in love with him, whatever the psychiatrist might say. She hated the imperfections of her body after the accident and had to find someone on whom to vent the bitterness of her wounded pride. In choosing Oliver as her scapegoat she tortured herself as much as him. Beneath it all she still loved him; of that I was certain. But I still asked myself: did she kill him? It was possible.

There was a ritual for dealing with Marion's outbursts of weeping and I followed it now. I brought a glass of water and a couple of aspirins from the bathroom and laid them on the table by her bed. After a moment or two she swallowed the aspirins and took a sip or two of water. She was already calmer.

When I judged the time was ripe, I asked her, as casually as I could:

'When did you last see Oliver, Marion?'

Her face was blank. 'What did you say?'

I repeated the question.

'Oh! at dinner last night. I came up here immediately afterwards – I had a headache, I remember. Wait a minute, I did see him after that. He popped his head round the door just before he went out and said he was going to be later in getting back than he had thought. He had just had a phone call. As if I cared when he got back,' she added bitterly.

'He didn't phone you during the evening, I take it?'

'Well, if he did, he was unlucky. I was out.'

'You were *out*?' I gasped. She couldn't have said anything more astonishing.

'Yes, Simon, even I go out occasionally, preferably in the dark.'

I knew that Marion hadn't been out of the house more than a dozen times in the past three years.

'Where did you go?'

She was angry. 'What is this, an inquisition? Do you think I killed Oliver?'

I looked at her steadily. 'I think it's quite possible. Whether you did or not, you'll certainly be a suspect and Inspector Kennedy will be here asking you questions.'

'We had a cosy chat before breakfast this morning, the inspector and I,' she answered archly. 'I told him I had to go out on personal business and I refused to tell him what that business was. Nor will

I tell you.'

'When did you get back?'

'11.55 p.m. precisely.'

'Good God!'

She smiled, a brittle, self-satisfied little smile which I recognized well. I knew it was hopeless to pursue the subject.

I asked her about the incident on Wednesday that Millie had recounted to me. Again, however, Marion was uncommunicative. I had a feeling that she knew more than Millie about this but she wouldn't say anything.

I turned to go. There seemed no point in continuing the conversation. For the moment at least Marion was in control of herself and had no need of my help.

But she called me back. Already her mood had changed and she was feverishly searching for her cigarettes. I tossed her my packet.

'Will you do something for me, Simon?' she said. 'Will you arrange for the – the funeral? And please, don't let them bring his – him – back here.'

'All right,' I said. I would need to see Kennedy first. I had no idea what the procedure was in circumstances like these.

She seemed to read my thoughts. 'The inspector told me the inquest is to be held tomorrow. Didn't you know? And the funeral can be any time after that. I suppose it had better be Monday.'

'All right,' I said again.

As I went out of the room she was lying back on the bed, puffing at her cigarette, her eyes fixed vacantly on the ceiling.

I went downstairs and back into the kitchen to pick up my coat and hat. Millie offered to make me a cup of tea, but I declined. It was getting late and I wanted to get back to the office. I was putting on my coat when the doorbell rang.

'That'll be another of them reporters,' Millie muttered peevishly.

'Don't bother, Millie. I'll send him packing,' I said.

I went to the front door and opened it. The light was so poor outside that for a moment I didn't recognize the slim figure in the dark raincoat and hood standing on the doorstep.

Then she spoke. 'Hallo, Simon,' she said.

It was Linda.

CHAPTER 5

I was so taken aback I stood there speechless.

Marion's voice floated down to us, 'Who is it, Millie? Who's at the door?'

'Quick,' said Linda urgently, pulling at my arm. 'We must get out of here. I don't want to meet Marion.'

We almost ran down the drive. A red Vauxhall was standing at the gate. I recognized it as Waterston's. We bundled into the car and Linda drove off. 'Where are we going?' I asked.

'Somewhere quiet,' she replied tersely, peering intently through the rain at the road ahead of her. 'Please don't talk to me while I'm driving, Simon.'

I should have remembered. She was not a good driver, or at least she was not a confident or relaxed driver. It was uncomfortable to sit beside her and see the fierce concentration on her face. It always put my nerves on edge, although in fact she was safe enough.

We turned along City Road and then swung left past the hospital. I studied Linda's face. It was thinner, I thought, thinner and harder; but it was a beautiful face. The pallor of her complexion set off the brown eyes with their long dark eyelashes and the richness of her hair. But some indefinable quality had gone, that delightful air of unsophisticated and almost childlike wonderment that had so bewitched me.

Linda stopped the car and switched off the engine. We were in the east end of the town, in a street of drab grey tenement buildings. A trio of school-children were making their way home through the rain, heads down into the wind. Otherwise the street was deserted.

Linda took out her cigarette case – a present from me last Christmas, I remembered – and lit up. Belatedly she offered the case to me. I had never liked these filter tips, but, having given the last of my own cigarettes to Marion, I accepted one.

We smoked for a bit in silence. I could sense that Linda was nervous and tense and was finding it difficult to start talking. To make it easier for her I asked:

'How did you know I was at Marion's?'

'I've been trying to get you all day. The last time I phoned the office I was told by Fergusson that he had dropped you at Marion's after lunch.'

The conversation died almost before it had begun. This time I felt no obligation to take the initiative. I waited.

Linda rolled down the window of the car and threw away her cigarette. As she did so, she pointed to the right at an intersection running off at right angles.

'That's Gribble Street, isn't it?' she remarked.

'Gribble Street? It may be. This is a part of the town I don't really know.' The confusion her question had thrown me into made my answer unconvincing, although it was true.

She showed her impatience. 'For heaven's sake, Simon, don't try to tell me that this is another of your brother's activities you know nothing about. I'm not so gullible as I used to be, you know.'

'I know Oliver had a flat there, yes. But what is that to do with me – or with you, for that matter?'

'I got an invitation from Oliver last night to spend a weekend with him in Gribble Street.'

'Oliver was joking,' I said angrily.

She sighed. 'Yes, I believe he was. Anyway, that wasn't what I wanted to talk to you about. You did know I saw Oliver last night?'

'I was told so by Inspector Kennedy.'

'Ah! yes, Inspector Kennedy. Did you offer to the inspector any explanation of why I should have been visiting your brother?'

'No.'

She gave an almost inaudible sigh. Her voice was more relaxed when she continued:

'All the same, I expect you have guessed why I went to see him?'

'I can only imagine you were trying to do a deal with him.'

'It's not a very nice way of phrasing it. But – yes, I was trying to persuade him to return the papers.'

'You should let your father do his own dirty work.'

'Don't let's quarrel again, Simon,' she said in a weary voice. 'It wouldn't do any good. I want you to say nothing to the inspector about these papers. My father hasn't mentioned them, nor will I, but before I tell my story to the police I must be sure that you won't blurt it all out.'

'But Linda, this isn't just a question of your father's reputation any longer. It's murder. You can't keep this back from the police.'

'This had absolutely nothing to do with the murder. That I swear. I was back in the hotel by half-past ten and my father was already there.'

'The hotel?'

'We stayed overnight at the Station Hotel.'

I was finding the strain almost intolerable. This was the first time I had spoken with Linda alone since that terrible night when a quarrel – our first serious quarrel – suddenly blew up into something so big that our marriage crumbled and disintegrated before our eyes. Here I was sitting beside her in the car, almost in physical contact with her, experiencing once again the subtle fragrance of the perfume she always used. I believe that if I had got one look or word of tenderness from her, I would have promised anything she asked. But her expression was cold and distant, her voice matter-of-fact.

'Don't you realize, Linda,' I said, 'that the police will find these papers anyway and when they find them they are bound to put two and two together? Oliver kept them in his safe, you know. Do you imagine they won't examine the papers in the safe?'

'The police will not find them,' she said softly.

'You mean that Oliver let you have them?' I asked incredulously.

She hesitated. 'Yes,' she said finally.

She was lying. I think that hurt me more than anything, that she should lie to me.

We sat there without speaking for a long time. The implications of what Linda had just said to me were frightening.

'Well, Simon?' she said at last.

I felt tired and dispirited. 'I can't promise, Linda,' I said flatly. 'I'll think about it, but I can't make any promise just now.'

She made one more effort. 'You realize that if this dirty linen gets washed it will ruin you as well as my father?'

'Oh, hell, Linda, that's rubbish and you know it. Or if you don't, it's time you learned. Why do you think your father is so desperate to get these papers back? I don't believe he's ever told you the truth about them. It's a discreditable story, let me tell you. And if you think that—'

'Simon,' she interrupted, 'I'm not prepared to go into all that again. I'm asking you a simple question, and all I want is your answer to it. Are you going to tell the police why I visited Oliver last night?'

'I can't make any promises, Linda,' I repeated.

'Very well.' She started up the engine. 'I'm going to your office to see Inspector Kennedy. Shall I take you there?' She was only just able to control the anger in her voice.

'Yes, please.'

As we drove through the rain-washed streets my mind turned back from the depressing and somehow degrading conversation we had just had, right back to my first meeting with Linda. It was at the office dance again, that same function at which, a year later, there was the ugly scene between Oliver and Fergusson.

She was at my table at the dinner. As I sat down I was relieved to see that my right-hand neighbour was a woman whom I knew and liked, a sensible, jolly woman, the wife of a shipping agent from the office below ours. I barely observed the girl on my left whom I had never seen before.

I talked so long with the shipping agent's wife that I felt guilty as I turned round to do my social duty with my left-hand neighbour. She was gazing apprehensively at her wine-glass which had just been filled.

'I'm wondering whether I should try this,' she remarked.

'Oh, I think so. I'm not an authority on wines but you can be sure that the Chilton won't supply anything cheap or nasty.'

'It's not that,' she said. 'I'm not supposed to drink alcohol. In fact—' she giggled nervously – 'I've hardly ever been at a dinner like this before – or a dance.'

I looked at her with more interest, not yet certain whether she was pulling my leg or not. I saw then that she was not the un-attractive mouse I had imagined. She could be beautiful, I thought, with her brown eyes and creamy skin, if she would do her hair in a more adult style and if someone could advise her about clothes. She was wearing a flowered dress, all frills and flounces at the neck and arms, that did nothing for her slim figure.

She followed my eyes. 'Do you like my frock?'

'It's very unusual,' I replied.

'That means you don't like it.' She looked hurt.

To change the subject I asked, 'And why have you lived this cloistered existence – no dinners, no dances, no alcohol? Is it from choice?'

'Daddy is very strict about these things. You see, my mother died when I was quite small and Daddy has brought me up. He thinks that for a girl a sip of sherry is the first step towards a fate worse than death.'

Her eyes were twinkling as she said this. At least she's got a sense of humour, I thought.

'Who is Daddy, may I ask?'

She pointed to a table on our right. 'That's him over there talking to the woman with red hair.'

'*Waterston?*'

'Yes, Professor Waterston. Do you know him? He's only here tonight because Mr Barnett (that's his partner) persuaded him to come. From all I hear he's a real horror, is Mr Barnett. And I'm only here because I positively begged Daddy to take me.'

'My name's Barnett and I'm a partner of your father. But I think it was my brother you were referring to.'

I was smiling as I spoke but it didn't lessen her discomfiture. She put her hand to her mouth and turned a rich crimson. Then we both began to laugh.

That was how it started. I discovered that she was twenty-two – eleven years younger than myself – and that she had been running her father's house since leaving school. She had not exaggerated the strictness of her father's discipline. Waterston was a pompous little man of singularly unpleasing appearance. He was not more than five feet five inches in height and he had a small birdlike face with a prominent nose and a weak chin. Like many of his physical type he hid his inferiority complex in an aggressive air of self-importance. Not that he hadn't reason to be satisfied with himself. He was an able lawyer and in his own field an acknowledged authority. His book on *Conflict of Laws*, first published thirty years ago, was the first systematized treatment of the subject and had by now run into many editions. That book was the foundation of his reputation and it had led to his appointment to a university chair and, eventually, to a knighthood.

Until I met Linda I had seen little of Waterston, for he rarely came to the office. He was not the sort of man one could readily like, but I had no particular antipathy to him. I now began to take more interest in him and what I saw I liked less and less. He was the worst kind of possessive father. Linda was completely dominated by him; she was not encouraged or even allowed to develop a personality of her own. Not that he was openly unkind to her; he was too subtle for that. But if ever she did anything of which he disapproved, he had the faculty of touching her conscience on the raw by letting her see how hurt and disappointed he was. He didn't really want Linda to grow up at all: he treated her still as if she were a schoolchild.

I knew I would have trouble with Waterston before long, but my first difficulty was with Linda herself. It took all my patience and diplomacy to convince her that her father was not inevitably right in everything he said or thought, and that it was not necessarily sinful to enjoy some of the things other girls enjoyed. Her first visit to the cinema with me was a major adventure for her. I don't know what catastrophe she feared might befall her, but I had endless arguments on the telephone before I could persuade her to come.

Once she made the first break, however, her progress was rapid. Indeed, it was almost frightening how completely she put her trust in me. I became her mentor in everything, even in matters of dress and make-up and hair style. I had to tell her more than once not to set me up as a father-substitute, for she would soon discover my imperfections. On the night I first kissed her, however, the passion with which she returned my kiss was not that of a daughter. It was hard to believe (as she told me herself) that this was the first time she had ever been kissed. In this, as in other things, she was an apt pupil.

We met surreptitiously to begin with. Almost from the night I met her I knew that Linda was the girl I was going to marry, but I didn't want to provoke the inevitable clash with Waterston until Linda was surer of herself. Curiously enough it was not from Waterston that the first salvo came, but from Oliver. He strode into my room one day and said in his usual direct way:

'I hope this affair with Linda Waterston isn't serious.'

How Oliver had heard of it I don't know. He had his sources of information.

'Yes, it's serious,' I replied. 'I mean to marry her.'

'Don't be a fool, Simon, Linda isn't the girl for you. I thought you had more *savoir faire* than to be taken in by that air of dewy-eyed innocence. No girl of twenty-three, is it? is as naïve as all that. Look at her father and you'll see what she's really like.'

'Mind your own bloody business, Oliver,' I shouted at him.

He laughed and went out. But he came back at me again, more than once. It was only when I told him one day of our engagement that he capitulated. He never criticized Linda again.

By this time the battle with Waterston had been joined. I broke the news to him myself and he laughed in my face, so confident was he of his power over Linda. But Linda never wavered, not even when Waterston threatened to drive her out of the house forthwith. She had transferred her affections completely to me and nothing her father said had any effect on her. There was one terrible scene when he came to my flat late one night in a state of hysteria and hurled wild accusations and threats at me.

Then suddenly, and astonishingly, he too gave in. He called me into his room one morning, apologized for his previous behaviour, and said he now gave the wedding his blessing. Not only so, but he announced that as a wedding present he and Oliver together proposed to buy us a house. There was a house on the market which I had mentioned to Oliver might suit Linda and me, although I would have to borrow pretty heavily to buy it. This was the house we were now to get as a gift.

Linda regarded this *volte-face* of her father's as one more manifestation of my power to get things arranged as I wanted them. To me it was charged with suspicion. That Oliver was behind it I was certain. Just what his hold over Waterston was I did not know, but I knew I ought to find out. I had a presentiment that to accept the position without question would not only be morally wrong but would have evil consequences in the future. But the bait was too tempting, the immediate prospect too rosy. I let things slide. Seeing now what had come of it all I bitterly regretted my weakness.

'Are you going to sit there all afternoon?'

Linda's voice brought me back to the present with a start. The car was parked outside the office and Linda was already out on the pavement. I climbed out slowly and joined her and we walked into the building together. She caught her foot on the step of the doorway, stumbled, and would have fallen had I not gripped her arm. I did not release her arm immediately and I felt a tremor go through her; and for a brief moment the mask of hard indifference on her face was down. Then she recovered her composure and said lightly:

'Thanks, Simon.'

We didn't speak again as we went up in the lift. I went off to my own room and I saw Linda walk briskly down the corridor to see Inspector Kennedy, a trim figure, still in her dark raincoat.

CHAPTER 6

Joyce was hammering at her typewriter when I went in. She looked up briefly.

'You might have told me you were going to be out all afternoon,' she said.

I looked at my watch. I was surprised to see it was ten to five.

'Why? Who's been wanting me?'

'A certain Mr Gatherer.'

'Oh! God, yes. I had completely forgotten about him.'

Gatherer was a client of some substance for whom we were negotiating a lease of his house during his forthcoming business trip to South Africa. A lessee had been found, and I had promised to have a draft missive of let ready for Gatherer to see that afternoon. He was not a man who brooked delay.

'I can't possibly manage it today,' I said wearily. 'It's quite a tricky thing. You should see that letter of his with all the conditions he wants put in.'

Joyce smiled at me more kindly. 'This is it I'm at now. When Mr Gatherer called, I dug out the file and got Alan Kelly to draft it. I promised we'd send it round to the old boy tonight.'

I looked at her in admiration. 'The show must go on, eh?'

'Yes, the show must go on.'

'Well, anyway, thanks, Joyce. That's put an idea into my head – but you'd better finish that thing first. How long will you be?'

'Ten minutes if you give me peace.'

While Joyce was finishing her typing I phoned the undertakers.

I intended simply to let them know that I would be calling later in the evening to see about the funeral, but the man who spoke to me was efficiency itself: before I put down the receiver everything had been arranged. I had even given him the list of people to be invited to the private funeral service. I then rang Marion and told her what arrangements had been made.

By this time Joyce was finished and was putting on her coat and hat.

'I'll take that round to Gatherer myself,' she said. 'I didn't like to ask Tom to wait all this time. But you'd better read it over first.'

'If Kelly did it, it will be all right. But sit down for a minute, Joyce. I want to talk to you.'

She sat down and waited. Again I observed how relaxed and composed she looked. No jagged edges about her, I thought.

'You know that Mrs Grassie is having a baby?' I asked.

She smiled. 'Twins, more likely, by the look of her.'

Mrs Grassie was the third secretary I had had since Joyce transferred to Oliver. None of them had been satisfactory, Mrs Grassie least of all.

'She's off just now, taking a week in bed on her doctor's orders, so she says. I doubt if she'll be back, and anyway it can't be for long. What I wanted to ask you, Joyce, is – would you come back and work for me again?'

She took her time before she answered. 'I was asked the same question by Mr Fergusson a couple of hours ago. But – yes, I think I would like to work for you again, Simon—'

'Fine. Well, let's go out for a drink to celebrate. I could be doing with one.'

'—But on one condition. I will be secretary to you but there our relationship ends. I will not go out for a drink with you.'

'Good heavens, Joyce! Do you think I'm planning to seduce you? All I wanted was to relax over a pint of beer.'

'No. We'll start as we mean to go on, Simon.'

This seemed an unreasonable compunction and I was irritated.

'You didn't have these delicate scruples when you worked with Oliver,' I said.

'I could cope with your brother. I'm not certain that I'm equal to coping with you,' she replied calmly.

There was an uncomfortable pause and then suddenly Joyce grinned mischievously and added:

'As a matter of fact, one time when Oliver invited me for a drink, he *did* try to seduce me.'

I was surprised to feel a pang of jealousy.

'Tell me about it,' I said, trying to keep my voice unconcerned.

'Well, he took me out for dinner once or twice and to the cinema occasionally. I suppose I shouldn't have gone, but – well, I knew about his home life and I was sorry for him. And, frankly, I enjoyed it. He was good company. A beautiful dancer, too . . .'

She sighed, her mind reliving the past. Then she continued:

'One night we were at a play in the town hall. You remember the local dramatic society's performance of *The Cherry Orchard*? Excruciating, wasn't it? Far too ambitious. Anyway, on our way home, Oliver was in wonderful form, impersonating some of the ham performances we had just seen. I was laughing so much that it wasn't till the car stopped that I realized we were way off course. We were in a street somewhere in the east end—'

'Gribble Street,' I interrupted.

Her eyes widened. 'You know about it? Yes, I think it was Gribble Street. Oliver asked me to go in for a drink. I'm not a child, Simon: I knew what this meant. But I went in. I was intrigued and I wanted to see the inside of the place. I knew I could handle Oliver.

'It's quite a place – but perhaps you've seen it?'

'No,' I said. 'Go on.'

'It's on the ground floor of a four-storeyed tenement. Not very romantic from the outside, but snug inside, very snug. Oliver had obviously put out some money on furnishing it. There were just two rooms and a bathroom. I never saw the kitchen properly, but Oliver assured me it was well-appointed. The other room was a bed-sitting-room, with emphasis on the bed.

'I got my drink and almost at once Oliver started to make overtures to me. I stopped him firmly and as soon as he saw I wasn't just being coy he desisted without, so far as I could see, any embarrassment or rancour. He was a remarkable man in some ways, your brother.

'We sat and talked till late that night. He spoke to me quite frankly about the set-up but said he relied on me not to let it go any further. He had taken elaborate precautions to keep it secret – of course a cloak and dagger intrigue like that was something after his own heart. He rented the flat under an assumed name – Smith or Jones or something like that. And he never went there except after dark. So he told me, anyway: how he managed it in the summer I don't know.

'You know how he used to be away every second weekend in the city to attend board meetings? He was supposed to have one meeting on the Friday afternoon and another on the Saturday and he was away from midday Friday until Sunday morning. Well, he always went to the Cameron and Forsyth meeting on the Friday, but the Saturday meeting was entirely fictitious.'

This I knew and I had been pretty sure that Oliver was having an affair with some woman; but I had always assumed it was in the city. It seemed crazy – and yet somehow characteristic of Oliver – that he should bring her back to his home town where the risk of being discovered was so much greater.

Joyce went on, 'Oliver used to bring his girl (who didn't, so he told me, even know his real name) to the flat late on the Friday night and they stayed until Oliver drove her back to the city in the early hours of Sunday. It wasn't always the same girl, of course: I gather there was quite a succession of them. In fact I think Oliver was getting a bit tired of the whole business and was contemplating a more permanent relationship. That's why he invited me there that night. And, after I let him down, I believe that he did find someone.'

'Who?' I asked.

'I don't know,' said Joyce slowly. 'He became very reticent about the whole subject and I suspect it must have been someone known to me. But I may be quite wrong. Anyway the fortnightly weekends at the flat continued – I do know that. I don't think he went there much at other times. You can't be secretary to someone like Oliver without finding out a good deal about his movements, even out of office hours.'

'Do you think this had something to do with his murder?'

'Well, if Marion ever learned of what was going on, it's difficult to guess what her reaction would be. But, frankly, I can't see her as a murderess. She hasn't the guts.'

Remembering Marion's tirade of hate earlier in the day, I wasn't so sure.

Joyce stood up. 'I really must go, Simon,' she said. 'Gatherer will be waiting. I've cancelled your appointments for tomorrow morning, by the way. You'll have to be at the inquest. It's at ten-thirty in the court-house. I gather they are just taking formal evidence tomorrow and they're going to ask for an adjournment. There has been a great flap on here all afternoon. Some startling new evidence has turned up and the CID is being called in. I got all this from a young bobby who should have kept his mouth shut. So don't let Inspector Kennedy see that you know.'

'I've no intention of seeing Kennedy again tonight.'

'I'm afraid you'll have to. You've still to read over your statement and sign it. He asked me specially not to let you go until you had seen him.'

'Oh, lord! I wonder if he's free now?'

We were out in the corridor by this time and, as if in answer to my question, Oliver's door opened and Linda came out. I had thought she was gone long since. Her face was ashen and she looked desperately tired. She walked unseeingly past us along the corridor to the exit. I called out to her but she didn't answer, didn't even look up.

'Poor Linda,' I muttered, more to myself than to Joyce. Joyce stood for a moment without saying anything. Then she turned and walked slowly away.

I went in to see Inspector Kennedy.

CHAPTER 7

Joyce was right. The inquest was little more than a formality and lasted less than an hour. I was the first witness and I described, as concisely as I could, the events leading up to the discovery of Oliver's body. The coroner, a dapper little man and himself a prominent solicitor in the county, asked me a few questions about the revolver which had been found beside the body. It was a Webley automatic and was similar to the one which Oliver had brought home as a trophy from the war. Where he got it I don't know. I couldn't swear, however, that it was the same gun. At one time Oliver had kept it in a drawer in his desk and he used to show it with some pride to his visitors. But that was years ago and I hadn't seen it for a long time. When asked if Oliver had a licence for the gun I had to say that I didn't know but that I suspected not. The coroner pursed his lips but refrained from comment.

When I had finished my evidence I found that the only seat left for me was beside Waterston, on whose other side sat Linda. Waterston gave me a curt nod; Linda stared straight ahead and ignored me.

We now got the medical evidence from the police surgeon. Oliver had died from a bullet wound. The bullet had entered his chest from the front and to the left and had travelled on a slightly downward path, piercing both heart and left lung and lodging in the spine. Death had been instantaneous and had occurred some time between nine-thirty and eleven-thirty p.m. In reply to a question from a member of the jury the witness said that the angle of entry of the bullet made it improbable that the wound had been self-inflicted, especially since he understood that Oliver had been left-handed. At this point I was recalled to testify to Oliver's left-handedness.

I was surprised to hear Linda called next, until I remembered that she was the last person known to have seen Oliver alive. The black suit and black hat that she wore emphasized the pallor of her face. She seemed composed, however, and gave her evidence in a low, but firm monotone. She said that she had called to see Oliver by appointment on a matter of private business. (A woman member of the jury half rose in her chair and embarked on a question; but she was quelled by an angry frown from the coroner and subsided.) Oliver had been dictating on the dictaphone when she arrived, Linda continued, but had immediately switched it off. He had seemed much as usual and after their business was concluded they had chatted for some time and smoked a couple of cigarettes. Latterly, however, Oliver had shown some signs of restlessness and had glanced surreptitiously at his watch once or twice. Taking the hint, Linda had left – about nine-forty-five, she thought it would be. Her appointment had been for eight-thirty, but because of the fog, she hadn't got there till nearly nine o'clock. Her father had driven her to the office in his car but she had walked back to the Station Hotel, where she was staying the night. She reached the hotel about ten-twenty-five.

'Thank you, Mrs Barnett,' said the coroner swiftly, 'That will be all.' Linda stepped down.

The woman juror again showed signs of wanting to ask a question, but thought better of it. I was sure that she was longing to know the nature of Linda's business with Oliver and that the coroner, no doubt on advice, was determined not to give her the opportunity.

While Linda was speaking I was conscious of Waterston beside me fidgeting in his chair and crossing and uncrossing his legs. Eventually I looked round at him. He was staring fixedly at Linda, his hands tightly clenched and beads of perspiration on his brow. My God, I thought, the little man's in a panic. Is it his precious reputation still or has he something worse on his conscience now? When Linda rejoined him his body went limp and his head fell forward as if he were asleep.

Inspector Kennedy was the last witness and his evidence was brief. He told of the telephone call he had got from me and described the scene that the police had found on their arrival. The police were pursuing certain inquiries, he went on, and he would like to request an adjournment of the inquest so that fuller evidence could be gathered.

'Granted,' said the coroner without hesitation and rose to his feet. 'Adjourned until this day fortnight at 10.30 a.m.' He was out of the room before the rest of us grasped what was happening.

Linda took her father's arm and pushed her way through the crowd. By the time I got out to the street they were already climbing into Waterston's car. The doors were slammed and the door drove off, with Linda at the wheel and her father slumped beside her in the front seat. I gazed after it until it turned the corner and disappeared from sight.

'Still pining, Simon?'

I swung round. It was Marion. She must have been at the inquest, although I hadn't seen her there. Dressed in conventional widow's black and with a veil half obscuring her face, she looked mysterious and attractive. She was conscious of it too and was more cheerful than I had known her for a long time.

'I want to ask you a question, Simon.'

'Well, get into my car. Here's the Press descending on us.'

I didn't use the car much during the week except when I had to go into the city, but I had felt too tired or too lazy that morning to walk the half-mile to the court-house. It was a 1958 Ford Anglia. Oliver had never approved of it, believing as he did that it was important to make a show of prosperity by running a large car (his own was a Wolseley). But the Ford suited my purposes admirably.

We got into the car and I drove off. Marion snuggled up close to me and leant her head on my shoulder. I swore under my breath. Of all Marion's moods this was the one which most disgusted and embarrassed me, especially as I had never learned the best way to deal with it. If I brushed her off too abruptly it was liable to lead to one of her nervous tantrums. On the other hand the slightest encouragement, or even passive acquiescence, was a worse blunder, as I knew from past experience.

'What was the question you wanted to ask me, Marion?' I said, in as casual a voice as I could achieve.

Fortunately she responded. She took her head off my shoulder and slowly straightened. She must genuinely want to know something, I thought.

'Who is Mrs Cargill?' was the question.

'Mrs Cargill?' For a moment the name didn't register with me and then I remembered. 'She's the widow of Thomas Cargill, the shipowner. At least I suppose that's the Mrs Cargill you mean. She's the only one I know of.'

'Yes,' said Marion. 'I've heard of her, but surely she's old. Millie said it was a young woman's voice on the phone and I thought . . .' Her voice trailed off into silence.

'Marion, what is all this about?'

'Well, you remember I told you that Oliver got a phone call just before he went back to the office on Thursday night. It was Millie who answered the phone and the woman who spoke said she was Mrs Cargill and asked to speak to Oliver. And it was immediately after he got that call that Oliver came up and told me he wouldn't be home till late. I thought . . .' Again she didn't complete the sentence.

We had reached Oliver's house by now and I stopped the car outside the gate. But I made no move to get out. My mind was racing furiously, trying to recall every detail of an incident that had occurred a few days before.

Oliver had come into my room to discuss something with me and while he was there my telephone rang. When I picked up the receiver I heard a woman's voice, low-pitched and with an attractive huskiness, say, 'Is that Mr Oliver Barnett?'

'It's for you, Oliver,' I said, passing over the phone. The girl on our exchange must have known that Oliver was in my room and had switched the call through to my extension.

While Oliver was speaking, I was idly speculating about that voice. I was sure I had heard it somewhere before but I couldn't place it.

When Oliver put down the phone, he was rubbing his hands in glee.

'Do you know who that was?' he said. 'Mrs Thomas Cargill. The Cargill Shipping Company, you know. And do you know what she wants to see me about? She wants me to draw up a new will for her.'

'But Oliver, you can't,' I protested. 'Henderson is her solicitor, always has been. There will be a frightful stink about breach of professional etiquette if you entice her away.'

'Who said anything about enticing her away? She can change

her solicitor if she wants to, surely. I won't do anything to influence her, you can depend on me for that.'

I doubted it. 'Well, anyway,' I said, 'you'll have to tread pretty warily in this. When are you seeing her?'

'She's coming to the office to see me at ten o'clock on Friday night.'

'Ten o'clock at night? There's something fishy about this, Oliver.'

'Well, you see, her brood are gathered round her, I understand, and she doesn't want them to get any inkling of what she's up to. She goes out to see a friend every Friday evening and she wants to call in and see me on the way home.'

It still sounded extraordinary to me and I wasn't happy about it but there was no damping Oliver's enthusiasm. It wasn't so much the prospect of acquiring as a client the richest woman in town that appealed to him as the thought that he would be putting one over Henderson, his great rival. He made no attempt to keep it dark: everyone in the office heard about it.

The whole incident had slipped from my mind after Oliver's murder. After all, Oliver had been killed on the Thursday night and his appointment with Mrs Cargill had been arranged for the Friday. I had no reason to connect them. But now Marion had thrown a new light on it. It sounded as if Mrs Cargill had phoned to bring the appointment forward by twenty-four hours. And was it really Mrs Cargill? That husky voice was still ringing in my head. Where had I heard it before?

Marion hadn't told the inspector about the telephone call and didn't know whether Millie had. I knew this was something Kennedy ought to hear about at once and so, declining Marion's pressing invitation to stay for lunch, I drove off to find him. Knowing that the police had now vacated their temporary headquarters in our office, I went straight to the police station. Kennedy wasn't in, but I left a message for him to phone me as soon as possible.

CHAPTER 8

That was the longest weekend I can remember. On the Saturday afternoon I stretched out on a sofa trying to make up on my sleep, but my brain was too active and restless. Eventually I got up and switched on the radio and endured ten minutes of a football commentary before turning it off again. I spent the rest of the afternoon doing some minor repairs about the house; not very successfully, for I am no handyman, but it did keep me from brooding for an hour or two. The evening was even more frustrating. When I tried to settle to some work I had brought home with me I found I couldn't concentrate. My thoughts kept sheering off to fruitless speculation about the murder of Oliver. I think I missed Linda that night more than I ever had before. I needed someone to talk to, someone to help me get things in proper perspective. The feeling was strong in me that somewhere in the jumble of half-formed impressions and recollections that were chasing each other through my head there was a fact or facts of significance. But try as I might, they eluded me.

Inspector Kennedy did not phone me on the Saturday, nor did I hear from him on the Sunday morning. Sunday was a typically boisterous, gusty April day, with sunny periods in between heavy showers. After lunch (my usual Sunday lunch these days of tinned soup followed by a couple of boiled eggs), in desperation for something to occupy myself with, I got out a spade and started turning over the vegetable plot in the back garden. It should have been done weeks before but since Linda had left me I had lost interest in the garden as in other things.

I hadn't dug more than a couple of rows when I heard the front-door bell ringing. When I went through the house and opened the door I found two strangers on the doorstep, both tall men, the younger one exceptionally so, and wearing, as far as I could see, identical light raincoats and soft hats. The older man introduced himself as Detective-Superintendent Garland from Scotland Yard and his companion as Detective-Sergeant Baker. I took their hats and coats and showed them into the sitting-room.

As they sat down I studied my visitors more closely. Superintendent Garland was a man who would have stood out in any company. He carried himself well and with an air of easy authority. His features were regular and handsome and were saved from conventionality by the depth of his brow and the resolution and intelligence of his eyes. His companion was very much younger – still in his twenties, I estimated – and with his height and thinness looked a little ungainly. But he too had a certain indefinable distinction about him, and even before he opened his mouth, I guessed – rightly – that he was a product of a public school. Both were dressed in sober, but expensive, lounge suits and I was acutely conscious of the grubbiness of my gardening flannels and pullover.

Superintendent Garland seemed in no hurry to get down to business. He discomfited me at once by discussing gardening, a subject of which he clearly had expert knowledge. He appeared to assume that I was a fellow enthusiast and tactfully hid his surprise as my ignorance was revealed. Whether or not this was a deliberate technique, its effect was certainly to give him the initial advantage and to put me on the defensive.

They refused the cigarettes I offered them. Garland, however, took out a pipe and filled it unhurriedly. Only when he had his pipe going to his satisfaction did he begin.

'The local police have asked the CID to assist them in this case, Mr Barnett. I know you have already made a very full statement to Inspector Kennedy which I have of course read. Sergeant Baker and I have spent most of the last twenty-four hours going over with the inspector all the statements that have been lodged. But I'm sure that you won't mind filling in a few details for me even if it does mean a certain amount of repetition.'

Since he seemed to expect an answer I said 'Of course not,' and waited.

'Good. Well, now, what I always like to do is to get my characters into focus before I get bogged down in a morass of detail. Would you try to tell me all you can about your brother – give me his *curriculum vitae*, as it were; more than that, his character, his interests. What made him tick, in other words.'

I was tempted to say that it would be more to the point if I could tell him what made Oliver stop ticking, but I stifled the cheap retort.

I did what I could, but it was impossible to convey in mere words the extraordinary vitality and force of personality that Oliver possessed. From his earliest days it was the same. 'He has an agile mind and boundless energy but lacks application,' was a typical comment in his school reports. He was not the sort of boy that school masters like as a rule, for, although intelligent, he was not notably studious and, although athletically gifted, he had little interest in games or in any organized activity that had not been organized by himself. Despite all that he was a natural leader and since his interests tended to conflict with the ordained pattern he was regarded by his teachers as a pernicious influence on his fellows.

All the same he did creditably enough at school and in his last year surprised everyone by putting on a spurt and winning an open exhibition to Balliol. I think nothing ever pleased my father more than this success of Oliver's. However, he didn't sustain the effort; the temptations of Oxford were too great for him. Not that he ever got into serious trouble, apart from one occasion when he was nearly sent down for organizing an undergraduate prank that went a little too far. But he just didn't do any work.

For Oliver, as for some others of his generation, the war proved a steadying influence. It came at the end of his second year at Balliol, when he was twenty. He enlisted at once in the ranks but very soon got his commission. The Army in war time brought out the best in Oliver, for here at last he found a niche where his exuberance and love of adventure were not only tolerated but were an asset to him. When he came out in 1945 he held the rank of Lieutenant-Colonel and he had an MC and a DSO to his name.

He seemed much the same when he returned; handsome, debonair and inclined to be domineering. But in one respect he was changed: he had acquired a sense of responsibility and he was prepared to settle down to do some work. He didn't go back to Oxford but elected instead to read law at the red-brick university in the city. He was in his last year there when I returned from National Service in 1947 and joined him at the university. Oliver got a very creditable first and then completed his apprenticeship in our father's office, where I followed him two years later. We both stayed on in the office as Father was obviously failing and would soon have to retire.

As soon as his father did retire, Oliver let his latent organizational talents loose. The office itself was reconstructed, modernized and extended. He threw himself into the task of attracting clients, especially wealthy clients, and even if some people might raise an eyebrow at his methods, he did keep within the law and he did achieve results. He also strengthened our reputation and standing by bringing into partnership first Waterston and then Fergusson.

As a lawyer Oliver was brilliant but erratic. Unless something specially interested him he hadn't the patience for long, slogging work; but on the other hand he had occasional flashes of real inspiration, as when he discovered a loophole in the income tax laws that everyone else had missed. The case went to the House of Lords and was won by his client, and amending legislation had to be rushed through. This was a great fillip to our firm and a huge delight to Oliver.

He relied a great deal on others for keeping him right on points which he was too lazy to check for himself. Especially he relied on me. He treated me with the tolerant affection due to a younger brother. I was in point of fact eight years younger and I had been schooled from birth to being junior partner. Realization had only come to me gradually in recent years that I was more mature than him and in some ways the better lawyer. I made no attempt to change our relationship, however, and still came at his bidding and helped him with his difficulties whenever, as happened half a dozen times a day (and often enough in the evening too), he lifted his telephone and summoned me. The truth was, I liked Oliver and had no wish to hurt him.

Suddenly realizing I had been talking about Oliver for rather a long time, I stopped abruptly.

Superintendent Garland echoed the phrase I had just used, 'You like your brother and you had no wish to hurt him. Would it surprise you to learn, Mr Barnett, that your brother was a blackmailer?'

Linda had been wrong, then. The police *had* found those papers. It was all I could do to keep my voice steady as I answered:

'No, it doesn't surprise me. I knew about it. But you must admit there are extenuating factors. Indeed, Oliver believed he was morally justified in doing what he did.'

'Well, go on. I'll be interested to hear your definition of morally justifiable blackmail. But tell me first how you found out about it.'

'I had always had my suspicions, of course. I wondered why Waterston had joined a parochial firm like ours and how Oliver had such a remarkable power over him. He could persuade Waterston to do almost anything he asked. I also wondered why Oliver made such a fetish of his office safe. As a rule he was careless about papers and would leave confidential documents lying openly on his desk. But that safe was kept religiously locked and no one but Oliver ever saw inside it, not even his secretary. His explanation was that it contained his files and papers dealing with his business interests outside the office. It's true enough that he had been spreading his wings a bit in recent years and held directorships in quite a number of businesses both here and in the city. But why these papers should have been so confidential I couldn't understand.

'The safe was an old one which had been used by my father. It had a combination lock of which, so far as I'm aware, only Oliver knew the combination. But it had one defect. Although it was self-locking when you closed it, it required a good hard push. I think there was rust in the mechanism or something. Anyway, one day when I went in to see Oliver the safe was open and he was putting some papers into it. He pushed it shut. I noticed, but he didn't, that the door was left ever so slightly ajar.

'That was my opportunity. I didn't like spying on my brother but I had to find out. I waited until I heard Oliver go out of his room. Then I nipped in and hastily raked through the papers in the safe. I very soon found the document involving Waterston.'

As I spoke I was reliving the scene in my mind. I barely noticed the startled glance which passed from Garland to Baker and its significance did not impinge on my conscious mind until later. And then it was too late.

I went on with my story. On opening the safe I had expected to find evidence of some discreditable episode in Waterston's past, but what I did find astonished and perplexed me. There was a single sheet of yellowing notepaper bearing the printed heading of the Faculty of Law of the neighbouring university and typed on it was a letter dated 11th October, 1926, in these terms, 'I am sorry to have been so long in dealing with Mr Barnett's manual on Private International Law, which I now return. He makes some interesting points but I am afraid his theories are too fanciful and far too remote from the law as it actually is. I strongly advise against publication.' The letter was signed 'Charles B Waterston'. Underneath the letter was a thick sheaf of manuscript pages. Although the writing was faded and indistinct I had no difficulty in recognizing the spidery hand of my father. It all meant nothing to me.

I was still studying the papers when Oliver came back into his room. I told him what I had done and showed him what I had found, and demanded an explanation. He flew into a rage and snatched the papers back from me. I stood my ground and repeated my question. He was always one to recognize when he was beaten and to cut his losses; and eventually he calmed down and told me the story.

In his younger days my father had had leanings towards the

academic life and for a number of years had combined a part-time assistant lectureship in the university with private practice. He used to tell Oliver and me that he had once written a legal textbook which had not been accepted for publication. He had always been reticent about the details and we had tended to assume it was nothing more than a short monograph.

However, when Oliver was clearing out my father's papers after his death he came across in the safe – that same safe – a dog-eared manuscript of many pages entitled 'Private International Law'. Oliver skimmed through it at first, but soon began to read it more carefully and with growing interest; for it was good, extremely good. He came to the conclusion that it had been rejected for publication because it was modelled too closely on Waterston's famous book on the same subject. There was a marked similarity of treatment and many of the cases cited were identical.

Then Oliver got a shock. Clipped to the manuscript at the back was a rejection slip from a well-known firm of publishers of legal works and the date on it was October, 1926. Waterston's *magnum opus* hadn't appeared until 1928.

Oliver was intrigued now and he made a close comparison of the manuscript with Waterston's book. While there were considerable differences in style and in treatment of detail, the similarities were too striking to be coincidental. He even came across a palpable error of fact in the manuscript which was faithfully reproduced in the book. He then went to see a friend of his who worked in the publishing firm and asked if they still had records of the affair after all these years. He was lucky. His friend was able to tell him that the manuscript had been received in December, 1925, and had been passed to 'some chap Waterston, a lecturer in the university' as reader; and he was able to produce Waterston's letter, dated nine months later, recommending rejection. Oliver somehow managed to persuade his friend to part with the original letter.

'That's the story, Simon,' said Oliver. 'Waterston knew Father and knew the sort of man he was defrauding. I doubt if Father suspected what had happened; and if he did, he wouldn't do anything about it. He was far too easy-going and unambitious. So Waterston went on from strength to strength. He got the chair, he got his rich wife, he got his knighthood. But, by God, he's paid for it this last year or two. He knows that I could ruin him if I informed the Law Society of what I know.'

'How much has he paid, Oliver?' I asked.

' So far about £4,000 to each of us.'

'To each of us?'

'Well, he put £2,000 towards your house, didn't he? And I put £2,000, which you can chalk up against his payments to me. And I've had another £4,000 or so besides. I've always intended we should share equally in this. We are both his victims.'

I was horrified. I couldn't put all the blame on Oliver, for I was morally implicated too. I had suspected that the gift of the house from Waterston and Oliver was in some way tainted but I had accepted it all the same.

I tried to persuade Oliver that this blackmail must stop, that what he was doing was wrong, no matter how outrageously Waterston had acted in the past. But it was hopeless. Oliver's ethical code and mine were poles apart: his attitude to the mulcting of Waterston's ill-gotten gains was almost that of a religious crusader. Besides, he knew that I would never turn informer against him.

When I told Oliver that I was having no part in this and that I wouldn't rest until I had returned all the money that had been put up for my house, both his contribution and Waterston's, Oliver laughed and said, 'What about Linda? Are you going to tell her this pretty story about her father and her brother-in-law – and her husband for that matter?'

Oliver's attitude to Linda was always equivocal. On the surface they appeared to get on well enough, but I sometimes suspected that he was ill at ease in her company, and not only because she was Waterston's daughter. He was shrewd enough at reading her character, however, to understand that it would be no easy matter for me to explain this business to her without losing some of the respect, the hero-worship almost, that she had for me.

As I recounted this story I became so engrossed in it that I almost forgot who it was I was telling it to. Now the memories became too painful for me to continue and I fell silent.

Eventually Superintendent Garland interposed a question.

'Did you repay the money to Waterston?' he asked quietly.

'Yes. I had to take out a mortgage on my house to do it, though, and it was too late anyway.'

'Too late?'

'I had already lost my wife,' I said shortly.

He looked at me thoughtfully for a moment, but didn't pursue the subject. Instead he said:

'When you went through your brother's safe that day did you find anything else beside the Waterston papers?'

'There was a lot of stuff about the companies Oliver had an interest in – agenda, minutes, balance sheets and whatnot. I didn't look at it very closely.'

'Then you didn't find these?' The superintendent fished in his inside pocket and produced an envelope, which he handed to me. I could see that it contained photographic negatives, and I was taking them out when Sergeant Baker broke in. It was the first time he had spoken.

'We've had prints made of these, sir. I think you would find it easier to look at them.'

He in his turn took an envelope from his pocket and passed it over to me. He did it a little awkwardly and the envelope fell on the floor, spilling out some of its contents, which I saw were postcard-size photographs.

As I stooped to pick them up I saw what they were and recoiled in shock.

'Have you ever seen these before, Mr Barnett?' asked Garland, who had been eyeing me closely.

'No. Where did you get them?'

'In an envelope in your brother's safe marked "Messrs Cameron and Forsyth: Balance Sheet, 1960". Take a good look at them. You might be able to identify some of the people.'

There were about two dozen of them altogether. Anyone who practises law gets involved from time to time in unsavoury cases and is not easily shocked. But the obscenity of these photographs made me almost physically sick. I took my time before I spoke again. I was thinking hard.

'There must be some mistake here, Superintendent,' I said slowly. 'Oliver was not that type of man at all. He wasn't interested in pornography.'

'Perhaps not. But I don't think you quite take the point. These aren't professionally posed photographs, you know. Look at that one again. Do you recognize anyone there?'

I looked closely at the print he was pointing to. I saw at once that the man in it was one of our local aldermen, a pillar of respectability.

'Yes,' said Garland, 'that's Stroud. And we've already identified one or two others, although they are not from Brickfield. Now do you see what your brother was up to?'

'If you are suggesting, Superintendent, that Oliver was black-mailing these people, then you are making a terrible mistake.'

'You've told me yourself, Mr Barnett, that your brother was blackmailing his partner. Why should he stop there? Incidentally, we knew nothing about this Waterston business. The papers you spoke about were not in the safe.'

The telephone rang. I went out to the hall to answer it. It was Inspector Kennedy asking for the superintendent. Garland was away for quite some time, and while he was out I tried desperately to think of some rational explanation of what I had just heard. But I couldn't.

Garland looked pleased with himself when he returned. He resumed where he had left off.

'We are not merely guessing that your brother was blackmailing some of these people. We know he was. Stroud for one. And another man in the city has admitted it. The others we've traced so far say they have had no demands from him, and they are probably speaking the truth. He would have to pick his victims carefully.'

'How did he do it?' I asked dully.

'The machinery seems to have been rather elaborate. The victims didn't actually know who was blackmailing them. They got an unsigned letter enclosing a print of the relevant photograph and telling them to send a certain sum in cash (£10 in Stroud's case) each month to a Mr C. V. Jones, care of a Mr James Robertson at an address in the city. The threat was that if they didn't, the photograph would be sent to the wife or to the mayor or to the employer or to whatever person the victim would least like his indiscretions to become known to.'

The superintendent's pipe had gone out. He made a great show of relighting it, but all the time I was conscious that his eyes were on me. He was still wondering how much of this was known to me.

'Did you know that your brother rented a flat in this town under an assumed name?'

'Yes. In Gribble Street. I heard about it only on Friday.'

'Really? Then you may not know that he took it under the name of C. V. Jones?'

I was past feeling any surprise. I merely shook my head. The superintendent turned to another point.

'This accommodation address – James Robertson – interested us. Robertson is well known to the police in the city, although he has never actually been in trouble. He skates on the fringes of the law. He has a pawnbroker's business and has been suspected more than once of reset, but nothing has ever been pinned on him.

'I asked Inspector Kennedy to go over to the city today to interview Robertson. That was the inspector phoning his report a few minutes ago. He had some interesting things to say.

'Robertson got a letter a few months ago from someone who signed himself C. V. Jones. A five-pound note was enclosed. The writer said that a number of letters would arrive for him at Robertson's address from time to time. All that Robertson was required to do was to forward these in a bunch on the first Monday of each month to Jones at the Gribble Street address. Great stress was laid on the date: nothing was to be posted except on the first Monday of the month. If Robertson did this satisfactorily, he could expect further remittances of £5 every quarter.

'Well, Mr C. V. Jones, or Mr Oliver Barnett if you prefer it, chose his man well. Robertson asked no questions about this extraordinary transaction but did as he was told.'

Garland hesitated momentarily before he continued. Then he said, 'Robertson told Inspector Kennedy something else. I'm not sure that I ought to disclose it to you but I'm going to all the same, for I think you may be able to help. When you were looking at these photographs I noticed you studied one of them – number eighteen – for a long time before you passed on. Did you recognize someone in that photograph? Look at it again, please.'

He picked it out and handed it to me.

While I was still gazing at it and before I had made up my mind what to say, Garland went on:

'Don't say anything yet. Let me tell you Robertson's story first. About a fortnight ago a young woman called at his shop and asked him who C. V. Jones was and where she could find him. When he refused to tell her she pulled a gun on him. According to Robertson she had a wild look in her eye and he decided to take no chances. The plain truth is that, like most of his type, Robertson is yellow. Anyway, the upshot was that he gave her the Gribble Street address and she went away. He couldn't, of course, give her Jones's real name because he didn't know it.

'As you would expect, Robertson didn't go to the police. He didn't do anything, as a matter of fact, for more than a week. But eventually – last Tuesday, it was – whether out of a belated interest in his employer's welfare or whether he thought the incident might be turned to his own advantage, he wrote to Jones and told him what had happened. He also, Kennedy gathered, made it quite clear in the letter that he had a good idea of what Jones was up to and hinted pretty broadly that £5 a quarter was inadequate remuneration. That letter was not found by the police at the Gribble Street flat; so presumably your brother got it.

'Inspector Kennedy had a set of these photographs with him this afternoon and he showed them to Robertson. Although Robertson wasn't absolutely positive in his identification, he thought the woman in number eighteen was the person who visited him. Now you can see why it is so important that we should identify her. Can you help us?'

'The face looks familiar, Superintendent, but I can't place it,' I said, with as much nonchalance as I could muster. I was appalled to find myself lying to the superintendent, especially as I was none too sure of my motives for doing so. It could hardly be to protect a girl whom I hadn't seen for five years or more.

Garland exchanged a glance with the sergeant. The superintendent was no fool and I think he knew I was holding back information. But before he could press me, I hurried on to tell him the story about Oliver's appointment with Mrs Cargill, leaving out only the fact that her voice had seemed familiar to me. I knew now whose voice that was, and it was not Mrs Cargill's.

'Now, that's interesting,' said Garland. 'We're really beginning to get somewhere. It's just a pity you can't identify that woman for us. It looks as if she was "Mrs Cargill". Still, it shouldn't take us long to find her.'

He stood up. 'There were one or two other points I wanted to ask you about, Mr Barnett,' he said, 'but they'll have to wait for another occasion. Come on, Baker, we've got work to do.'

'Before you go, Superintendent,' I said, 'would you tell me one thing?'

'Yes?'

'Where were these photographs taken and how did Oliver manage to get hold of them?'

'That's two questions, not one. I thought you would have guessed the answer to the first. Do you remember the Merriman case? Even I, living in London, read about it. It must have been a nine days' wonder up in these parts.'

I remembered the case vividly now. It had indeed been a *cause célèbre* and it had rocked the city to its foundations. Merriman had been manager of a night club in the city, a reputable establishment in a respectable neighbourhood. The food and wines were excellent, there was a good band and a good floor for dancing, and the floor show was always entertaining and in unexceptionable taste. It was an expensive place but it was well patronized and by the right sort of customer. 'Superior' and 'exclusive' were the adjectives often applied to it. What ninety per cent of the habitués didn't know was that there was an even more exclusive club in the back premises. It wasn't simply a brothel, although that would have been sensation enough. The newspaper reports of the trial referred obliquely to 'obscene orgies'; and those who were present in court and heard the evidence were able to say that this was no journalistic exaggeration.

Merriman himself got five years, and some of his associates got lesser sentences. There was a rumour that Merriman was no more than a pawn in the game and that someone higher up had directed it and taken most of the profits. But the rumour had never been substantiated and Merriman himself had made no such allegation.

'That's where these photographs were taken,' said the superintendent. 'If you look closely at one or two of them you can recognize bits of the background. As for your second question, do you know who owned the Polygon Night Club?'

'I seem to remember it was one of a group of restaurants and small hotels.'

'Precisely. Northern Hotels Ltd. And your brother had a seat on the board of that company. Oh! I'm not suggesting that that explains how he acquired these photographs. There was no breath of suspicion that any of the directors knew what was going on at the Polygon. But it is a connexion at least, however tenuous.'

I showed them to the door. As they were going out I called Garland back again. He looked impatient this time and glanced ostentatiously at his watch.

'I won't keep you a minute,' I said. 'I just want to say one thing. You started off this afternoon by saying that you like to begin a case by getting your characters into focus. I have known Oliver all my life, you have not. The picture you have just drawn of him is not my brother as I knew him. Either I am more of a fool than I thought or there is some flaw in your evidence.'

'Yes,' said the superintendent, smiling as he turned away. 'I think I would accept that. Good day.'

CHAPTER 9

I stood at the door and watched the two detectives walk briskly down the path to the gate. Then I turned and went slowly back into the house.

What had possessed me to withhold Sheila's name from them? It couldn't do any good. She was too well known to too many people and it could only be a matter of time before they got on to her. It had been an instinctive reaction, springing, I think, from my distrust of the line the police inquiries were taking. The evidence that Oliver had been a blackmailer on a large scale was formidable and seemed to admit of no other interpretation. While Garland was making his case I had been convinced, or almost convinced; and yet a nagging doubt remained. It wasn't in character. Also I found it hard to accept Sheila in the role of murderess, which seemed to be the inevitable inference from the facts as they had been presented. I wanted time to think and I had therefore done the only thing I could to slow up the wheels of the law. It had been a futile gesture all the same, and ill-advised too, for the superintendent had not believed me and would be suspicious of anything I said from now on.

Anyway, the die was cast now and I decided I might as well increase the stake. I would telephone Sheila.

For the life of me I couldn't remember her married name and in the end I had to ring up Marion to find out. Marion sounded nervous and excited and was almost incoherent on the phone. Brushing aside my question about Sheila, she started talking feverishly about the arrangements for the funeral. I tried to calm her down and assured her that everything was in hand but she went on and on. Then suddenly she switched to something else.

'I'm so worried, Simon. The police have been back at me again, two new ones this time. They keep asking questions, questions, questions. Do I have to answer them, Simon? Do I have to tell them where I was that night? I didn't kill him, I swear I didn't kill him. But what else was I to think? I had to go there. I had to find out. But they keep on asking me. They . . .'

'For God's sake, Marion, pull yourself together. You're raving.'

There was silence at the other end of the line. She would be hurt by the brutal tone of my voice, I knew, but she would be calmer. This was not the first time I had metaphorically slapped her face.

I took the chance to slip in my question again.

'Tell me, Marion, what is the name of the man Sheila Cox married? You remember – he's got the big farm up at Lagside.'

As I expected, she had herself under control and spoke rationally, if rather petulantly.

'Roger Grant. Why?'

'I just wanted to phone her and I didn't know what name to look up in the directory.'

But Marion had already lost interest.

'Simon,' she said plaintively, 'won't you come along to see me this evening? I'm terribly lonely. I think I'll be all right after – after tomorrow, but I can't bear to be alone tonight. Please come, Simon.'

'You've got Millie there, haven't you?' I began. Then I had a sudden wave of pity for Marion. Life had been hard to her and she was not of the stuff that thrived on adversity.

'Very well, Marion,' I said gently. 'I'll come.'

As I looked up Sheila's number in the telephone directory I wondered how I came to forget Roger Grant's name, unless it was that he had always been so self-effacing. I had played a lot of tennis with him six or seven years ago until persistent cartilage trouble forced me to give up the game. He was the best player in the club – surprisingly, because he was heavily built and already running a bit to stoutness. He was about ten years older than me, and nearly fifteen years older than Sheila whom, even in those days, he worshipped with a devotion that was almost pitiful to see. We used to have a doubles every Saturday evening, Marion and I against Roger and Sheila. As soon as the game had ended Marion would go off with Oliver, who was a member of the club but had no pretensions to being a player, and the ill-assorted trio of Sheila, Roger and myself were left.

Sometimes my conscience made me invent some excuse to go home, but not often. I enjoyed flirting with Sheila – who didn't – and I couldn't really believe that I was playing gooseberry. It was inconceivable that Sheila had any romantic feelings for Roger. So the three of us used to go for walks on these summer Saturday evenings, Sheila playing each of us off against the other, all in the most good-humoured way. Sometimes we would go to the local dance hall and here I had the advantage of Roger, who was no dancer. And it was on these occasions that I used to feel stirrings of an emotion that made me wonder if Sheila wasn't worthy of more than a flirtation. She danced passionately and without inhibition. It was a unique experience to be her partner. Roger would stand looking on, benignly sipping a glass of lemonade. He seemed to bear no malice.

After I left the tennis club I saw little of Sheila. We had never been closely attached and she had many other admirers. The faithful Roger remained on the sidelines. Sheila tolerated him partly because of his tennis prowess and partly also, I think, because she was touched by his dog-like devotion. A year or so later Sheila's father, who was a schoolmaster, obtained a new post in a town some twenty miles away and Sheila moved from our ken. Two years later again – early in 1958 it would be – I was astonished to see in our local newspaper the announcement of her marriage to Roger Grant. I sent a congratulatory letter and a belated wedding present, I got a brief acknowledgment, and that was all. Although Roger's farm wasn't much more than ten miles away, they never seemed to come into Brickfield. At any rate I hadn't set eyes on either of them since their marriage.

It was Roger who answered the telephone. I didn't say who I was but merely asked to speak to his wife. As I waited for Sheila to come to the phone I was surprised to hear the thumping of my heart.

'Mrs Grant speaking.' There it was, that warm, musical voice, with the curiously husky undertone. How could I ever have been in doubt about it?

'Sheila, this is Simon Barnett.'

The silence at the other end was so complete that I said anxiously, 'Are you still there, Sheila?'

'Yes, but I'm wondering whether I shouldn't hang up.' There was a sound like a suppressed giggle and then she went on in an artificial voice, 'And how are you, Simon? It seems such an age since I saw you.'

'I think we'll do without the social chit-chat, Sheila. This is serious. You must know why I've called.'

She laughed outright this time. 'Still the same solemn Simon. The cares of the world on his shoulders. Yes, I can guess why you've called, but I'm not sure that I want to continue the conversation.'

'Sheila, I must see you. Can I meet you somewhere tonight?'

'I'm afraid not. Roger's got friends here for the weekend and I simply couldn't get away.'

'Tomorrow, then?'

'Look here, Simon, what good do you think this is going to do? I know what I'm doing and nothing you can say will influence me. Unless, perhaps, you want to blackmail me too?'

There was a tension in her voice which told me that she was much more worried than she was trying to appear. Before I could answer, she hurried on:

'Sorry, Simon, I shouldn't have said that. All right, I'll see you tomorrow. I think we'd better meet on neutral ground. Can you go to the city tomorrow afternoon?'

'Yes – damn it, no.' I remembered Oliver's funeral.

In the end we arranged to meet at seven o'clock the following evening at the Central Station in the city.

When we rang off I saw that it was well past six. I had had nothing to eat since lunch. On an impulse I phoned Marion again and asked her if she could give me a meal. It would keep her occupied and even give her pleasure, because one of the few things she was still proud of was her cooking.

I spent four hours with Marion that evening. She talked incessantly, but except briefly once or twice she never really lost control of herself. I must have made the correct responses, for she was pathetically grateful to me when I finally left. But her spate of words made no real impact on my consciousness. My mind was on Oliver and Sheila and the photographs.

CHAPTER 10

The office was officially closed on the Monday, the day of Oliver's funeral, but I went in that morning all the same. Joyce was there, and Fergusson, but nobody else.

Fergusson greeted me as if it were any ordinary day and plunged at once into a discussion of work. He was wearing a new grey pin-stripe suit and a bright red tie. I wondered if he intended to go to the funeral like that.

'You and I must have a talk,' he said, 'about the reallocation of work. We may have to take someone else on.'

'The first thing, surely, is to deal with the things Oliver was actually working on. We'd better go through his files and see what he had in hand.'

'Now?'

'Why not?' I was restless and had been wondering how to occupy myself. This was as good a way of putting in the time as any.

With Joyce's help it took less time than I had expected. The police had already been through all the papers in Oliver's room and had also, Joyce told us, looked through her files. Whether they had taken anything away or not, I don't know, but nothing appeared to be missing.

I was impressed by the acumen with which Fergusson could skim through a complex volume of correspondence, grasp the essential points of it and decide what was to be done. I prided myself on my own quickness in separating the wheat from the chaff, but I couldn't compete with him. Only once did I disagree with him and that was when we came to the mass of papers about the case under the Town and Country Planning Act.

'I'll write to Green tomorrow,' he said briefly and without glancing at the papers, 'and advise him to sell.'

'We can't just turn right round like that,' I protested. 'Oliver's been encouraging him for years in a crusade of resistance to the oppression of bureaucracy. You'll find that phrase in one of the letters here.'

'More fool Oliver,' said Fergusson. 'Green will lose his property in the end, anyway, and he won't get as good a price for it.'

But Joyce supported me. 'Oh! that poor little man,' she said. 'It would be like amputating a leg to take the fight away from him. He loves it.'

'Very well,' said Fergusson, dismissing the subject. 'You can handle it, Simon. I'm no sentimentalist.'

Indeed he was not. There was an uncompromising realism about him – ruthlessness, almost – that was chilling and rather frightening.

When we had finished our task, Fergusson's eyes surveyed Oliver's room and he remarked unexpectedly:

'Why don't you move in here, Simon? The king is dead and so on.'

I had been thinking about it myself, for I needed more space. But it seemed somehow indecent haste to establish myself in Oliver's room before he was even buried. However, Fergusson's gibe about my sentimentality had riled me. I said I would.

Fergusson strolled off to his own room and left Joyce and me to the task of moving my effects. We spent the rest of the morning at it. Joyce was unusually taciturn and eventually I asked her what was wrong.

'I can't put it into words, Simon,' she replied. 'Partly, I suppose, it's the thought of the funeral this afternoon. But it's more than that. I don't like to think of you moving into Oliver's room. It's symbolic, somehow. I'm afraid you are going to become *like* Oliver.'

'Well, what's so terrible about that? I thought you liked Oliver?'

'Oh, yes, I liked him! But he got out of his depth a bit, you know. He had too many big ideas and a finger in too many pies. This room had something to do with it. I never liked this room. It's too – too opulent, somehow.'

I could see what she meant. Even stripped of its carpet, which had been sent away to have the bloodstains removed, the room had a richness more appropriate to the office of a film magnate than of a small-town lawyer.

Joyce's eyes, which had been roving round the room, lighted on the safe, now firmly closed, and she asked:

'Simon, do you know what Oliver kept in that safe?'

I was taken off my guard by this sudden question. I wasn't sure whether I ought to reveal what I knew myself and what the police had told me. To stall for time I said:

'Do you?'

'No,' she said slowly, 'but it must have been some pretty ghastly secret. He guarded it like the crown jewels.'

I told her the whole story then, except that I didn't mention Sheila's name. I hadn't been pledged to secrecy and I wanted to get Joyce's reaction to the idea of Oliver as a blackmailer.

She was non-committal. 'It's not impossible, Simon,' she said. 'Oliver had an elastic conscience. He usually did what he wanted to do and then persuaded himself that it was morally right. All the same . . . Blackmail. That I wouldn't have expected.'

We were still discussing it when Fergusson came into the room. He was wearing his hat and coat.

'I presume it is your intention to attend the funeral this after-noon. If so, you might care to note that it is now ten minutes past one.' He stalked out again without waiting for an answer.

He had spoken more stiffly than usual and he was undoubtedly annoyed about something. Had he overheard any of our conver-sation, I wondered?

'He's not pleased that I agreed to become your secretary,' Joyce remarked. 'We had a row about it before you came in this morning. He wanted me to go to him.'

'But why? He's got a good secretary.'

'Yes,' said Joyce absently.

We had invited only relatives and a few intimate friends to the funeral service, which was held, in deference to Marion's wishes, in the undertakers' service room in City Road. Marion was there, and Linda and her father, and Fergusson, and Joyce, and Millie. These were all, apart from one or two cousins whom we saw only at weddings and funerals. Marion bore up well during the service but suddenly collapsed when it was over. I thought at first it was another display of histrionics; but no, she was out cold, in a dead faint. She quickly came round, but didn't accompany us to the cemetery.

When we came out of the undertakers', the street was lined with people and there were two or three policemen keeping them back to the far pavement. Cameras flashed once again as we climbed into the leading cars. Behind the official cortège there stretched a line of private cars and many more people followed the procession on foot to the cemetery, not all of them, I believe, inspired by morbid curiosity. Whatever his faults, Oliver had had friends, good friends.

It was a fine, clear day, warmer too, with the first hint of summer in the air. It somehow gave added poignancy to the scene. As the vicar intoned the words of the committal service I felt rage welling up in me at the wantonness of Oliver's murder. I studied the faces of those gathered round the graveside, etched clearly against the bright skyline: Joyce, Waterston, Fergusson, all inscrutable. Only Linda showed some emotion. Her expression was hard and set, but I could see a tear trickling down her cheek.

After it was over, one or two people came up to shake my hand and make the conventional noises of commiseration. While I was talking to them I became conscious of someone standing a little way off on my right and I got the impression that he was trying to attract my attention. As soon as I tactfully could, I broke away and turned round. It was Roger Grant.

At first I didn't recognize him, so much had he changed. He had put on a lot of weight and he looked much older. His face, although weather-beaten, was puffy, and there were pouches under the eyes. The clothes, I think, accentuated it. His morning-suit and black coat were obviously too tight and in any case appeared incongruous on him. He was a farmer and looked like a farmer; formal clothes did not sit easily on him.

His expression, however, was the same as it always had been – good-natured and slightly foolish; except that at the moment there were creases of worry in his brow. It was easy to underrate Roger Grant. I knew that he was not so naïve or unintelligent as he let himself appear. When he took over Lagside it was a small marginal farm, always threatened with failure. Roger had borrowed heavily to modernize and mechanize it and he had also purchased two or three neighbouring properties at prices which he could only afford by large mortgages. Within a few years he had paid off his debts and Lagside was now one of the most productive and prosperous farms in the country. Roger had also won Sheila, which was a tribute to his good sense as well as to his persistence.

'Can you spare a few minutes, Simon?' he asked.

'Yes, I've got to go home and change. Why don't you come with me? I'll rustle up a cup of tea for you.'

'No, I've got to get back to Lagside. But I'll drive you to your house and we can talk on the way.'

We got into his car, a grey Rover, and he drove off.

'You phoned Sheila last night?'

It was a statement, an accusation almost, rather than a question. However, I merely nodded assent.

'Simon, what is the matter with Sheila? What's worrying her? Is it something to do with Oliver's murder?'

'Sheila hasn't told you?'

'Not a word. She pretends to treat it all as a huge joke, but she's all tensed up and on edge. I've never seen her like that before and I don't like it.'

'Well, I'm sorry, Roger, but this is between Sheila and you. If she hasn't said anything to you, I can't.'

He braked sharply and went round a corner too fast. It was the only indication that he was angry.

His voice was as quiet and amiable as ever when he went on:

'You're seeing her tonight, aren't you?'

'Yes.'

'Well, Simon, please try to persuade her to confide in me. I want to help her. Whatever it is, it can't be so bad that she can't tell me about it.'

'It's bad enough,' I said.

We were now at the gate of my house. I got out and shut the door of the car. Roger leaned out of the window and started to say something else, thought better of it and slumped back in his seat. He looked worried and despondent.

He didn't respond when I called goodbye to him. He let out the clutch and drove away.

CHAPTER 11

Sheila was late. Unpunctuality had always been one of her more exasperating traits. I stood outside the station for more than twenty minutes and was wondering how much longer I should give her when I saw a gloved hand waving to me from the window of a car across the street.

'Hop in,' said Sheila, when I crossed to her. 'You're taking me for dinner.'

'My car is just round the corner—' I began.

'My car is right here,' she interrupted. 'Hop in.'

It was a pale blue Morris Minor.

'Is this your own car?' I asked as I settled myself.

'In a manner of speaking. Roger hardly ever uses it. He has first claim on the Rover.'

She threaded her way expertly through the traffic.

'Where are we going?' I asked.

'Patience, Simon. We're nearly there.'

She turned into a side street and parked the car. As we walked the few yards back to the main road I suddenly realized where we were and what she was up to.

'Sheila, you're not—' I began.

'Yes, why not?' she said. 'It will set the right atmosphere for our talk.'

There it was, in glittering lights above the marble entrance: POLYGON RESTAURANT. They had closed the night-club immediately after the scandal and had reopened the place some months later as a restaurant, retaining the name Polygon for publicity purposes.

I laughed. Only Sheila could have thought of so bizarre a notion as having our talk at the scene of the crime, as it were.

I had never been inside the Polygon before, either in the night-club days or since its conversion. It was quite a place; one had only to glance into the dining-room to know that the meal was going to be expensive. It was a spacious and magnificent room, dominated by an immense crystal chandelier in the centre. Discreet wall lamps provided the only other illumination. There was an immediate impression of spotlessly white table linen and gleaming cutlery and of waiters moving silently and unhurriedly about their business. I was relieved to see that only a few customers were in dinner dress.

'It hasn't changed much,' Sheila remarked, as the head waiter showed us to a table. 'Take away the carpet and clear a space for dancing and there you have it as it was four years ago.'

When we sat down I had my first real chance to look at her. Unlike her husband she had changed very little. In repose her face was conventionally pretty; but it was seldom in repose. Emotions played on it like wind on the leaves of a tree. Even now, as she studied the menu, concentration was written on her brow and she had wrinkled her nose in an oddly attractive way. She had had her hair cut short, I noticed, and this enhanced the general effect of mischievous vivaciousness which she created. She wore a jade-green cocktail dress which seemed just right with her auburn hair and hazel eyes.

When I had ordered, Sheila went back to what she had been saying.

'No, it hasn't changed much. You miss the band, though.'

'Did you come here often?' I asked.

'Good heavens, no. Once was quite enough, considering what happened.'

She was toying with a spoon, her head bent. Then she looked up at me quizzically. 'You've seen that awful photograph, haven't you, Simon?'

I admitted it.

'And you're shocked?' I could have sworn there was a smile lurking about her lips.

' "Surprised" would perhaps express it better.'

'Don't be so stuffy and pompous, Simon. You look just like Roger. It was all perfectly innocent, or at least it was to begin with, only I got tipsy.'

'Don't you think you'd better start at the beginning?'

She laughed, that infectious, husky laugh that I remembered so well.

'I'm not so clever as you at marshalling my facts and presenting them in a logical order. I'm a scatterbrain. I always was. But I'll try.'

She took a deep breath and began again.

'Well, you remember Joe Barrington? Oh! no, you wouldn't. That was after I moved to Endsleigh. Anyway Joe and I became very friendly. I suppose you could describe him as a flash type. A very smooth character he was, hair sleeked back, toothbrush moustache, positively oozing shaving lotion. He father owned a couple of garages and seemed to be in a good way. Not quite top drawer, of course, but the money helped. Joe was supposed to be learning the business but he seemed to have plenty of free time. I don't think I really liked him much – he was too obviously a phoney – but he had his points. He had a little racing-car that he used to drive me around in, and he danced divinely.

'Roger, of course, absolutely loathed him. I couldn't bring myself to break with Roger completely. I had known him too long. But I saw less and less of him. Joe made it quite clear that he wasn't sharing me with anyone.'

She broke off and a faraway look came into her eyes.

'Do you remember, Simon, how you used to let Roger tag along when we went dancing?'

'Stop romancing, Sheila, and get on with your story. I was the odd man out in that trio. You were Roger's girl. Remember?'

Her eyes widened in genuine amazement.

'But Simon, I was crazy about you. Didn't you know? The one time in my life I've been head over heels in love with a man and he didn't even know it! Lord, I thought I made it obvious enough. Did you think I danced with everybody like that?'

She was quite angry. Anything I said could only make matters worse; so I kept silent. We concentrated on our food for a few minutes.

Then Sheila laughed again. She was a volatile girl and her spirits were never dampened for long.

'I must say it's a chastening experience to know you, Simon. Anyway, to get back to my story. Joe's sister got married towards the end of 1957 and Joe and I were at the wedding. Roger was there too – he was a friend of the bridegroom. Well, after the wedding was over, some of us were feeling a bit flat because no entertainment had been laid on for the guests for the evenings. Then somebody, I don't remember who it was, suggested going to the Polygon.

'You couldn't just walk in in those days; you had to be introduced. But Joe was a member and so were one or two others, so it was all right. About a dozen of us went altogether. As luck would have it,

Joe and Roger and I landed at the same small table, just we three. Well, it wasn't really luck. Joe chose it so that he and I could be by ourselves, and Roger simply walked over and sat down beside us. Joe was furious but there wasn't much he could do about it.

'We had had quite a few drinks at the wedding and now Joe kept plying me with more. If Roger had kept his mouth shut it would have been all right. I knew I had had enough – I don't really like the stuff anyway. But in that exasperating, patient voice of his he kept saying, "Do you not think you've had enough, Sheila? I wouldn't take any more, Sheila," until I could have screamed. Just from sheer perverseness, I kept on drinking. It was gin and tonic mostly, although latterly I seem to remember knocking back some whisky.

'I felt on top of the world, and everything Joe said seemed uproariously funny. I laughed a lot. I even laughed at poor Roger's miserable face and made some coarse joke about it. We got up to dance, Joe and I, and I remember remarking on how unsteady the floor was. I must have made an exhibition of myself at that dance. When we got back to the table Roger had disappeared. I suppose he had gone home in disgust. It was then that Joe said he knew a much better place for dancing upstairs. He went off and spoke to a weedy little man – Merriman, the manager, as I discovered later. They had quite an argument and Merriman kept glancing over at me and shaking his head doubtfully.

'But he must have given in, for Joe came back to the table beaming. He led me – half-carried me, I expect – out that door there—' Sheila pointed to a door at the back of the room – 'along a corridor and up a flight of stairs. We could hear dance music coming from behind a door at the head of the stairs. There was a bit of a fuss about getting in – some special pattern of knocks which Joe didn't get quite right the first time. When we did get in, we found about half a dozen couples dancing a fox-trot to a gramo-phone. The only odd thing (and it didn't seem odd to me at the time) was that none of the people had a stitch of clothing on. There was a lot of queer-looking furniture around the room but I didn't really take it in.

'Well, Joe was already taking off his jacket and he told me to hurry up. I know this must sound absolutely disgusting and shock-ing to you, Simon, but it seemed the most natural thing in the world. I remember having difficulty with the zip of my dress and having to get Joe to help me.

'And that's all I remember, absolutely all.'

She stopped abruptly and started to push food into her mouth.

'And then?' I said gently.

'Then? Oh! well, I have a hazy recollection of sprawling on the seat of Joe's car and being bumped about with the movement of the car. But I didn't really come to until the next morning. I was in Joe's flat, in his bed, wearing a pair of his pyjamas. And I felt like death. My head! God, I can feel it now. All that alcohol . . .

'Joe wasn't any more pleased with me than I was with him. I was told I had been sick all over his precious car, which was just about the worst thing you could do to Joe.' She giggled at the thought. 'Anyway, I gather I had been too far gone in drink to be very co-operative the night before. I hadn't been – what's the polite phrase? – interfered with.'

'You weren't too far gone', I said, 'for the photograph to be taken.'

'Oh! that. Please believe me, Simon, I've no recollection of that at all. I don't even know who the man is. It isn't Joe.'

She gave me a coquettish smile and added, 'Did you like me in it? I've got a nice figure, haven't I?'

'Please be serious, Sheila,' I said, but I couldn't help smiling.

She sighed with relief. 'Thank the Lord you're not going to play the heavy father, Simon. There's a spark of humour in you after all. I'm not a bad girl really, you know. I've only gone off the rails that once, and I learned my lesson.

'I felt really chastened that day and disgusted with myself. I saw Joe for the heel that he was. As soon as I had dressed I told him in a few choice words what I thought of him and marched out. I've never spoken to him since. I went straight to a phone box and rang up Roger and asked him if he still wanted to marry me. He used to propose to me about twice a month. And – well, that's that, I guess.'

'Did you tell Roger what had happened?'

'Good heavens, no. He thinks I've led a life as pure as the driven snow. He never asked me what happened after he left here that night.'

A waiter came with our coffee. As Sheila poured out I asked casually:

'And how has it all worked out?'

'Between Roger and me? Oh, well, we don't scale the heights, you know, but we rub along well enough. There's a lot to be said for security and comfort. There are times when I wish I could have had something more, but I was never one to cry over spilt milk.'

There was a lull in the conversation. Sheila sat there sipping her coffee and looking perfectly composed and happy, as if this were an ordinary casual meeting of acquaintances.

'When did the blackmailing begin?' I asked.

'Oh, Simon! must you? I don't like to *think* about it, especially just after I've got that awful story off my chest. Do you realize that I've never told it to a soul before? I don't think I *could* tell it to anyone else but you. You—'

'When did blackmailing begin?' I repeated.

Her face broke into a grin. 'This is as bad as being cross-examined in the witness box. About three months ago, it was – the middle of January. It was the biggest shock I've ever had in my life. It was lucky Roger wasn't there when I opened the envelope. My face would have given the show away.

'It was simply the photograph and a note saying, "You will send £25 in single notes to Mr C. V. Jones, c/o Mr James Robertson" – the address was given – "before the end of each month. If the money is not received by the last day of any month, a copy of this photograph will be sent forthwith to your husband." There was no signature.'

'What was the handwriting like?'

'It was typed. Rather badly typed, by somebody not used to a typewriter, I should think.'

'Why didn't you just show it to Roger and then take it to the police?'

'Mercy on us, you don't understand Roger. Oh! I know he seems so meek and undemanding. But he's as jealous as hell. I daren't so much as look at another man.' She spread her hands in a gesture of mock despair. 'And I'm such an incorrigible flirt. I just can't help myself. It's all very innocent, but not to Roger. He frightens me sometimes. If he were to see that photograph . . .' She left the sentence trailing.

'Anyway,' she went on, 'I paid the twenty-five pounds in January, and again in February. By March I was at my wits' end. My dress allowance for the year was gone already and there was nothing for it but to dip into my own bank account – a few hundreds I had saved against a rainy day. But that couldn't go on. Roger would be bound to find out. However, I paid the money in March too.

'But I'd been making plans. I had found out a bit about Robertson. He has a pawnbroker's business in the city and he's a pretty shady character by all accounts. I decided to frighten him into giving me Jones's real name and address. The funny thing is, it worked. At least I got the address – he didn't know the name. So—'

'Where did you get the revolver?' I interrupted.

'Oh, of course, the gun! That was Daddy's. He used to keep it in a drawer in his study and I knew it was still there, for I'd seen it not long ago. I just drove into Endsleigh one afternoon and picked it up. Mummy would never notice it had gone.'

'Didn't your father miss it?'

'Daddy? Didn't you know? He died last year.'

'Oh, I'm sorry! I hadn't heard . . . Well, what sort of gun was it?'

'It was black.'

'Most of them are. Couldn't you describe it a bit better than that? Where is it now, anyway?'

'I'm sorry, Simon, but it just seemed an ordinary sort of gun to me. And it's at the bottom of the river now.'

Before I could comment on this she hurried on, 'Don't ask me about that just now. I'm coming to it later.'

'Well, then,' I said, 'where did you get the ammunition?'

She gaped at me. 'Oh, Simon! you surely don't think it was loaded. I would have been scared to death.'

I gave it up. 'All right,' I said, 'you've got Jones's address. Gribble Street, Brickfield, wasn't it? What next?'

She had gone in the very next day to the Gribble Street address. She got no reply, of course, when she knocked at the door, but that didn't daunt Sheila. She spoke to all the neighbours, both in that tenement and in the adjoining properties. The mysterious habits of Mr Jones had naturally aroused a good deal of curiosity and the purpose for which he kept the flat was well known. But he had been very circumspect in his comings and goings and Sheila could get no more than the vaguest description of his appearance; and no one could describe the woman, or women, at all. It was common knowledge however, that the flat was never used except at the weekends. Jones and a girl would arrive, sometimes together, sometimes separately, about ten o'clock at night, on a Friday (usually every second Friday) and they had on occasions been heard to leave at three or four a.m. They were always gone by the time the neighbours got up in the morning. The performance would be repeated on the Saturday nights. That at any rate was the recent routine. In earlier days – up till about last November – Jones and his mistress had usually remained in the flat continuously from the Friday night until early on the Sunday morning. Even then they had managed to avoid recognition, for they never opened the door or showed themselves at a window in the daytime. The only indication that they were still there was the occasional sound of gramophone music on a Saturday afternoon.

Sheila next tried the owner of the property, a Mrs McConnell, who lived in some comfort on her unearned income in an expensive apartment in the city. But Mrs McConnell was unco-operative – she clearly thought that Sheila was up to no good – and in any case she didn't appear to know much about her tenant, whom she had met only once. The rent was posted to her regularly in advance and that was all she cared about. If she knew the purpose for which the flat was being used, she shut her eyes to it. She was obviously much more concerned with some of her other tenants who were not so punctilious in their payment of rent.

Sheila had one more string to her bow. She drove into Brickfield the following Friday evening (six days before the murder), parked her car in Gribble Street across the road from the flat, and waited. She waited from eight o'clock until nearly eleven, and was on the point of abandoning the vigil for the night when a couple appeared out of a side street, the man with his hat pulled well down and both with their coat collars up. It would have been too dark to recognize them anyway but, observing their furtive approach, Sheila was not surprised when they disappeared into the entrance of the tenement. A door banged and a few moments later a light went on in one of the ground-floor windows. Sheila walked back the way they had come. It didn't take her long to find the car, parked on a bit of waste ground a few blocks away. It was a dark green Wolseley, almost new, and obviously didn't belong to that neighbourhood. She had no doubt that it was Jones's car. She took the registration number and had little difficulty the following day in tracing it to Oliver.

I interrupted at this point. 'You took it for granted that Oliver must be the blackmailer?'

'What else was I to think? It was a bit of a shock, I admit. I had known Oliver slightly in the old days and I always rather liked him. He was good fun. But I suppose even a blackmailer can have a sense of humour. Anyway, Oliver was quite definitely C. V. Jones.'

'Yes, but—' I began, but decided not to argue the point for the present. 'All right, go on with your story.'

Sheila had by this time been enjoying her Sherlock Holmes act and she now thought up an elaborate plan for getting Oliver to disgorge the negative and any other prints of the photograph. She was convinced that if her personal charms didn't work she had only to produce the revolver and Oliver would react as Robertson had reacted. She didn't know Oliver: he would have laughed at her and called her bluff.

Since it was essential to her scheme that she should see Oliver alone, she had somehow to contrive an appointment with him in the office late in the evening when no one else would be there. And, of course, she couldn't let him know in advance who she was. That was why she put across the Mrs Cargill act. It was a brilliant improvisation, for it touched Oliver's vanity and so blunted any suspicions he might otherwise have had about this odd arrangement. Her only piece of bad luck was that I spoke to her on the phone the first time and recognized, or half recognized, her voice.

She chose the Friday night for the interview because her husband had said he was going up to London on business that day and wouldn't be back until lunchtime the following day. Roger had been inquisitive about her absence on the evening she watched Oliver's flat and they had quarrelled when she refused to tell him where she had been. Since then he had been moody and suspicious and she didn't dare embark on another unexplained journey unless she could be sure that Roger wouldn't find out about it.

On the Thursday afternoon Roger suddenly announced that he had changed his plans. He would drive up to London after tea, do his business the following morning, and be back at the farm before dinner on the Friday. And off he went in the Rover at five o'clock.

This wrecked Sheila's timetable and at first she thought she would have to abandon or at least postpone her visit to Oliver. It was almost too late when the possibility occurred to her of bringing it forward. She phoned Oliver at his house about eight o'clock, again in her role of Mrs Cargill, and asked if he could see her that night instead of Friday. Again her luck held. Oliver was going back to the office anyway that night and was quite willing to wait on till ten o'clock to see her.

Up to this point Sheila had told her story fluently and even with relish. But now she began to hesitate.

'I hate to think of that night, Simon,' she said. 'I'd like to shut it out of my mind for always. The drive itself was a nightmare. I couldn't see a foot ahead of me for the fog. I was crazy even to attempt it, but I was all keyed up for the big scene with Oliver and I just couldn't bring myself to put it off.

'Well, by God's good grace I got there, but I was more than an hour late – it was nearly a quarter past eleven. I was sure Oliver would never have waited all that time, but when I peered up through the fog I thought I could see a dim glow from one of the third-floor windows. I hoped it was Oliver's room. I went upstairs.'

Her face was white and strained now, and she continued with difficulty.

'The light was from Oliver's room. I knocked and went in. I was shaking with nerves. I suddenly felt I had been an awful fool to come here expecting to get the better of Oliver with the help of an empty gun; and of course the drive had made me more jittery than ever. It was quite an anti-climax to find the room empty. I sat down on a chair and almost wept with relief. And then – oh! God, Simon, it was awful – I saw the hat and coat on the chair and then . . . the hand on the floor. And when I went round and looked . . . all that blood . . . and the face—'

She broke off and groped blindly in her handbag for a handkerchief. I gave her a minute or two to recover her composure.

'And then?'

She managed a tremulous smile. 'You're an unemotional character, aren't you, Simon? I might be describing a Sunday School picnic for all that you're affected.

'I screamed. I'm sure I heard myself scream. Then I hopped it out of there as fast as my legs would carry me. I got back into the car and made for home. The fog was even worse then. I was off the road half a dozen times. But I made it.

'Oh! I forgot,' she added. 'About halfway home I stopped the car and flung the gun into the river.'

'What on earth made you do a crazy thing like that?'

'Well, I was almost out of my mind with terror. I knew I would be suspected if it ever came out that I was at the office that night and I just felt I had to get rid of that gun at once. It was burning a hole in my pocket.'

'But you saw the other gun lying there beside Oliver. It would have *helped* your case if you could have produced your gun.'

'I know, I know,' she said irritably. 'But I've told you before, I haven't got a logical mind. And besides, I was upset. And don't speak of my "case",' she added fiercely, 'as if I were on trial for murder.'

'By God, you soon will be,' I muttered, 'unless you're damned lucky.'

She chuckled. Her mood had changed again like quicksilver. 'What a pity you're not a barrister, Simon,' she said. 'It would be lovely to have you as my defending counsel. Anyway, I feel much better after getting all this off my chest. I hate bottling things up inside me. Look, Simon,' she added, 'I think some pressure is being put on us to leave.'

It was true enough. We were the only diners left in the room. Three waiters were lined up against the wall within our view, looking ostentatiously bored.

As we rose to go, I said to Sheila, 'Don't think I'm finished with you yet. We'll continue this confession in the car.'

She grinned mischievously at me. 'And such a cosy little car, too! Think of the opportunities you must have missed in life.'

We didn't talk during the drive back to the station. There was a lot of traffic about and I didn't want to disturb Sheila's concentration. But more than that, I wanted time to think. I was convinced that Sheila was in appalling danger and that she herself had no appreciation of the seriousness of her plight. I believed she had told me the truth; but it would be hard to convince anyone else that she hadn't murdered Oliver. Motive was there, and opportunity – and, most damning of all, the fact that she had previously produced a gun and threatened to use it. I tried desperately to think of some fact that was in her favour. If she was the murderer, why hadn't she removed the photograph from the safe, which was supposed to be the motive for the murder and which was bound to cast suspicion in her direction if the police found it? The answer, I supposed, would be that she hadn't time; that she was actually raking through the papers in the safe when she was interrupted by my arrival. Well, then, what about the gun? If it could be shown that the revolver found beside Oliver's body, the revolver with which the murder was committed, was not the one that had belonged to Sheila's father, that would be some help. But not much, I had to admit. Why should the police believe her story about where she had obtained the gun? If only she hadn't been such a damned fool as to throw the thing away.

I came back to this point now. Sheila had stopped the car beside mine in the station car park.

'Do you remember', I asked, 'exactly where you threw that gun into the river?'

'Heavens, no. The road runs alongside the river for more than three miles. It would be somewhere about the middle of that stretch. But it was thick fog, remember, and in any case I wasn't in any condition to take in the geographical details.'

I sighed. This was hopeless.

Sheila sighed too, a contented dreamy sigh. 'Isn't this romantic, Simon? Look at the moon. In books the moon is always shimmering on a lake or silvering the leaves of a forest. But this is where I like it best, in a big city, shining on the rooftops and the church spires and the factory chimneys. It seems to transform everything. Look at—'

I interrupted her. For the first time I was really angry with her.

'If this is intended to be the prelude to a petting session, you can save your breath,' I said brutally.

My anger was nothing to Sheila's. If she hadn't been in so restricted a space I think she would have slapped my face.

'Get out,' she hissed.

'I'm sorry, Sheila, but—'

'Get out, damn you.' This time it was a shout.

'Listen to me!' I was shouting too now, to drown her protests. 'Unless a miracle happens, you're going to be arrested in the next day or two and tried for murder. And all you do is to sit there and babble about the moon. I had to do something to bring your predicament home to you.'

She was in tears now and made no further move to eject me. I continued more gently, 'All the same, I'm sorry for what I said, Sheila. I know it was unjust.'

She sobbed quietly for a moment or two. Then in a small voice she asked, 'What am I to do, Simon?'

I had been thinking about this ever since we left the Polygon. I was in no doubt about the answer now.

'In the first place you must tell Roger. He's your husband and you owe it to him. And secondly you must go straight to the police station tomorrow morning – tonight, if you like – and tell them the whole story exactly as you've told it to me. You should have done that last Thursday night. But better late than never.'

'But, Simon, they would arrest me.'

'They might. I'm not sure. What I do know is that they certainly will arrest you when they ferret all this out for themselves.'

Sheila sat silent for several minutes. Finally she said firmly:

'I can't do it. Don't interrupt.' She held up her hand to silence my protest. 'I'm not as irresponsible as you think. I've given this a good deal of thought already. I realize that the police will probably discover I'm the woman in that photograph and that Robertson will identify me as the person who threatened him with a gun. I'll admit that if I have to but that doesn't prove that I killed Oliver. I'll deny that I was the woman who impersonated Mrs Cargill and I'll deny that I went anywhere near your office on Thursday night. I'll say that I sat at home knitting. Nobody could possibly have seen me in that fog. The police can suspect as much as they like: they won't be able to prove anything.

'There will be no fingerprints, either, for I wore gloves,' she added triumphantly, as if that clinched the matter.

'What about servants?' I asked. 'They are bound to know you were out that night.'

'We've only got a daily woman for the house and the farm workers don't live anywhere near.'

'Sheila, I can only repeat that you are playing with fire. Don't underrate the police. I recognized your voice when "Mrs Cargill" phoned. Someone else may have recognized it too. And there are all sorts of other ways in which the police may find out – little things that you would never think of. For instance, somebody may have phoned your house that night and got no reply. Don't be a fool, Sheila. Go to the police now. Get in with your story first.'

But her mind was made up. I was astonished once again by her resilience. She sounded quite cheerful and unconcerned again.

'I can't even promise to follow your other bit of advice about telling Roger,' she said. 'Roger would have a fit if he saw that photograph. He really has the most Victorian notions about the chastity of women and especially about the spotlessness of the woman he selected as his soul mate.' She couldn't repress another giggle.

We talked for a few minutes longer. As I was opening the door of the car to get out, I remembered something that had been niggling at the back of my mind.

'When you ran out of Oliver's room, did you switch off the light?'

'I don't think so. No, I'm sure I didn't. I was too hell bent on getting out of the place to bother about economizing on electricity. Anyway, I remember the light from his door showed me my way down the corridor. Why do you ask?'

'The light was off when I arrived. In fact I heard the murderer leave, although the police seem to be sceptical about it. But the point is that Oliver's killer must still have been in the building all the time you were there.'

'What a horrible thought,' said Sheila, shivering.

'Never mind about that. Think hard, Sheila. Did you notice anything, anything at all, to indicate that there was somebody else there? A coat or a hat, a sound, a smell of perfume even?'

'Well, there was a coat and hat lying on a chair,' she began, 'but—'

'Those were Oliver's. Nothing else?'

Her brow furrowed in concentration. 'I'm sorry, Simon, I can't remember anything like that. All I could take in was the body on the floor.'

'Never mind. It was just an idea. Well, I think it's time we were going, Sheila.'

'You're not angry with me any more, are you, Simon?' she asked anxiously.

She looked so vulnerable sitting there that I had to laugh.

'Of course I'm angry with you,' I said. 'I've never come across such a pig-headed nitwit in all my life. Still, I think Roger is a lucky man.'

I got out of Sheila's car and went back to my own. I heard her start her engine and watched her drive off. I followed the tail lights of her car until it turned a corner and disappeared from view.

CHAPTER 12

Tuesday and Wednesday passed quietly enough. The lull was an uneasy one, though, and did nothing to reassure me. Superintendent Garland appeared at the office on the Tuesday afternoon and spent more than an hour with Waterston, who had for some reason taken to coming in daily. I met the superintendent as he was coming out of Waterston's room and found myself saying fatuously to him:

'Well, no arrest yet?'

'Give us time, Mr Barnett, give us time,' he replied blandly, and walked on. I was not encouraged by this cheerfulness.

Waterston, curiously enough, seemed to have a weight lifted from his shoulders after Garland's visit. As he was leaving that night, he looked into my room – Oliver's room – and said affably:

'Nice chap, Garland. Educated, too. He's got his eye on the ball, all right. We had quite a long chat about these – er – papers of mine that your brother kept. It was naughty of you to tell him. Gave me quite a turn when he grilled me about them. Still, perhaps it's all for the best. The superintendent doesn't think it need ever come out. Not that I've done anything to be ashamed of. Still, it could have been embarrassing. Damned embarrassing.'

He gave me a sly look and added. 'Yes, perhaps it's all for the best. But Linda won't be pleased when she hears you told the police why she came here that night. Not pleased at all.'

Now was my chance to have it out with him. There was still much that was unexplained about Linda's sudden decision to leave me. I knew that her father was behind it in some way but I had never discovered just how he had poisoned her mind against me. I had never been able to see him alone. From the day Linda left me until this past week he had kept away from the office. I had gone twice to his house to see him but both times Linda had insisted on remaining with him. With Linda present I could employ the only tactics that were likely to succeed against him – straightforward bullying. Even the return of the £4,000 had made no impression on Linda: she had described it as an attempt to buy her back.

However, I let the present opportunity pass. I had a presentiment that a better one would come along presently.

Waterston's parting shot was, 'I won't be back for some time, Simon. Term starts next week. And in any case I think it's time that we parted company. The firm can struggle along without me from now on, eh? I'll write to you about it.'

He made as if to hold out his hand, changed his mind, and turned to go. As he did so, Joyce came through the communicating door from her room. She made a face at Waterston's retreating back and remarked:

'Slimy little slug! Carry on without him, indeed! Much help he's been to the firm.'

She put some letters on my desk for signature. She hesitated for a moment and then she said:

'Simon, I don't want to interfere, but isn't it time you got down to some work? Look at the pile of stuff waiting for you and you've done nothing but moon about all day and smoke cigarettes.'

It was quite true. I had let the hours slip away while I went over and over in my mind everything that might have a bearing on Oliver's murder. And I had nothing to show for it. The more I racked my brain the more confused I became.

I worked till after ten that night, and on the Wednesday I slogged away for nearly twelve hours in the office. When I finally left, my brain was tired, but agreeably so, and I had a sense of well-being and optimism. I remember thinking as I climbed into bed that I had allowed myself to get things out of perspective, that I had exaggerated Sheila's danger, that the police would probably never trace her at all and even if they did they would accept her explanation. I had my first good sleep that night for a week.

The first thing I saw when I opened my newspaper the next morning was a photograph of Sheila splashed on the front page. A banner headline proclaimed: 'BARNETT CASE: NEW DEVELOPMENT.' 'Police inquiries' (the text ran) 'into the murder of Mr Oliver Barnett in Brickfield last Thursday took a dramatic turn yesterday afternoon, when Superintendent Garland of Scotland Yard and Inspector Kennedy of the local police visited Lagside Farm, about ten miles north-east of the scene of the murder. They spent several hours interviewing Mr Roger Grant, the owner of the farm, and his young and attractive wife, Mrs Sheila Grant. (See picture.) Later Mrs Grant accompanied the detectives to the police station in Brickfield to give further assistance in the investigation. She was still there at a late hour last night.' The story went on to give potted biographies of Roger and Sheila and then to recapitulate the circumstances of the murder. It was mainly padding, and it ended with the customary statement that 'an arrest was believed to be imminent'. Obviously the reporters knew they were on to a hot story but had little real information to give. Or if they had, they dared not give it.

I was just about to put the paper away when my eye caught a paragraph in heavy black type in the stop press column. 'BARNETT

Murder Arrest – The police announced late last night that a woman had been arrested and charged with the murder of Mr Oliver Barnett. She will make a formal appearance in court this morning.'

I pushed my breakfast away untasted. I couldn't get Sheila's face out of my mind. I felt that in some way I had let her down, that I should have been able to protect her from this.

The telephone rang. It was Roger. His voice was slow and slurred like the voice of a man who has had a stroke. He started to talk incoherently about Sheila's arrest, but I cut him short.

'Look, Roger,' I said, 'I'll have to see you about this. But first I want to have a word with the police. It won't do any good but I must try. Come and see me at my office at eleven o'clock.' I rang off before he could reply.

I went straight to the police station and asked to see Superintendent Garland. The sergeant on duty eyed me doubtfully but lifted the telephone and dialled through. To my surprise Garland agreed to see me at once.

It was an unsatisfactory interview. Garland was seated at a desk, with Inspector Kennedy beside him, studying a great mass of papers. The superintendent was polite, but brisk, and made no attempt to disguise the fact that he was a busy man and that I was interrupting him.

I told him he was making a colossal blunder – his second; that Sheila was no more guilty of murder than Oliver had been of indiscriminate blackmail.

'Have you any evidence for these statements?' he asked. 'Or is it simply that the murder and the blackmail are not "in character"? I'm afraid that in our profession we have to pay more attention to facts than to psychoanalysis.'

'Well,' I retorted, 'the facts, as you call them, are not convincing. Mrs Grant wasn't the only one who was being blackmailed. If that was the motive, there were many others with the same motive and the same opportunity. Anybody could have walked into the office that night and killed Oliver.'

He didn't even bother to argue with me. Instead he said, 'You know Mrs Grant well, don't you?'

'It's five years since I saw her last. But I did know her, yes.'

'Why didn't you tell me on Sunday that you recognized her in that photograph?'

'Because I knew you were on the wrong track.'

His voice was cold as he replied, 'That is a very arbitrary and dangerous line to take, Mr Barnett. I thought that you as a lawyer would have known better than to conceal material information from the police.'

He stood up. The interview was at an end. I knew better than to antagonize him further by continuing my protest.

As I was going out the superintendent added in a more friendly tone, 'We're not out to victimize anyone, you know. We don't make an arrest unless we're sure of our ground, but even so, we haven't completed our investigations yet, and if anything turns up that is in Mrs Grant's favour her advisers will be told of it.' It was cold comfort.

Roger was waiting for me when I got into the office, although it was nearly an hour before the time I had suggested. He was in a state almost of collapse. His face was an unhealthy grey and his eyes were bloodshot. He wouldn't sit down but paced restlessly about the room all the time he was talking. He had been drinking, too; I could smell whisky from his breath.

He spoke in rambling and disconnected sentences and was

constantly shooting off at irrelevant tangents. It was only with difficulty and by the exercise of much patience that I was able to piece together what had happened.

After she got back from her meeting with me on the Monday night Sheila had gone to Roger and told him the whole story. My advice must have carried some weight after all. Roger frankly admitted that he had taken it badly; in fact there had been a scene. From what he said I got the impression that he had been more upset by the evidence of Sheila's indiscretion at the Polygon Night Club years before than by her present danger. His excuse was the terrible shock it had been to find that the woman he had placed on a pedestal had feet of clay; and the jolt of his self-esteem to realize that she had only married him on the rebound from the despicable Joe Barrington.

When they had calmed down a bit, Sheila announced that she now wanted to go to the police with her story. What had held her back before had been mainly the fear of Roger's reaction to learning the truth. When he heard this, however, Roger flared up again and declared he wouldn't permit it. He might just be able to live with the knowledge of Sheila's guilty past but he could not contemplate the scandal if she became involved in a murder case, especially since the unsavoury details of her visit to the Polygon Club would then inevitably come out in open court. So he persuaded Sheila to do exactly what she had said to me she was going to do – to volunteer no information, to admit nothing that she didn't have to admit, and above all to deny that she had ever left the house on Thursday night.

As I had foreseen, it proved the worst possible course to take. Roger had been present, at Sheila's request, when she was inter-viewed by Superintendent Garland and Inspector Kennedy at the farm. They ought to have realized that the police wouldn't be there at all unless they had some information that pointed to Sheila; but Sheila, faithful to the letter of her husband's instructions, at first denied all knowledge of the photograph or the blackmail. Both she and Roger maintained that the woman in the photograph, although resembling her, was not Sheila. Not until Garland offered to arrange an identification parade to be attended by Robertson and some of the Gribble Street tenants did Sheila retract her denial. She then admitted that she had been blackmailed, admitted the visit to Robertson and the inquiries about C. V. Jones but maintained that she hadn't yet discovered who C. V. Jones was and certainly hadn't visited Oliver's office on the Thursday night. She had stayed at home all night.

Garland pressed her on this and only when she persisted in her story did he produce his trump card. It was bad luck, I suppose, but when a person tampers with the truth there is nearly always some unexpected little detail to trap him up. When Sheila went to see Oliver on Thursday night she parked her car in Church Street just around the corner from the office. Whether absentmindedly or from some vague desire for secrecy she switched off the lights. While she was in the office a policeman happened to pass up Church Street on his rounds and, seeing a car parked without lights and being a conscientious man, noted its number. It was as simple as that. It was some days before the local police got round to tracing the owner of the car and issuing the routine summons. By the time that they did, Sheila had already been recognized as the woman in one of the blackmail photographs and the significance of finding, near the scene of the murder and at the time of the murder, a car registered as belonging to her husband was at once apparent.

This revelation, of course, upset the whole apple-cart. Roger was still for blustering it out and maintaining that the policeman had made a mistake in the number, but Sheila, who was a realist if nothing else, brushed him aside and announced that she was now going to tell the whole truth. The superintendent cautioned her and said that if she wished to make a statement it might be better if she accompanied them to the police station. Off they went, and several hours later Roger got a phone call to say that his wife had been placed under arrest and charged with Oliver's murder.

While Roger was telling this dismal tale I could hardly contain my fury.

'My God,' I said, when he had finished, 'if you wanted to put a noose round Sheila's neck you could hardly have done it more effectively. What a bloody performance.'

'Oh! but she won't hang, surely. Think of the provocation. Blackmail's a filthy game.'

I stared at him, speechless.

When I found my voice it was all I could do to control it.

'Roger, do you believe that Sheila killed Oliver?'

'Well,' he said uneasily, 'you must admit the case looks pretty black against her. I wouldn't have believed it a week ago, but I find now that I don't really know her at all. To think that she could behave like a woman of the streets – worse than a woman of the streets – and deceive me all these years and—'

'Listen to me, Roger,' I interrupted quickly. 'Sheila is no murderer. And I'm going to prove it. I thought I could count on your help but in your state you would be a liability. You'd better get on with arranging for her defence. Who are your solicitors?'

He told me.

'Well, see that they get a top-rank counsel. Cramond, if he's available. And the defence must be a straight denial of the charge, none of this provocation nonsense. And see that they find that gun even if they have to employ every diver in the country to search the river. And another thing,' I added, 'forget what happened at that night-club years ago. It never did mean much and it's of no consequence now at all, if only your suspicious mind would stop dwelling on it. Sheila's your wife and a damned sight better wife than you deserve. This is the time you must stick by her, when she's in trouble. If you let her see that you think she's guilty, I'll break your silly fat neck for you.'

It was difficult to know how much of this had penetrated. He seemed in a daze. He muttered something intended as an apology and shambled slowly out. He was unrecognizable as the man I had played tennis with a few years earlier.

CHAPTER 13

As soon as Roger was gone I told Joyce to see that I wasn't disturbed and that no calls were put through to me. When I had said to Roger that I was going to prove Sheila's innocence, it wasn't much more than a fine-sounding phrase designed to put some guts into him. But as soon as the words were out I had begun to wonder whether I shouldn't have a shot at it. The obstacles were formidable, I knew: it seemed presumptuous to pit my wits against all the resources of Scotland Yard. But I did have two advantages not enjoyed by the police. Firstly, I had personal knowledge of the *dramatis personae* and of their character and background; and secondly (this was really a consequence of the first) I was virtually certain that Oliver had not been a professional blackmailer and absolutely certain that Sheila was incapable of murder. If the police were committed to a theory which I was convinced must be false, surely it could do no harm, putting it at its lowest, for me to try to demolish that theory and replace it by the true solution.

To clarify my thoughts and to get into some sort of pattern the miscellaneous and undigested mass of data I had gathered over the past week I took a sheet of paper and began to scribble down some notes.

'Assuming Oliver did not use the photographs for blackmail,' (I wrote) 'who did? Call him X for the moment. X was someone with an intimate knowledge of Oliver and his habits. He knew about the Gribble Street flat and he knew that Oliver used it only at weekends. That was why Robertson had instructions to forward mail to the flat only on a Monday, so that it would arrive at a time when Oliver would not be there. (No doubt the police explanation is that Oliver wanted the stuff to arrive on a Tuesday so that there would be no danger of his mistress seeing the envelopes and becoming curious.)

'More than that, X must somehow have acquired a key to the flat, to get in and collect the mail each month. He must also have had some connection with the Polygon Night Club or must have got the photographs from someone with such a connection.

'X must have put the negatives in the safe after Oliver's death, for it is scarcely credible that that is where he normally kept them or that he would have put them there while Oliver was alive; even if he had access to the safe, the risk of Oliver's discovering them would have been far too great. Now there was no opportunity for anyone to get to the safe after I arrived on the night of the murder, for Oliver's room was under continuous police surveillance between then and the discovery of the negatives. Therefore they were planted between the time of the murder and the time of my arrival. And that means that failing some fantastically improbable coincidence, X, the blackmailer, is also the murderer.

'Motive? Clearly X intended the police to infer, as they have inferred, that Oliver was the blackmailer. But there must have been some desperate crisis to compel the blackmailer to part with the photographs, which were so lucrative a source of income to him. The explanation must be that X knew that Sheila had arranged to see Oliver and knew that as soon as she accused him of the blackmail and showed the threatening letter Oliver would tumble to the truth.

'X was therefore aware of Sheila's appointment for the Friday night or at any rate knew she was hot on Oliver's trail. But he did not know that the appointment had been brought forward to

Thursday; otherwise he wouldn't have dared to leave the murder so late. If Sheila hadn't been held up by the fog, she would have been at the office by ten o'clock, at least three-quarters of an hour before Oliver was killed. That would seem to let Marion out, for she did know that "Mrs Cargill" had changed her appointment to the Thursday night.

'To sum up, X *must* be somebody fairly close to Oliver, quite possibly someone in the office. Remember that the person I disturbed when I arrived that night was able to find the fuse-box on the landing without delay and in semi-darkness.'

As I read over what I had written I felt a surge of rising excitement. The investigation didn't seem quite so hopeless now: a number of ideas were forming in my head about the lines it should take. But first I must get some help. I rang for Joyce. There was no reply, and when I looked at my watch the reason became plain. It was one-forty. I had been too absorbed to notice the time passing. I went out to see if there was anywhere I could still get lunch.

When I got back I at once asked Joyce to come in and phoned for Kelly.

Over lunch I had been thinking hard and I had decided that Joyce Carruthers and Alan Kelly were the two people whose help I needed; Joyce because I liked and trusted her and because as his secretary she knew a great deal about Oliver and all his affairs; and Kelly because, young though he was, I valued his intelligence and his judgment and could rely on his discretion. Kelly had served his apprenticeship with the firm and was now being groomed for a partnership. Despite his name he had no Irish blood in him and had been born and lived all his life in the North of England. He was a powerfully built young man and looked more like a professional footballer than a lawyer; and indeed he did play football for a local club, although as an amateur. He showed promise of becoming a good lawyer for all that.

When they were both there I asked them to sit down and began:

'I expect you have both heard of the arrest of Mrs Sheila Grant for the murder of my brother. I want you to hear the substance of the police case against Mrs Grant and I want to know your reactions to it. Joyce knows some of the story already, but I'm sure she won't mind if I tell it in full for your benefit, Alan.'

They heard me through without interruption. It took a long time to tell. I spoke slowly, picking my words with care and trying to be detached and unbiased. I said nothing of my own views on the case.

There was a long silence when I had finished. They were obviously wondering why I had told them all this and what emotion they were expected to register. Then Kelly ventured:

'I don't envy the defence counsel if that's the case he has to answer. It all hangs together and there is no other reasonable explanation. And yet . . . I don't know . . . One thing sticks in my throat and that is the idea of your brother as a blackmailer, and a blackmailer of such an unsavoury type. I would have said that was preposterous. It just goes to show that you never know what a person is really like under the surface.'

'Joyce?'

'I agree with Alan,' she said. 'It's hard to accept that Oliver was so depraved, but the facts speak for themselves.'

'Do they? Listen to this.' I read over to them the notes I had written that morning.

'Isn't that another possible explanation of the facts? And one that doesn't conflict with what we know of Oliver's character?'

'Yes,' said Kelly slowly, 'but it does postulate a coldblooded monster among your brother's close circle of friends. And that is nearly as hard to believe. Still,' he added, 'it is possible, I grant you.'

Joyce was still less encouraging. 'It's too fantastic, Simon. You've been carried away by your loyalty to Oliver. And I suspect you've fallen under the spell of this Grant woman. You never see straight when you're dealing with women; you're like clay in their hands.

'Anyway,' she went on, 'what do you propose to do about it? Put on a Lord Peter Wimsey act?'

'Something like that,' I replied. 'And I want you both to help me. Suppose for a moment my theory is right, fantastic or not. We know already so much about X, the blackmailer and murderer, that it shouldn't be impossible to identify him. A little private investigation can do no harm, even if the only result is to prove me wrong.'

'What do you want us to do?' asked Kelly. There was a ring of interest in his voice which had been absent before.

'Well, the first pointer we have is X's connection with the Polygon Night Club. In other words, how did he get those photographs? I thought I might tackle that end myself. Then there's the Gribble Street flat. How did X know so much about Oliver's arrangements there and, more important, how did he get a key? He must have called there once a month to collect his spoils. Was he ever seen by any of the neighbours? That's your department, Alan.'

'And mine?' asked Joyce in a flat voice.

'To reduce the list of suspects by eliminating all those with an alibi for last Thursday night. X is someone who knew a great deal about Oliver and his movements. So start with the office staff. Find out where everyone was between ten-thirty and eleven-thirty that night, from the office boy upwards. Better still, cover the period from nine-thirty to midnight. You've got the tact to do it without arousing suspicion.'

'I don't like it, Simon,' said Joyce. 'This is a police matter. I can't believe we could possibly do any good by interfering. And especially I don't like spying on my colleagues here, because that's what it amounts to, you know.'

'If I'm right, Joyce, Sheila Grant is in danger of being convicted of a murder she didn't commit. Surely that's enough to allay your scruples.'

She pondered for some time before she spoke. 'Very well,' she said at length. 'I'll do what I can to help. But I'm still uneasy about it. Once you start raking up muck you may not like what you find.'

'And you, Alan?'

'Oh, I'm all for it! I've always had an ambition to play the amateur sleuth. Mind you, I'm not at all convinced that the police are wrong. But even so, I don't quite see what Joyce is worrying about. Nobody is going to be any worse off if it's a red herring we're chasing.'

'Well, that's settled, then. I think we should start right away. I'm going over to the *Herald* office to dig out the files about the Merriman case.'

'Just a moment,' said Kelly. 'Before we break up this conference there are one or two points I want to raise. First have you any reason to suppose that X, as you call him, is not a woman?'

'None. I used the masculine merely for convenience.'

'Right. Now one other thing we know about X which you didn't mention is that he (or she) must have known Mr Barnett was to be in his office that Thursday night. If you are right, this was a planned murder and the murderer obviously wouldn't wander into the office at ten-thirty or later on the off chance of finding his victim sitting there waiting to be shot. Yet you say that X didn't know of Mrs Grant's appointment with your brother for that night.'

'That's a point,' I conceded. 'I don't know the answer to it. He may have known of Linda's appointment with Oliver for eight-thirty.'

'Even so,' said Kelly doubtfully, 'he could hardly have been so sure that Mr Barnett would still be there two hours later. Still, leaving that aside, what I'm driving at is this.' He hesitated, then went on with some diffidence: 'If we are to investigate this case, we must do it thoroughly. Your wife knew that your brother was in the office that night, Mr Barnett. She actually met him there at nine o'clock and so far as I know we have no proof of when she left or whether she returned later. I'm not suggesting that she had anything to do with the murder but I do think that Joyce's inquiries should not be confined to the office staff.'

'Linda wouldn't . . .' I began angrily, then stopped. They were both staring at me. I felt I was on dangerous ground.

'I agree that we should cover every possibility,' I said shortly. 'Find out what you can about Linda's movements, Joyce, and Marion's too for that matter. She was out somewhere that night and wouldn't tell me where.'

There was a perceptible slackening of tension in the room. Joyce remarked lightly, 'What about me? Shouldn't somebody investigate me or am I automatically eliminated as too unintelligent to contrive a murder as ingenious as this?'

'Indeed, no. We'll grill you now. Where were you, Miss Carruthers, on Thursday of last week between the hours of 10.30 p.m. and midnight?'

She fluttered her eyelashes and said coyly, 'I was in my flat with Mr Fergusson, sir.'

'What!'

Joyce laughed. 'I thought that would shake you. It was really rather an extraordinary incident, although very fortunate for both of us, because I suppose it gives us an alibi. I left the office at five o'clock that evening and went out for a meal and then on to the cinema. I got back about half-past ten – perhaps twenty to eleven. I had the devil's own job finding my way back in the fog. I made myself a cup of coffee and was just sitting back with my feet up when the doorbell rang. There was Fergusson on the doorstep. I was utterly astounded. He had never been to my flat before although he lives only a couple of blocks away. I couldn't imagine what brought him there at that time of night. And I'm still not much the wiser.

'I invited him in. He wouldn't take his coat off and he wouldn't sit down. He just stood there twisting his hat round and round in his hands. He spent about five minutes apologizing for disturbing me. Then he began to talk about Oliver. Have you ever noticed what a prude Fergusson is? He won't call a spade a spade at all. He kept speaking about Oliver's "unfortunate home circumstances" and his "unconventional private life" and he referred more than once to "that other establishment which he keeps". This was clearly the Gribble Street flat. He was angling for information of some sort and I even got the impression at one point that he was implying that I was Oliver's kept woman. But he couldn't bring himself to put any direct questions and I didn't volunteer anything. Not that I could have helped him much anyway. If he only knew it, I was as curious as he to know who Oliver entertained in his flat every other weekend. However, I just acted dumb and pretended not to know what he was talking about. Eventually he gave up the struggle and went away.'

'Did he seem nervous or excited?' I asked.

'He didn't look like a man who had just committed murder, if that's what you mean. But then he wouldn't anyway. He's the phleg-matic type. He was embarrassed, though. His manner of speech was even more stilted than usual. You know these long, rounded periods that he indulges in when he is uncomfortable about something.'

'When precisely did he arrive and when did he leave?'

'I couldn't say exactly. But I remember eleven o'clock struck soon after he came in, and he wasn't away until nearly half-past.'

That seemed to let him out. Even without the fog to contend with he could scarcely have had time to commit the murder either before or after his visit to Joyce.

At this point Kelly broke in. 'Sorry to change the subject, but something has just struck me. How could the murderer hope to pin his crime on Mrs Grant if he didn't know that she was due to call that night?'

'I don't think he had any such intention,' I said. 'He wanted it to be read as suicide. The photographs would be found in the safe and it would come out that Oliver was about to be exposed by Mrs Grant as a blackmailer. Suicide would be the obvious explanation. That plan went wrong, but the actual course of events proved still more favourable to the murderer.'

'But the murderer, you say, is someone who knew your brother well. Surely such a person would have known that he was left-handed and wouldn't have made the blunder of planting the gun by his right hand?'

'It wasn't really a blunder, you know; it was forced on him. You didn't see the body. Oliver's left hand was clutched to his chest and was covered in blood. The murderer couldn't have got the gun into that hand to press the fingerprints on it without giving the show away. He would be forced to put it in the right hand and hope that nobody spotted the discrepancy.'

Kelly and Joyce got up to leave. As they did so, Joyce's eye fell on the newspaper – an early edition of the evening paper – which I had bought after lunch. The entire front page was given over to the arrest of Sheila and the brief proceedings that morning at the Magistrates' Court. But it was at a small photograph near the foot of the page that Joyce was gazing.

'That's the husband, is it?' she said. 'I've seen him in the office here two or three times. He used to call and see Oliver. I never got his name.'

'I think you must be mistaken, Joyce. They used to know each other slightly years ago. But I'm pretty sure there has been no contact since.'

She peered at the photograph again. 'I don't think I'm mistaken,' she said.

CHAPTER 14

The *Brickfield Herald* was printed and published in a dingy and decaying building off City Road. The newspaper occupied the first and second floors; below it were some shabby little shops – a greengrocer, a tobacconist and a second-hand clothes dealer. To get to the *Herald* office you went through a narrow close and up a stone stair whose steps were hollowed by the passage of generations of feet. The premises hadn't changed since I was a boy, nor had the plant. Even to the uninitiated like myself a glance into the machine room disclosed how antiquated were the processes by which the paper was produced.

Yet somehow the *Herald* survived and even prospered. For that much of the credit was due to its editor James Devlin. He had taken over the paper thirty years ago and had moulded it into what he thought a local newspaper ought to be: not merely a purveyor of local news and gossip, but a forum for serious discussion of matters of public interest. He had fallen foul of authority on more than one occasion for the forthright views his paper expressed, but he was impervious alike to intimidation and to bribery. The *Herald* came to be respected and even feared by local councillors and others in authority and the effect was wholly good for the community. It was also good for the circulation of the paper: there was scarcely a household in Brickfield or in the neighbouring villages that didn't get its *Herald* every day.

Devlin and my father had been firm friends for many years, and I had no hesitation in going to him now with my problem. He was astonishingly well informed about the background to stories which had appeared in his paper – about the facts that couldn't be published or that he had refused to publish. I knew too that anything I said to him would go no farther.

I never know what are the busy hours for a newspaper editor. If I called at an inconvenient time, however, Devlin gave no sign of it. He greeted me warmly, led me into his sanctum, as he called it – a tiny little room on the second floor – cleared some proofs from the only chair and told me to sit down. He himself perched on the end of the desk.

Coming straight to the point, I said that I wanted to consult the *Herald* files for the period of the Merriman trial but that in addition I would be glad of any information Devlin could give me about the trial that hadn't appeared in the Press.

He pressed a bell on his desk. Almost at once a girl appeared in the doorway.

'Get the bound volume for February 1958,' he said. The girl went out.

All this time his shrewd eyes were studying me from behind the shaggy white eyebrows. It was a formidable face, forbidding almost, until you saw the kindliness of the mouth.

'This has something to do with your brother's murder, hasn't it?' he said. 'Shocking business. You should have married that girl, you know. I always thought so.'

The transition was so sudden that I didn't follow him.

'I'm speaking of Sheila Cox,' he added testily, seeing my blank look. 'Sheila Grant, I suppose I should call her now. There was fine stuff in that girl. I was at school with her father. Yes, you could have had her for the asking and you would never have regretted it. And look what she got – Roger Grant—' he gave an exclamation of disgust – 'a walking jellyfish.'

'How much do you know about the case against Sheila?' I asked curiously.

'Oh, we hear things!' he said vaguely. 'Can't publish them, of course. Prejudicing the trial and what not. It's some pickle she's got herself into, God help her.'

'Mr Devlin,' I said. 'I don't believe that Sheila killed Oliver. I'm going to try to prove that she's innocent.'

The girl came back into the room, holding one end of a large tome. Gripping the other end was a perspiring small boy, who looked as if he should still have been at school. They laid the volume carefully on the desk and scuttled out.

Devlin was gazing quizzically at me, drumming his fingers on the edge of the desk. He took out a dog-eared packet of cigarettes and offered me one. He didn't speak until we had lit up.

'Let me give you a bit of advice, Simon,' he said at length. 'I've had my brushes with the police in the past. They make mistakes occasionally and sometimes they can be a bit high-handed. But by and large they are efficient and they are never – or hardly ever – corrupt. When it comes to a serious crime like murder you can depend on it that they won't make an arrest unless they are absolutely satisfied they've got the guilty party.'

'These are almost the identical words Superintendent Garland used when I went to him. I don't deny that the police are satisfied Sheila is guilty and I don't deny that they've got strong reasons for it. But I believe they are wrong all the same.'

He was silent for a moment. Then he laughed.

'All right, go ahead. I must say I hope you are right. I like Sheila. She's got a bit of spirit, unlike most of her generation. What is it you want to know about the Merriman case?'

'I believe there is a connection between someone in Oliver's circle and the Polygon Club. I want to find out who that person is and what the connection is.'

'That person would be the murderer, I suppose?'

'Yes.'

'Well, if there is such a link, I don't know of it. You'd better read up these files. We gave the case quite a splash. One thing I can tell you, though. Although Merriman took the rap, there was somebody behind him who got off scot free.'

'Who was that?' I asked.

'Oh, I don't know *who* it was. I only know there must have been somebody. You see, I attended the trial and had the chance of studying Merriman. He was only a lick of paint above the moron level and it was standing out a mile that he couldn't have organized a mothers' meeting, far less a highly efficient show like that. But whoever it was covered his tracks well. And Merriman was loyal too.'

'Is Merriman still in prison?'

'He's in Broadmoor. Quite gaga, I believe.'

Devlin told me I could take the *Herald* file home with me. He helped me to carry it down to my car. As we were parting, he said, 'One other thing. The present manager of the Polygon is a friend of mine, a chap called Grandison. He was with the company at the time of the scandal as assistant manager of one of their hotels and they put him in charge of the Polygon when it reopened as a restaurant. He's got inside information about the case and if I have a word with him he'll tell you what he knows.'

I thanked Devlin and said I would call on Grandison the following day. Devlin promised to ring him up at once.

That night I read every word of the *Herald* reports of the

Merriman trial, which had lasted three full days in February 1958. Although I didn't get the clue I was looking for, by the time I had finished I did at least have a clearer picture of what had been going on. The prosecution case rested largely on the evidence of four or five girls who had been employed as professionals at the debauches. It was one of these girls who had started proceedings by going to the police. She had misunderstood the extent of her duties when she was engaged. As she quaintly put it, she 'had earned a respectable living on the streets for years and she didn't approve of indecency, however high the wages.' The other girls, while less willing witnesses, largely corroborated her story. No doubt they preferred to give evidence for the prosecution rather than to be in the dock themselves.

None of the clients gave evidence and their names were not revealed. Indeed, what had given the case much of its savour were the constant hints that notable persons were involved. Merriman was the only one of the defendants to plead not guilty. The three underlings who were charged along with him – waiters at the night-club – admitted their complicity but maintained that they had played a very subsidiary part in the organization. Merriman's defence was a denial of all knowledge of what had been going on and a claim that it was a conspiracy against him. His counsel, in cross-examination of the prosecution witnesses, made a virulent attack on their character and credibility; and it was true enough that some of them had a pretty unsavoury past. But the mass of evidence against Merriman, not only of the girls, but also of his co-defendants, was too great. And any lingering doubt about his guilt must have been removed when he went into the witness box himself. He convicted himself out of his own mouth with almost every sentence. I could see what Devlin had meant when he referred to Merriman's low intelligence.

There were one or two references to the photographs. I was
astonished to find that these formed an integral part of the entertainment. Apparently the clients – or some of them at any rate –
liked to take away pictures of what they had taken part in, to gloat
over in private, presumably. So they were supplied for an extra
charge. Merriman was said to have taken and developed the photographs himself, although this too he denied. It was all rather nasty
and one couldn't feel much sympathy for the victims of the blackmailer. If ever anyone invited blackmail, these people did.

I spent the following morning in the office, where I had one or two
appointments that I couldn't cut. I was interested to notice that
Joyce was out for most of the morning and that Kelly didn't appear
at all. Presumably they were busy on their respective tasks.

I drove into the city after an early lunch. It was a glorious
spring day and I found my spirits rising. Even the thought of
Sheila languishing under a charge of murder didn't depress me.
I was supremely confident that I was going to get her out of her
troubles.

However, my interview with Grandison, the manager of the
Polygon Restaurant, was at first disappointing. Anxious though he
was to help, he had little to add to what I already knew. He did
take me upstairs and let me see the room in which the orgies had
taken place. It was now tastefully furnished as a lounge and was
part of Grandison's private apartment. I asked him whether
Merriman had lived on the premises too.

'Yes, they had this same flat. The room was officially part of it,
but, of course, as you know, it was used for other purposes.'

'They? Was he married, then?'

'Oh, yes! His wife was a very retiring sort of person. Hardly anybody knew her. She must have had some idea of what was going on, but I don't think she was implicated. At any rate the police didn't seem to think so.'

'Where is she now?'

'Mrs Merriman? I really don't know. I seem to remember hearing that she went abroad soon after the trial.'

I asked him about the photographs. He knew that the police had made a great fuss about the absence of the negatives and that Merriman had been grilled again and again. But they had never got them.

I thanked Grandison for his help and held out my hand to say goodbye. But he was gazing abstractedly out of the window. Finally he turned to me and said:

'I don't know what the purpose of your inquiries is, Mr Barnett, and I don't want to pry. But James Devlin asked me to let you have all the information I have about this business and if he trusts you I know I can too. There is one thing more I can show you.'

He led me into another room, unlocked a safe and brought out two foolscap envelopes. He handed me the bulkier one first.

'There's nothing particularly private about that,' he said. 'It's a list of the members of the Polygon Night Club, dated January 1958. It was a perfectly respectable club in its own right and not simply a façade for the goings on upstairs.'

He was still holding the second envelope irresolutely in his hand.

'Some months after I came here I discovered, quite by accident, that there was a false bottom in one of the drawers of the desk Merriman used and a secret compartment underneath. In it I found this. It's a list of the members of the inner club. I suppose I should have given it to the police but – well, the case was over and done with and I thought it was better not to stir up the mud again. I couldn't quite bring myself to destroy it; so in the end I just kept it. I've never shown it to anyone before.'

He parted with the envelope reluctantly. I started to open it but he stopped me.

'No, no,' he said. 'Take it away with you and bring it back when you've finished with it. I don't want to know what all this is about and I don't want to be asked questions about people whose names appear on that list.'

I put the envelopes in my pocket. Grandison offered me a drink before I left and I felt it would be churlish to refuse, although I was longing to get a sight of the contents of that envelope. I was convinced it held the key to the whole mystery.

We chatted for some minutes over a glass of whisky. It was a strain for both of us. Grandison, I could see, was an abnormally sensitive man and was having a struggle with his conscience over what he had just done. It was as great a relief to him as to me when, as soon as politeness allowed, I got up to leave.

I got into my car and drove to Clitheroe Park, where I found myself a seat in the sunshine. I lit a leisurely cigarette and with exquisite self-torture opened the larger envelope first. It contained six foolscap sheets of names and addresses, perhaps 200 in all. I ran my eye down the list and recognized quite a few of the names. I was surprised to find that Waterston had been a member of the Polygon Club and even more surprised to see Roger Grant's name there.

However, I could contain myself no longer and ripped open the other envelope. This time there was a single sheet of paper, headed simply 'Members', and containing about twenty-five names, without addresses, typed on it. I read the names through twice, a chill of disappointment gradually spreading through me. A number of the names were familiar to me. There was Stroud, for example, and there were one or two others whose faces I had recognized in the photographs that Superintendent Garland had shown me. But there was no one who could be described as a friend or associate of Oliver. It was a bitter anti-climax. I had had high hopes that the blackmailer had himself been a member of the 'inner club', as Grandison termed it.

After a bit my spirits began to revive a little. There were, after all, one or two crumbs of comfort, even if only of a negative sort. Oliver's name was not on the list, so that at least this provided no confirmation of the police's case either. Nor was Sheila's, which tended to support her statement that her visit to the place was an isolated occasion. Thinking of Sheila brought me back to a name which *was* on the list and which hadn't registered until now, 'Joseph L. Barrington'. This was the oaf who had enticed Sheila into the place.

On an impulse I decided to try and see Barrington, with no clear idea of what I wanted from him. Remembering that Sheila had said he used to work for his father, who owned two garages in Endsleigh, I went to a post office and looked up the telephone directory. Sure enough there was a J. L. Barrington with an Endsleigh address. When I rang the number, a woman's voice answered me. She told me rather curtly that her husband was out and that I could get hold of him at the Central Garage; and she gave me the number.

However, I decided to call on him instead of phoning. Endsleigh was only fifteen miles away and I was there in less than half an hour. When I asked at the Central Garage for Mr Barrington I was directed to a figure in overalls bent double over the open bonnet of a battered old Austin.

As soon as he straightened up I recognized him from Sheila's description. There was the toothbrush moustache, the sleek hair and the shifty eyes. 'A flash type,' Sheila had said. The slang phrase summed him up admirably.

'Yes, sir?' said Barrington, an ingratiating smile on his lips, while his eyes looked me up and down to assess my potentialities as a customer.

'Is there anywhere I can have a private talk with you?' I asked.

The smile vanished from his face and he looked more wary. 'You'd better come into my office,' he said grudgingly and led me through a door at the back of the garage and into an untidy room where a buxom blonde was seated at a desk, a cup of tea at her side and a newspaper spread over her typewriter.

'Out, Flossie,' said Barrington, jerking his thumb towards the door.

The blonde flashed an angry look at him, swept up her newspaper and flounced out.

'How's business?' I asked.

He didn't know whether to answer or not. He was still eying me watchfully.

'Oh, well,' he said eventually, 'you know how it is. It's hard to make ends meet, with overheads going up all the time. I had to sell our other place last year. And you can't get the staff to do an honest day's work. When the old man retired two years ago I got rid of all the old dough-heads he had gathered round him. But, by God, I sometimes wonder if they wouldn't have been better than this lot.

'But I'm on to a good thing now – second-hand cars. You saw that old jalopy I was working on? Five quid I paid for her. And, by

God, a lick or two of paint and she'll go for fifty, you mark my—'
He broke off in the middle of his sentence.

'Haven't I seen you somewhere before?' he asked thoughtfully.
He snapped his fingers. 'Now don't tell me. I never forget a face.
Got it!' – he smirked triumphantly – 'You're the brother of that
chap that was murdered. I've seen your picture in the paper. The
murder that they've arrested—' Again his voice tailed off in mid-air.
It was obvious that his thoughts had taken an uncomfortable turn.
His mind was as easy to read as an open book.

I finished his sentence for him: 'Yes, the murder that they've
arrested Sheila Grant for. But she was Sheila Cox when you knew
her, wasn't she?'

'I don't know what you're talking about,' he growled truculently.

I knew how to deal with the Joe Barringtons of this world.

'Look here, Barrington,' I said. 'You could have got two years
for what you did that night. And it's not too late yet. If you've got
any sense, you'll answer my questions.'

He continued to bluster, but his face had gone pale.

'I never even heard of your perishing brother until I picked up
my paper one morning and read that he had been bumped off. If
you think I—'

'That's not what I want to ask you about. I want you to tell me
all you know about the Polygon Club. I mean the club within a
club, Merriman's little show.'

'And suppose I tell you to go and chase yourself?' he said
belligerently.

'That would be a mistake, Barrington. The police would be
interested to hear how you got Sheila drunk and then inveigled
her into that hotbed of vice. And you're married now, aren't you?
How would your wife react to that story?'

It was blackmail again, but I felt no compunction. And it was effective. Barrington folded up completely.

What he told me confirmed the evidence that had been given at the trial. In particular he was quite emphatic that it was Merriman who took the photographs. He was pathetically anxious to convince me that he was not himself perverted and that he had only attended these sessions for the fun of 'watching other people making fools of themselves'.

'Besides,' he added, 'I wasn't a proper member anyway. I had a free pass, so to speak. I knew the boss.'

'Merriman?'

'Him!' He gave a contemptuous snort. 'God, no. Merriman was only a stooge. No, I mean the real boss. Claire, his wife.'

'But I thought she was a quiet little woman who kept in the background?'

'Oh! She kept in the background all right. But she wasn't so quiet when you got to know her. She was hot stuff, that one. A good looker, too. And she was the brains of the show, although I doubt if any of the fashionable queers that paid out their money so lavishly even knew she existed. Even the pros didn't know that she wore the trousers. But I knew. You see, I had privileges.' He gave me a horrible, knowing leer. He had quite recovered his composure.

I tried to keep the disgust out of my voice. 'Who was she? Where did she come from?'

'It's funny you should ask that,' he said. 'She was always very cagey about it. They hadn't been married very long. I believe her father had a good job in the city, a doctor, or a banker or something, but she never mentioned him. Not until they arrested Merriman. She was in a flap then, all right. I think her old man used his influence to keep her in the clear. You see, the police had their suspicions, she told me.'

He grinned complacently. 'I didn't do so badly out of it either. I was the one she had to fear. I could have given the game away any time. But the very day Merriman was arrested she came along and planked down fifty quid. She didn't say a word. She didn't have to.'

'Where is she now?' I asked.

'She's dead.'

'Dead?'

'Yes. She went off to Canada as soon as the trial was over and I read of her death in the paper not many months later. A car accident in Toronto.'

There was nothing more to be got out of Barrington. I was glad to get away from him and into the fresh air. He nauseated me.

I looked at my watch. Five-fifteen. There might just be time to do what I had in mind. I drove to the nearest telephone kiosk and put through a call to the Admiralty in London. I was in luck. My friend was still in his office.

'Peter,' I said, 'would you do me a great favour? I'm trying to get particulars of a marriage. The man's name is Henry John Merriman; all I know about the wife is that she was called Claire. They are both from this part of the country. They were married almost certainly between 1950 and 1957. Could you possibly get someone to go along to Somerset House to ferret it out for me? I expect I could trace it locally here if I spent long enough at it. But it's important and urgent, and I think you could get it for me quicker. What I want to know is the full name of the wife and the full name and occupation of her father.'

Peter said good-humouredly that he would get the whole resources of the Admiralty on to it first thing in the morning and ring through the result to my office.

I drove slowly home. I was tired and dispirited. If this hunch didn't come off, I decided, I would drop the whole thing.

CHAPTER 15

I called in at the office when I got back. Everyone had gone, but there was a note on my desk, 'Please phone me as soon as you get in – A.K.'

I rang Kelly. There was a note of suppressed excitement in his voice.

'I think I'm on to something,' he said. 'Can I look round and see you?'

'Well, I must get a meal first. Come to my house about eight o'clock. And see if you can round up Joyce and bring her too.'

I deliberated whether to go out for a meal or to cook myself something at home. The thought that if I went home I could get a shower and a change of clothes finally decided me. But I regretted the decision as soon as I turned the car through the gate, for there was Marion ringing the doorbell. My heart sank. It was too late to turn back, for she had already seen me.

'Oh, there you are, Simon!' she called. 'Where on earth have you been? I've been trying to get you at the office all afternoon.'

'I was in the city on business,' I said shortly, as I got out of the car. 'You'd better come in.'

'What a shambles,' she remarked, as she glanced into the kitchen. 'Is this not Mrs Kettles's day? Let me wash up these dishes for you.' I hadn't had time to wash the breakfast things before I left that morning.

'It would be more to the point if you made me something to

eat while I go upstairs and change,' I said. 'I'm tired and I'm hungry.'

She brightened visibly and set to work at once. When I came down, bacon and eggs were sizzling in the frying-pan.

She talked to me while I ate.

'What's that girl Carruthers up to?' she said. 'She's been nosing around and asking Millie questions about where I was last Thursday night. What's it got to do with her? Anyway, it's all finished and done with now, isn't it? They've got the woman who did it.'

I thought it wiser not to reply. I continued eating steadily.

This exasperated Marion. 'You're at the back of this, Simon, I know it. Why is it so important to you to know where I went to that night? I've told you before, I didn't kill Oliver. I've nothing to hide.'

'If you've nothing to hide, Marion,' I said gently, 'why don't you tell me where you went? You haven't been out alone in the evening for years. It's curious you should choose that particular night for a solitary stroll in the fog.'

Her mouth was set in a petulant line and she didn't answer.

I had a sudden inspiration. I recollected that just before he went out that night, Oliver had got a phone call from 'Mrs Cargill' and had immediately afterwards told Marion that he wouldn't be home till late.

'You went to the Gribble Street flat, didn't you, Marion? You thought you would surprise Oliver there with his mistress?'

Her face was contorted with fury. 'Damn you, Simon, do you have to humiliate me like this?' She burst into a frenzied sobbing.

'Get me a drink,' she shouted at me hysterically.

I went over to the sideboard and poured her out a neat brandy. She swallowed it over at one gulp and held out the glass for more.

I put water in with the brandy this time.

She was calmer now and began speaking in a flat lifeless tone. 'I used to tell you that I didn't care about Oliver's affairs with other women. Well, it wasn't true. I was as jealous as hell. It wasn't so bad when he picked them off the streets. But these last few months – God, I could have strangled the woman if I could have got my hands on her. Worst of all was not knowing who it was.

'Many a time, at the weekends, when I knew he was with her, I was within an ace of going along and bursting in on them. But my pride held my back. Yes, pride. I still had a little of that. And also there was Oliver to think of; he needed that outlet. In my more rational moments—' she smiled without humour – 'I recognized that.'

This was certainly one of her more rational moments. I think she was being as honest with herself as she was capable of being. As so often before, my exasperation with her turned to pity.

'But that night,' she continued, 'I just boiled over. The thought that that woman would have the effrontery to phone up to my house and make a date with my husband almost within earshot of me was too much. Yes, I went to Gribble Street. And I've been ashamed of it ever since. And still more ashamed of snooping around the flat when I found he wasn't there.'

'You mean you went into the flat?' I asked in surprise.

'Yes.'

'But how did you get in?'

'Oh, I – I had taken Oliver's key!'

There was something odd about this.

'But Marion,' I protested, 'if you were able to take Oliver's key, you must have known he couldn't have gone to the flat.'

She took a long time to answer. 'Well,' she said, 'he had a spare key which he kept in the dressing-table drawer in his bedroom. That's the key I took.'

This was a patent lie, thought up on the spur of the moment. I couldn't understand it, for I was convinced she had been speaking the truth up to this point.

I decided not to press the point for the moment. Instead, I asked her when she had got to the flat and how long she had spent there.

'Well, I left here about half-past nine and I managed to get a bus. The fog wasn't quite so thick at that time. I would be there by ten to ten. And I know I left at twenty-five to eleven. I had to walk back and I got utterly lost. It was five minutes to midnight when I got in. Millie was nearly out of her mind with Oliver and me both missing.'

'And did you learn anything about Oliver's mistress from your snooping?'

'I couldn't positively identify her, but there were some indications. Quite a selection of night attire she had there. And it's a very unusual perfume she uses.' She fell silent. She seemed disinclined to pursue the matter further.

'How's Linda?' she asked suddenly.

It was the sort of malicious question she indulged in that never failed to irritate me.

'How should I know?' I answered shortly. 'I haven't been seeing her.'

It was after seven-forty-five and I was wondering how I could get rid of Marion tactfully, when she suddenly glanced at the clock and exclaimed, 'Lord, look at the time. And I promised Millie I would be in for dinner by seven-thirty.'

I had to drive her home, and when I got back it was Joyce and

Alan Kelly this time who were waiting on the doorstep. Rather wearily I let them in and showed them into the sitting-room.

Kelly was obviously bursting to get something off his chest, but with his customary good manners insisted that Joyce tell her story first. She produced some typed sheets and handed copies to Kelly and me.

'It was quite a task,' she said. 'It was easy enough to get people to say where they had been that night: the real headache was verifying their stories. I don't think I would be cut out for the CID – I haven't enough patience. This painstaking checking of every detail goes all against the grain for me. I prefer to rely on my intuition to decide whether a person is speaking the truth or not. However, I've suppressed my instincts on this occasion and looked for independent corroboration wherever I could get it – and I've trodden on a few corns in the process, I can tell you.

'Anyway, the upshot is that nearly all the staff can be completely wiped off. Most of them were home long before nine-thirty – remember it was a filthy night – and didn't stir out again. And some of the ones who *were* out late have unshakeable alibis. Incidentally, Alan—' she turned to Kelly – 'your alibi was a surprising one. Who is this Susan Ross?'

Kelly blushed. 'I'm hoping to pop the question to her next week. I didn't want it to get around until she had accepted me.'

'Well, well, you're a dark horse. Anyway, you're out. We're left with only a handful. I've put down on that sheet what they *say* they were doing at the relevant times. For the sake of completeness I've covered the whole evening and not just the period between nine-thirty and midnight. I've included myself and Fergusson because our alibis depend on each other and I suppose we could have been accomplices. I've also included you, Simon. Your story's a pretty thin one, when all's said and done.' She grinned at me.

'By all means,' I said.

'Oh, and one other thing,' she added. 'You know Ethel, the new junior typist? The toothy one. Well, her story of how she spent the evening reads like a Hollywood epic and is quite unconfirmed. But I just couldn't bring myself to put that down on paper. The idea of Ethel as a murderer and a blackmailer is too ludicrous.'

I studied the list. It was indeed a short one: six names in all. And one of these the name of a murderer, I thought, a shiver going down my spine. This was the list: –

Joyce Carruthers: – 5 p.m., left office; 5.15–6.15, high tea at the Chilton; 6.45–9.30, Rex Cinema; walked home (delayed by fog); 10.35, arrived at flat; 10.55 Fergusson called; 11.30, Fergusson left.

Simon Barnett: – (Here was reproduced an accurate statement of my movements from the time I got back from the city.)

Fergusson: – 6.20, called at the office on return from the city; 6.45 left office; 7–8.20, dinner at Club; 8.45–10.45 at home (unconfirmed); 10.55–11.30, at Miss Carruthers's flat; 11.40 home.

Mrs Oliver Barnett: – Until 9.30 home; 9.30–11.55 out (whereabouts not disclosed).

Mrs Simon Barnett: – 7.30, left the city by car with father; 9, arrived at office; 9–9.45, talked to Oliver Barnett; 9.45, left office (unconfirmed) and walked to Station Hotel; 10.25 arrived at hotel (confirmed); 10.25 onwards, in hotel (unconfirmed).

Waterston: – 7.30 left the city by car with daughter; 9, dropped daughter at office and drove to Station Hotel; 9.10

arrived at hotel; 10.40, left hotel; time of return not known, but was in for breakfast next morning.

The last entry of all pulled me up short.

'What's this about Waterston?' I asked sharply.

'Yes, it's curious, isn't it?' said Joyce. 'I nearly missed it, too. He told the police he was in the hotel all night from ten-past nine onwards, and the receptionist confirmed that. Her desk is just inside the door. It wasn't a busy night at the hotel and she said she couldn't have failed to notice either Mrs Barnett or Waterston if they had gone out again. But he went out all the same. He must have used the staff entrance. Anyway he was seen getting into his car and driving off at ten-forty or thereabouts by a porter who had been sent out to the car park by one of the guests to get something out of his car. It was Waterston's car all right, and, foggy though it was, the porter is absolutely certain it was Waterston who got into it. He was right beside him.'

'Now this is really significant,' I said excitedly. 'Waterston could easily—'

'Yes, no doubt,' Joyce interrupted. 'But don't jump to conclusions, Simon. Waterston might have been going anywhere – perhaps just up the street to get cigarettes. And he wouldn't think it worth mentioning to the inspector when he made his statement. And remember that there are others on the list with the opportunity. Your wife, for instance, could easily have slipped out of the hotel. And what about Oliver's wife? And for that matter my own alibi is largely unconfirmed. I doubt if anybody would remember seeing me at the cinema that night and—'

'I can corroborate part of your story at least, Joyce,' Kelly interrupted.

'What? Have you been checking up on me, Alan?'

'Not on you. On Fergusson. You see, I've discovered that he had a key to the flat in Gribble Street.'

He dropped the remark out quietly, casually almost, with the true instinct for dramatic effect. Our reaction must have gratified him. I leapt out of my chair, while Joyce, who had been unwrapping a piece of chewing gum – her cigarette substitute – dropped it and held her pose rigid, staring at Kelly.

'Well, don't sit there savouring it,' I said at length. 'Tell us about it.'

It was a simple enough story. Kelly had gone to the neighbours at Gribble Street and had asked them much the same questions that Sheila had asked them; and had got much the same replies. He asked them particularly about visitors to the flat during the week, and especially on a Tuesday, but drew blank. One woman did have a vague recollection of hearing someone open and close the door of the flat about breakfast-time on a weekday a couple of months before, but as she wasn't sure which morning and hadn't seen the visitor anyway, her evidence was of little value. Kelly did learn, however, from more than one source that a man had visited the flat about 8.15 p.m. on the Wednesday – the night before the murder – and also that there had been someone there lateish in the evening of the Thursday. One witness thought that the visitor on the Thursday was also a man but another was sure it was a woman.

Kelly, again following Sheila's footsteps, went next to the owner of the flat, Mrs McConnell. Here again he seemed to be making little headway at first. Mrs McConnell admitted she knew little or nothing of her tenant, Mr Jones, having met him only once. He paid his rent regularly each month by money order and that was enough for her. She had sent him two keys to the flat as soon as the tenancy was agreed on.

It was the words 'sent him' that put Kelly on the right track.

'I presume that your meeting with Mr Jones was when he called to arrange the tenancy with you?' he asked.

'Oh, no!' she said in surprise. 'That was all done by correspondence. I didn't meet him until much later – round about last Christmas.'

And then the story came out. A man describing himself as Mr Jones had called on Mrs McConnell one morning and asked if he could borrow her key to the flat. He explained that he had just got back after two or three days in London and had found he had inadvertently left in the London hotel a pair of trousers in a pocket of which were his keys, including the keys to the Gribble Street flat. Mrs McConnell was a gullible woman and, in any case, her visitor was obviously a man of 'good breeding', as she put it, and fitted her mental picture of Jones. She gave him the key, all unsuspecting, and when it was duly returned through the post two days later she dismissed the incident from her mind.

'The visitor made quite an impression on Mrs McConnell,' said Kelly, 'and she was able to give me a pretty detailed description of him. From what she said I am absolutely certain it was Fergusson. But in any case I've got corroboration from another source. I asked myself where Fergusson would go if he wanted a duplicate key cut. The obvious place is Smith & Chappell's. And sure enough old Sam Chappell remembers the transaction. He could even give me the date – 29th December last. Fergusson came in with a key – said it was his house key and he had lost the spare. Chappell cut a duplicate for him and gave it him the next day.'

I interrupted here. 'I wonder why he got it done locally. If he wanted to keep it dark, surely he would have been safer to go to a locksmith in the city where he wasn't known.'

'I'm not so sure,' Kelly answered. 'Some of these places refuse to make duplicate keys for a stranger until they've satisfied themselves of his bona fides. Whereas Sam Chappell, who knows Fergusson, would do it without question and would be most unlikely to think it worth mentioning to anybody. Anyway, the fact remains that it was to Smith & Chappell's that he went.'

Kelly had been so carried away by this success that he had started at once to check on Fergusson's alibi for the night of the murder. He tried to enlist Joyce's help, but she had been out on her own investigations. The main stumbling-block to the theory that Fergusson had committed the murder was Joyce's evidence that he had been with her from about ten-fifty-five to eleven-thirty. As Joyce had been none too certain of the exact times, Kelly wondered if he could in any way fix them more precisely. He had a nodding acquaintance with the woman who occupied the flat across the landing from Joyce, and, not very hopefully, he called on her.

It turned out that this woman, a Mrs Andrews, knew quite a lot. In the first place she was able to confirm that Joyce got back to her flat a few minutes after ten-thirty. Mrs Andrews had been putting out her milk bottles when she arrived. And she had heard Joyce's doorbell ring some time later. Being of an inquisitive disposition, she peered through her letterbox to see who was calling at that late hour. When she saw that it was a man and saw him being admitted to the house she was still more intrigued and hovered about until the door opened again and the man came out. She noted the times most particularly. Ten-fifty-seven he arrived and eleven-twenty-eight he left. She was also able to describe the man. It was undoubtedly Fergusson.

'Well,' said Kelly, 'that's the lot. It gives Fergusson two minutes more on both sides. But I still don't see how he had time to do the murder either before or after he called on Joyce. All the same, the whole thing's damned fishy.'

'Fishy? It positively stinks,' I said. 'But for that alibi, it all dovetails so well. I can tell you who the visitors to the Gribble Street flat were on the Wednesday and Thursday nights. The Thursday night one is really irrelevant – it was Marion, hoping to surprise Oliver and his mistress.' I recounted to them what Marion had told me earlier in the evening.

'Now, who was the man who went to the flat on the Wednesday evening?' I went on. 'Surely the answer is obvious. It was Oliver himself. We know he took the car out immediately after dinner that night and came back about an hour later, 'white and shaken', according to Millie. Why he went to the flat that particular evening I don't suppose we'll ever know, but there is no doubt about what he found there: the letter from Robertson which was posted the previous day. Now the police view would be that what upset him so much was to learn from Robertson that Sheila, one of his blackmail victims, was on his trail. But if we assume that Oliver was not the blackmailer, that letter would be no less of a shock to him. It would show him that somebody was making use of his flat and his assumed name, for a criminal purpose.

'What did he do as soon as he got back home? He phoned Fergusson and demanded to see him immediately. And when that wasn't possible he had lunch with him the next day and, even by Fergusson's own admission, made some odd insinuations. Why should Oliver go to Fergusson unless he had some reason to suspect him? It couldn't have been for advice, for they loathed each other. And there's one other thing. Fergusson's account of that luncheon with Oliver didn't ring true at all. He made out that Oliver was panic-stricken and hysterical. Knowing Oliver, I just can't believe that.'

'Why should Fergusson, if he's guilty', said Kelly, 'have gone out of his way to tell you about the conversation with your brother at all?'

'I think he knew I would find it hard to believe Oliver had committed suicide and this was an attempt to make suicide seem more plausible. Also, for all he knew Oliver might have dropped a hint to me about what he had discovered. When Fergusson gave me his version of the lunch with Oliver, I got the impression at one point that he was testing me out to see how much I knew and that he was relieved to find that I knew nothing.'

'Just a minute,' said Joyce impatiently. 'For a lawyer you don't show much respect for the facts. Half an hour ago you were all for Waterston as the murderer on one flimsy bit of evidence. Now you're building up a case against Fergusson. There are two serious flaws in it. First of all you say that when Oliver got back after finding the letter from Robertson at the flat he at once suspected Fergusson and phoned him to arrange to see him and have it out with him. That implies that he already knew that Fergusson had a key to the Gribble Street flat. Can you really imagine Oliver acquiescing in a situation like that? But the second objection is even more fundamental. Have you forgotten it was physically impossible for Fergusson to have killed Oliver? He couldn't be in two places at once, you know. All it boils down to is that Fergusson had a key to the flat and therefore *could* have been the blackmailer. Have you any proof that he was? Have you found any link between Fergusson and the photographs?'

'Not yet,' I had to admit. 'But let me ask you a question, Joyce.

Can you suggest any reasonable explanation of why, if it wasn't for the purposes of the blackmail, Fergusson went to these extraordinary lengths to get a key to the flat?'

'Certainly,' said Joyce. 'I described Fergusson some time ago as a prude. Some people who are prudish on the surface are prurient-minded underneath, and it's my belief that Fergusson is one of these. I've got an instinct for that sort of thing. It wouldn't surprise me in the least that his reason for getting a key to the flat was simply unhealthy curiosity.'

'You mean he's a sort of peeping Tom?'

'Exactly.'

I turned this over in my mind doubtfully. It was true that when Fergusson had spoken to me of Oliver's affairs with women I had got the impression once or twice of an unnatural morbidity about such matters. But it was almost beyond belief that he would go through these complicated manoeuvres to get a key to the flat simply in order to spy on Oliver and his mistress. After all, he could scarcely hope to conceal himself in the flat while they were there.

All the same, the basic difficulty remained – the question of time. Oliver had been alive at ten-forty-six, when he spoke to me on the phone. Fergusson had appeared at Joyce's door at ten-fifty-seven. That gave him eleven minutes at the very outside to shoot Oliver, plant the negatives in the safe and make his way from the office to Joyce's flat. In normal conditions it was just feasible, for it was a seven or eight minutes' drive from the office to the flat. But in the fog we had that night it was out of the question. It was even worse at the other end. Fergusson left Joyce at eleven-twenty-eight. I found Oliver's body about eleven-thirty-five. Again, seven minutes was far too short for Fergusson to do all he would have to do. In any case we had the medical evidence that Oliver had died not later than eleven-thirty and Sheila's evidence that he was already dead when she arrived at a quarter-past eleven.

And yet I had a conviction that somehow Fergusson had done it. The alibi was too neat and too artificial. As Joyce herself had remarked, for Fergusson to call on her at that time of night was astonishingly out of character; especially as he seemed to have no pressing reason for his visit.

We discussed the problem for some time but could make no impression on it. My brain was tired and I found myself wishing that the other two would go. I couldn't even bring myself to describe to them my own investigations that day, knowing that it would start a fresh discussion. I contented myself with saying that I was expecting a phone call tomorrow which would tell me whether I had made any progress or not.

It was half-past eleven before they left. I switched on the immerser and took a hot bath. I lay and soaked in the hot water for half an hour, easing the tiredness out of my back and legs. Then I took a couple of aspirins and went to bed. But I still couldn't sleep.

CHAPTER 16

I was finishing breakfast the following morning when Roger Grant arrived. He looked in even worse shape than before and this time there was no doubt he had been drinking. His walk as he preceded me into the kitchen was unsteady and he stumbled once and nearly fell. It was a miracle that he had driven in from the farm without an accident.

He more or less collapsed into a chair. I poured out a cup of black coffee and handed it to him. His hand trembled so much as he took it that some of the coffee spilled into the saucer.

He gave a feeble laugh. 'I'm in a bad way, aren't I?' he said.

I didn't reply. I was anxious to get to the office and I was annoyed by this intrusion.

But he seemed in no hurry to get to the point.

'God, Simon,' he said, 'these last few days have been hell. Sheer hell. Police nosing around all day long and eternally asking stupid questions. You'd think that I was the criminal.'

He drained his coffee in one gulp.

'Ah, that was good! Could I possibly . . . ? Thanks very much. And a roll and butter if you can spare it, Simon. Our woman hasn't come in since – since it happened, and I've scarcely had a bit to eat for three days.'

As I buttered a roll for him I couldn't restrain the acid comment, 'You haven't gone short on the liquid refreshment, though.'

'It's the worry, Simon. You can't imagine what it's like, just waiting, not knowing what's going to happen.'

He took a sip from his second cup of coffee and followed it with a large bite from the roll. Some colour was coming back into his cheeks.

I watched him for a moment or two. 'How is Sheila?' I asked.

'Sheila? She's surprisingly resilient, much more so than I am. Full of amusing anecdotes about prison life. She's not in the least interested in the details of preparing her case – she left it to me to fix up with the solicitors who are to represent her at the trial. She doesn't seem to have any doubt that she's going to be acquitted. She puts great faith in you.' This last remark was accompanied by a sly, sidelong look from under his eyelids.

I ignored it. 'Tell her I'll try to see her in the next day or two,' I said. 'Incidentally, who have you got for the defence?'

He looked uncomfortable. 'As a matter of fact, that's one of the things I wanted to see you about. I suggested Cramond, as you said, but the solicitors won't hear of it. They say he's too clever by half and anyway far too expensive. They want to get somebody called Weatherly. Do you know him?'

'By reputation only. A second-rater. His chief virtue is a gift for pulling at the heartstrings of the jury. If your solicitors want Weatherly, it can only be because they believe Sheila is guilty and intend to base the defence on provocation. Haven't you told them, Roger, that that won't do? That's no defence anyway. The most they could expect from that would be a recommendation for mercy.'

'Well,' he said uneasily, 'you know what lawyers are like. They won't listen to laymen. But I did ask for time to think it over. I've to phone them before ten this morning. That's why I came over to see you so early.'

'Well, go ahead and phone them. Right now. Tell them it's to be Cramond and a plea of not guilty, otherwise Sheila changes her solicitors.'

I fretted at the delay while he was on the telephone. It was already half-past nine. What if Peter rang through from London before I got to the office? Belatedly I picked up the office extension and got through to the girl at the office switchboard. I told her that if a London call came for me before I arrived it was to be transferred to Joyce. Roger had gathered the remnants of his self-respect together and was almost beaming when he came away from the telephone. 'I told them pretty sharply what they're to do,' he said. 'There will be no more trouble from that quarter.'

He showed no inclination to depart, even when I put on my hat and coat.

'There was one other thing, Simon,' he began hesitantly.

'Tell me it on the way to the office,' I said. 'I can't wait here any longer. You can drive me there.'

But when I looked at him shambling out, his eyes still bleary and bloodshot, I changed my mind.

'On second thoughts,' I said, 'I'll drive. You're not in a fit condition.'

He looked offended, but didn't protest when I got into the driving-seat of his Rover. He climbed in beside me.

It was a beautiful car, and handled well. We purred along in silence for some moments.

Then Roger started again. 'I just wanted to ask', he said, 'whether you are any further forward with your sleuthing. You said you had some idea yourself about who had shot Oliver.'

'I didn't say that, but as a matter of fact I do have one or two pointers now.'

Roger waited, but I didn't elaborate.

'I think you might tell me a bit more, Simon,' he muttered

sulkily.

'Why should I?' He didn't answer.

I drew the car up outside the office and made to get out.

'Simon,' said Roger, 'I'm feeling a bit sick. Do you think I might get a glass of water?'

He's just like a damned leech this morning, I thought irritably. However, he did look seedy and I told him to come in with me.

We went up in the lift and through the door into our offices. As we passed the little room housing the switchboard the girl popped her head out and said:

'Oh! Mr Barnett, your London call came through a few minutes ago. Miss Carruthers wasn't in, so I put it on to Mr Fergusson. I hope that's all right?'

I swore. Of all the damnable things to happen this was surely the worst. I felt a momentary blind rage at Roger, who had caused me to be late; and at Joyce, too – why did she have to be such a bad time-keeper, why couldn't she have got to the office at nine o'clock for once? But I knew at once that this was unjust. The fault was mine and mine alone. I should have made it clear to Peter that this was a confidential matter and that he mustn't leave a message with anyone else; and in any case I should have been more explicit in my instructions to the telephone girl. I apologized to the girl for my language and continued more slowly towards my room.

I passed Roger over to Joyce, who was now in her room, and asked her to get him a drink of water and let him have a seat for a few minutes. I wanted time to collect my thoughts.

However, I had scarcely sat down at my desk when Fergusson entered, closed the door carefully behind him, and walked ponderously over to the desk. He sat down opposite me and with maddening deliberation pulled a sheet of paper from his breast pocket.

'I have a telephone message for you, Simon. From a Mr Peter Graham of London. Rather a cryptic message, but no doubt it has some meaning for you. I have written it all down to make sure I would get it right.'

He now fished his spectacles from his pocket and unhurriedly put them on. He read slowly from the paper, 'Married in Manchester, 24th April, 1956. The bride's full name was Claire Trevor Fergusson, with two s's.' (Mr Graham was insistent on the two s's, Fergusson interjected.) 'The bride's father's name was Edward Ramsay Fergusson; profession, solicitor.'

I didn't know how to cope with the situation. Here was the very clue I had been looking for, the link between Fergusson and the Polygon Club, the demonstration of how he could have acquired – must have acquired – the blackmail photographs. But I was being forced into a showdown with Fergusson too soon – before I had had a chance to break his alibi.

The ringing of my telephone gave me temporary relief. It was a client asking advice about an accident his child had suffered in a public playground. The point was an elementary one which I could have answered off the cuff; but I wanted time to think. So, having asked him to hold the line, I went over to a bookcase and, pulling out at random a volume of law reports, I made a show of looking something up in it. As I did so I saw, out of the corner of my eye, signs that Fergusson's usually impregnable composure was wearing thin. He kept shifting about in his chair and his fingers drummed a restless tattoo on the desk. This show of nerves gave me a little more confidence. I went back to the phone and discussed the case at considerable length, asking for a lot of unnecessary details. When I finally gave my opinion and rang off, I felt somehow that the balance of power had shifted, that I was no longer on the defensive.

'If you are quite finished with these trivialities,' Fergusson began, with an edge of nervous irritation in his voice, 'perhaps you would explain the meaning of these inquiries about my daughter and her unfortunate marriage.'

I didn't answer him directly. Instead I said, 'Let me tell you some of the things I know. A number of people were being black-mailed on the strength of indecent photographs taken at the Polygon Night Club. The blackmailer used Oliver's flat at Gribble Street for receiving the money and must have had a key to the flat. There were originally three keys to the flat, one which the owner retained, and two which she gave to Oliver. A few months ago you acquired a fourth by extremely suspicious, not to say criminal, means.' Fergusson made as if to interrupt at this point, but restrained himself.

'Next,' I went on, 'Oliver received a letter, intended for the blackmailer, warning him that one of the victims was on his track. He didn't fully understand the letter but passed the gist of it on to you at lunch on Thursday of last week. That same night Oliver was murdered and the incriminating negatives were found in his safe, leading the police to believe, as the murderer intended them to believe, that Oliver was the blackmailer. Finally, I now know that the person who controlled the vice ring and who was therefore more likely than anyone else to have custody of these photographs was your daughter.'

'And you deduce from all this that I killed your brother?'

'Yes.'

He didn't speak for some moments. Outwardly he was as stolid and imperturbable as ever, but there was a tension in his attitude which told me that my attack had not misfired.

I sat back in my chair and lit a cigarette. The next move was up to Fergusson.

When he did speak, his tone was surprisingly mild. 'I could, of course, tell you to go to hell, Simon. I didn't kill Oliver, and no amount of snooping on your part will ever prove that I did. I could simply remind you that Oliver was murdered between ten-forty-six and eleven-thirty and that I can prove that I was elsewhere during that period. But I want no more muck raked up about my daughter. God knows, there is plenty if you dig deep enough. So I'm going to try to convince you that your theory is wrong and ask you to call off your bloodhounds. Give me a cigarette,' he added unexpectedly. 'I don't use them normally, but I could do with one now.'

When he had lit it, he continued, 'You never knew Claire and I find it hard to describe her. She just missed being beautiful; but she had that indefinable quality that many women, even beautiful women, lack, the quality of attracting – "mesmerising" would be an apter word – the other sex. I remember even at one of her school parties, how the boys buzzed round her like bees all night. She was blonde but certainly not dumb – highly intelligent, in fact. I flatter myself that she inherited that intelligence from me.'

Fergusson tapped the ash off his cigarette and turned his gaze to the ceiling. 'With all her assets Claire was rotten, rotten to the core. I realized it quite early on. Her mother never accepted it, never until the very end, and then it killed her. I won't bore you with the sordid details of her life history. She had an illegitimate child before she was twenty. That, incidentally, was her one mistake. She had plenty of men after that, but she had learnt her lesson. Men meant nothing to her except as a means to an end, but the poor unfortunate men never knew that. She could twist them round her little finger. Oh, she was plausible! If you met her today, Simon, you would think she was a nice girl, the sort of girl that it would be pleasant to take out for an evening. But by God, you would have to hold tight to your wallet.

'She left us when she was about twenty-three and went to try her luck in London. Her mother was distressed to see her go, but for me it was a relief. She prospered, as I knew she would. She wrote to me from time to time telling me with disgusting relish of her miserable ploys. She took a perverse pleasure in hurting me in this way, knowing that, for her mother's sake if for no other reason, I would never inform on her. It was a life of squalor, in the moral sense though not the physical. But the law never caught up with her: she was too clever for that. She always laid her plans so that if anyone had to take the rap it would not be she.

'Five years ago she came back to the city, married to that little squirt Merriman. My heart sank as soon as I heard of it. I knew she must have embarked on something big when she threw in her lot with a weed like that. As usual she had everything organized to the last detail and she played her part to perfection. She was the little mouse of a wife whose only function in life was to cater to the needs of her husband. She kept so much in the background that hardly anyone knew her by sight and none of my friends, so far as I'm aware, had any inkling that Mrs Merriman was my daughter Claire. It was she, of course, who was the brains behind that revolting setup. The husband was a mere cipher. She lost no time, as usual, in telling me all about it, daring me to go to the police. I was so horrified by what she told me that I nearly did, and I wish now that I had.

'When the racket was exposed, Claire got a real fright and for the first time in her life she needed my help. She had sailed too close to the wind and was in danger of foundering. She was terrified

Merriman might split on her (although he, poor man, like the rest of them, was completely bewitched by her) and she seemed to fear someone else as well. She apparently hadn't covered her tracks as thoroughly as usual. Although she exaggerated my ability to intercede for her, I didn't tell her so. I made a few discreet inquiries and learned that the police, while not entirely convinced of her innocence, had no evidence to justify a prosecution. What I told Claire was that I could, and would, keep her out of it if she promised to leave the country and never return. I allowed her to stay until after the trial, since it would have looked too suspicious if she had run off before then. But as soon as it was over and the unfortunate Merriman was convicted I packed her off. There was a fearful scene about it, for Claire had thought she could go back on her promise with impunity now that the case was officially closed. I finally convinced her that it was no idle threat when I said that unless she was out of the country within the week I would go to the police.

'She sailed for Canada a few days later. But not before she had committed her worst crime of all.'

Fergusson's voice was unsteady as he continued, 'She went to our house one afternoon while I was at my office and gave my wife the plain, unvarnished tale of her life over the past ten years. It was an act of unspeakable brutality, the sole motive for which was a desire to hurt me. My wife was a highly strung woman and had never been emotionally stable. She was in hysterics when I got home that night and never really got over it. She died in a mental hospital a few months later. Not long afterwards Claire herself was dead. I got a cable one morning and a letter a few days later. She had been killed in a car smash just outside Toronto. Even that was a sordid affair. The man she was with – but I won't bore you with the details.'

A look of pain crossed his face. He was silent for so long that I thought he had finished. But at length he went on:

'I've told you this story at some length, Simon, partly to let you see why I don't want you to dig up any more of Claire's past, but partly also to show you what my relationship with her was. You seem to think that Claire had the originals of these photographs. That is quite possible. But if there is one person she would not in any circumstances have given them to it is I, her father.'

It was an impressive performance which had me half convinced. Most of his story was true; of that I had no doubt. Fergusson was far too clever a man to tell a pack of lies that could easily be refuted. But I sensed, all the same, that there was a flaw in it somewhere. He was too persuasive, too anxious to have me believe him. He reached forward now and took another cigarette from my packet, which was still lying on the desk. This in itself was a sign that he was nervous. Apart from the occasional cigar, I had never known Fergusson to smoke.

'If you didn't get these photographs from your daughter,' I said, 'who did? And how did they get into Oliver's safe?'

'I should have thought that was obvious,' he replied. 'Claire would want to get rid of them when she left the country. I don't suppose the idea of carrying on a campaign of blackmail across the Atlantic would appeal to her. She would dispose of them to anyone who was prepared to pay her enough. I would hazard a guess that Oliver bought them. He had affairs with a number of women from the city and it wouldn't in the least surprise me if he got into Claire's clutches. Of course it is possible, I suppose, that Claire sold or gave the negatives to someone else and that this person made use of them in the manner that you suggested I did. But this seems to stretch the arm of coincidence too far. I prefer the simpler explanation.

Oliver got the photographs, Oliver was the blackmailer, Oliver was murdered by one of his victims.'

In other words, I thought gloomily, we are back to where we started, right back to the police theory of the crime, except that now, for the first time, we have been offered a plausible explanation of how Oliver might have acquired these photographs.

But I didn't give up yet. There were some other points that Fergusson hadn't answered.

'You admit that you had a key to Oliver's flat?' I asked.

He smiled briefly. He seemed more composed now, as if the worst hurdle had been surmounted. I had the feeling that I had missed my cue somewhere, that I had failed to pinpoint the weak link in his argument.

'There doesn't seem much point in denying it,' he answered. 'Your detective agency has obviously been too efficient. Yes, I acquired a key to the flat. Rather an ingenious way of doing it, wasn't it? I knew a good deal about the arrangement and I knew that Oliver had never met the owner. For all his secretiveness your brother really was rather careless about leaving his correspondence lying about. What intrigued me first was to see a letter addressed to "Mr C. V. Jones, c/o Messrs Barnett and Fergusson, Solicitors" lying open on Oliver's desk. I have to admit that I read the letter, which was from Mrs McConnell confirming the terms of the lease. I made some inquiries and was able to put two and two together.

'I seem to remember telling you about this before. I didn't see any reason to interfere until something came to light that suggested Oliver was having an affair with a certain woman, which, if it ever became public knowledge, would cause a scandal of the first order. I had my own position to think of; I didn't want the firm's reputation to be shattered by notoriety of that sort. Besides, I have rather old-fashioned views on these matters. My attitude has been conditioned, perhaps, by my experience with Claire.

'Well, as you know, I broached the subject with Oliver at the office dance last Christmas, and you saw the result. He told me to mind my own business, only in less polite language. I didn't let it rest there. I had to find out for myself whether my suspicions were well grounded. One way was to hang around Gribble Street on a Friday night in the hope of being able to recognize the woman when she arrived. I did in fact spend two hours one night doing just that and all I got for my pains was a cold in the head. They never turned up. So I thought up this scheme for getting a key. I was pretty sure that if only I could get into the flat I would soon find evidence of whether or not the current mistress was the one I feared it was.'

'And was it?' I asked.

'Oh, yes! There was no doubt about it. Having already tackled Oliver, I now tried to persuade the woman to give him up. But it was no good. The most I could get her to promise was that they would take even more stringent precautions to avoid being found out. There I had to leave it. Fortunately, although the affair continued all through the winter, it never did come to light.'

'Fergusson,' I asked, 'who was this woman?'

He gazed straight into my eyes. 'There are some things, Simon, that for your own peace of mind it is better you should not know. That is one of them. I will not tell you.'

I could see that he was firmly resolved not to give me the name. So I passed on to something else. 'What exactly did Oliver say to you at lunch the day he was killed?'

'Must we go over all that again? I've told you all I know. He was almost inarticulate, babbling incoherently about threats of disaster. He was terrified.'

'That doesn't sound to me like Oliver.'

'Well, I can only tell you what happened. If ever a man was frightened, Oliver was. So much so that it had me worried. I had an appointment in the city that afternoon and all the time I was there I kept thinking about what Oliver had said. When I got home at night I couldn't settle down. Eventually I got so restless that I felt compelled to do something about it. I phoned Oliver's house and was told by his maid that he was out. I phoned the office, but there was no reply. So I went down the street and called on Miss Carruthers.'

'A convenient alibi, as it turned out,' I remarked sourly.

He smiled. 'Very convenient. But an alibi all the same.'

As he spoke he knocked the ash off his cigarette into the ash tray. My eyes followed the movement of his hand automatically. The sight of the four or five stubs in the ash tray stirred a distant recollection and germinated the first seeds of an idea in my mind. It was an idea with exciting potentialities but I pushed it firmly to the back of my mind and concentrated on the business in hand.

'Why should you call on Joyce of all people?' I asked.

'It was one of those irrational things one does sometimes. I had an overpowering desire to discuss with someone Oliver's strange behaviour and incomprehensible remarks. I thought that Miss Carruthers, as his confidential secretary, might possibly be able to throw some light on it.'

'Yet Joyce tells me you didn't speak of that at all. You spent most of the time dropping dark hints about the Gribble Street flat.' An incredible possibility suddenly occurred to me. 'I take it that Joyce wasn't the woman who shared the flat with Oliver?'

He looked so startled that I was at once reassured.

'Good gracious, no,' he said. 'No, I was simply testing out the ground, trying to find out how much she knew about Oliver's affairs. She was so non-committal and unhelpful that I found myself floundering more and more. In the end I didn't get round to raising the matter I had come about. I felt an utter fool.'

There was a long silence. I could think of no more to say. Finally Fergusson rose and said with a return to his normal pompousness of manner, which had been markedly absent until now, 'Well, Simon, I am glad to have the opportunity of this little *tête-à-tête* with you. I feel it has cleared the air for both of us.' He made towards the door but I halted him.

'Fergusson,' I said, 'you have a persuasive tongue. But don't imagine you have convinced me. I'm going on with my inquiries.'

His face flushed with anger. He made as if to reply, thought better of it, and went out, closing the door quietly behind him.

I called Joyce in. 'Is it too late for a cup of coffee?' I asked.

'It's all ready,' she said. 'I've been waiting for the marathon to end. What was all that about? I just got snatches of it. I've been dotting in and out of my room, ministering to your precious Mr Grant.'

'Lord, is he still here?'

'Yes. He's in pretty poor shape, Simon. I don't think he's fit to drive himself home.'

She went out and returned a moment later with a cup of steaming coffee. She hovered while I drank it.

'There are two people waiting to see you,' she said. 'Old Mr McKellar and a man from the Sterling Insurance Company.'

'You'll have to put them on to Kelly. I can't see them now. I've just had an idea that may turn this case upside down and I must get peace to think it out. I know what I'll do,' I added. 'I'll run Roger Grant home. I can get the bus back.'

She looked at me doubtfully and glanced disapprovingly at the pile of unanswered mail on my desk.

'Well,' she said, 'it seems a shame. They've been waiting a long time. But whatever you say.' She went out.

CHAPTER 17

Roger was indeed in poor shape. Although Joyce's room was warm and there were beads of perspiration on his brow, he complained of feeling cold and shivery. I suggested I should take him to a doctor, but he wouldn't hear of it.

'It's just a chill,' he said. 'I'll be all right if I can get home and into bed. It's the worry and the lack of food and lack of sleep that have brought it on.'

'And the over-indulgence in drink,' I muttered under my breath.

I had never been to Lagside before and had to get Roger to direct me. It was a narrow, twisting road for most of the way, with a couple of really nasty hairpin bends. One of these was at the foot of a steep hill, and a sheer drop awaited the driver who didn't see the bend in time. A flimsy wooden fence at the cliff edge was the only protection. Not being familiar with the Rover's capabilities, I went right down to first to crawl round it.

'This must be quite a test at night,' I remarked. 'Or worse still, in the fog. How on earth did Sheila cope with it that night?'

'She is a first-class driver,' said Roger, a note of envy in his voice. 'I've never known a better.'

'Even so, the conditions on that night were appalling. Incidentally, that reminds me. You drove to London that night, Roger, didn't you? That was a pretty risky thing to attempt, surely?'

'Risky? It was crazy. I didn't get very far, though. I ran the car into a ditch not many miles down the road. It happened in a God-forsaken place too. I had to walk for what seemed like hours before

I came to the nearest village. I didn't get there till after half-past ten and there was no way of getting home that night. I spent the night in the local inn.'

He relapsed into silence. His head began to nod and I let him sleep.

A mile or two farther on the road ribboned down to the riverside and hugged the bank for a stretch of about three miles. 'River' was really too grandiose a term: at this point it wasn't much more than a broad stream, a stone's throw from bank to bank, although it was deep in places.

I nudged Roger and he sat up. 'What are all these men doing?' I said, pointing ahead.

'They're searching the river for the gun Sheila said she threw in. They've got a couple of divers and I believe they have borrowed a powerful magnet from the university as well. The police are co-operating with our people.'

That was something. I wished them success.

We reached Roger's farm a few minutes later.

The farmhouse was an impressive building. It had been extended and largely rebuilt since Roger took over the place and it was now in fine condition.

Roger invited me in. He offered me a drink, which I refused; and I dissuaded him from taking any. He obviously ought to have been in bed but he seemed reluctant to let me go. He begged me to sit down and talk to him for a few minutes, pointing out that it was nearly half an hour before I could get a bus anyway.

This was not at all what I had bargained for. However, Roger looked so miserable and so pathetically anxious for my company that I couldn't bring myself to refuse.

He talked for a bit about Sheila. Although he spoke of her in terms of almost maudlin sentimentality – 'a jewel among women' was one of his phrases – it was noteworthy that he used the past tense all the time. I asked him about this.

'Are you not expecting to get Sheila back?' I said.

He was evasive. 'Oh, well, one hopes for the best, of course! But things do look pretty black, don't they?'

'Not as black as all that,' I said, trying to cheer him up.

'But—' he said this with some diffidence – 'I couldn't help overhearing your conversation with that man Fergusson this morning. It's a very thin partition,' he added hastily and defensively, 'and every word comes through. I gather he is the one you suspect and he seemed to demolish your case pretty devastatingly.'

I should have let this pass, but I was nettled by the remark and more so by the tone, which was almost one of malicious satisfaction. It came to me that Roger didn't like me. He probably felt he had some scores to pay off from the days of our joint acquaintance with Sheila.

'Fergusson talked plenty and no doubt he sounded plausible,' I replied tardy, 'but when you boil it all down, there is a powerful case against him on every count except opportunity. Break his alibi and he has no defence.'

'But how do you break his alibi? I thought it was foolproof.'

'Well,' I said, 'suppose it can be shown that Oliver was murdered not between ten-forty-six and eleven-thirty, but some time before ten-forty-six: where is Fergusson's alibi then?'

The effect was all I could have desired. Roger was staring at me speechless, with gaping jaw. But I was annoyed with myself for having been stung into throwing out this dramatic suggestion before I had had time to examine it properly. In any case it had nothing to do with Roger. To prevent him asking awkward questions I changed the subject rapidly and made the first remark that came into my head.

'I didn't know you had kept up with Oliver,' I said. 'I gather you visited him several times at the office recently?'

He didn't seem to be paying attention. His answer was vague, 'Oliver? Oh, yes! I did see him once or twice. A small matter of business. But tell me, Simon—'

I stood up. 'I really must go, Roger, if I've to catch that bus. Get straight to bed and if you don't feel any better in an hour or two, ring for the doctor.'

I was out of the door before he could stop me.

It was about half a mile from the farmhouse to the main road, where I was to get the bus. It was a pleasant day for walking, quite warm but with a refreshing breeze. Lagside was on high ground north of the river and commanded a fine prospect of the surrounding countryside – acres of rich farming land here and there studded with belts of trees and with the thin silver line of the river traced across it. In the far distance you could just distinguish the spires and chimneys of the city.

However, as I walked down the road, my mind was not on the view. I was conjuring up the picture of Oliver's room as I saw it on the night he was killed. Something had struck me as incongruous about that room at the time but it was only in the course of my conversation with Fergusson an hour or two ago that I had suddenly realized what it was. In the last few years of his life – since the accident to Marion, in fact – Oliver had been a heavy smoker; not quite a chain smoker, but not far off it. When he had been back in his office in the evening the evidence was always there in the morning – an ash tray filled with the stubs of his cigarettes. The cleaners came in each night at five-thirty and cleared out all the ash trays and waste-paper baskets. On the night when I found Oliver's body there had been five cigarette ends in his ash tray, two of which, by her own admission, had been Linda's. Therefore between the time of the cleaners' visit at five-thirty and the time of his death Oliver had put out only three cigarettes in his desk ash tray. Yet he was supposed to have been there from not later than eight-thirty (the time of the appointment with Linda) until at least ten-forty-six. For Oliver to limit himself to three cigarettes for such a period was scarcely credible. It wasn't that he had run short, either. The half-full cigarette box on the desk proved that.

It was true that he might have disposed of them by throwing them in the fire instead of using the ash tray. I couldn't altogether discount that possibility; but, like most smokers, Oliver had certain fixed routines, and throwing the ends into a fire was something he never did.

All this had set me wondering whether Oliver hadn't been murdered much earlier than we had supposed. The medical evidence said that the time of death was between nine-thirty and eleven-thirty. The other limiting factors were the telephone call I had got from Oliver at ten-forty-six and Sheila's statement that he was already dead when she arrived about eleven-fifteen. I had asked myself many times whether the call I had received couldn't have been an impersonation. But I knew it was not; it was undoubtedly Oliver's voice I had heard. However, I now had another idea about this, the validity of which I could only test with Joyce's assistance.

I got the bus at twelve-twenty. It was only ten or eleven miles to Brickfield, but the bus crawled along, stopping at every farm track to lift and lay down passengers. I soon had to resign myself to the fact that the office would be closed before I got back.

It was in fact a quarter-past one before I reached the office, and everyone was away. I phoned first Joyce and then Kelly and asked them to meet me in the office at two-thirty. When I told them it was urgent they made no protest and agreed to come, although I did detect a hint of regret in Alan Kelly's voice. No doubt his plans for the Saturday afternoon had encompassed the girl Ross whom we had heard about the previous night.

After telling them what I had discovered about Fergusson's daughter and recounting my interview with Fergusson, I went on to report my observations about the cigarette ends and the deductions I had drawn from them.

They mulled this over in their minds. Then Kelly said, 'What you're suggesting is that Mr Barnett was killed at, say, ten o'clock and that the murderer rang you up three-quarters of an hour later, impersonating Oliver's voice, to make it seem that he was still alive then?' He sounded sceptical.

'Not exactly,' I said. 'It was much cleverer that that. Oliver's voice was most distinctive. No one could hope to deceive me in that way.

'Just consider for a minute what Oliver actually said. As far as I remember it was this:

"Simon? Look here, I'm at the office and something rather urgent has turned up. Could you possibly slip along for a few minutes?"

'Then there was a pause while I registered a token protest which he simply ignored as if he had never heard it. And his next sentence was:

"Well, this really is rather urgent.

So if you could just nip across . . ."

'Now does anything strike you about these words?'

'Nothing,' said Kelly, 'except that I've heard the same patter many a time before. He used to ring up on the least provocation to get somebody to help him. The formula he used was always much the same. A slightly ingratiating manner, but at the same time conveying the hint that he was expecting you to drop everything and come at the double. People usually did, too.'

'Precisely. I was the chief sufferer. The number of such messages I got from Oliver was legion. And as often as not it was in the evening when Oliver was working here and I was at home. I nearly always obeyed the summons, however inconvenient it might be. It was Oliver's way of working and it would have upset him if he had been resisted. However, you have grasped the essential point, Alan, that he had a formula for these requests which never varied much. Now do you see where this is leading?'

But they both looked blank.

'All right,' I said. 'Let's turn to something else.'

I glanced at the dictaphone, which had lain unused on Oliver's desk since I had taken over his room.

'You remember, Joyce,' I said, 'playing back to me what Oliver had recorded on the dictaphone just before his death? Right at the end he suddenly broke off what he had been saying and started a conversation with someone who had just come into the room. Linda, it was, as we discovered later. And all this was faithfully recorded on the machine up to the point where he remembered to switch it off.'

I could see that I had aroused their interest.

'I'm beginning to get your drift now,' said Kelly. 'But go on.'

'Well, the point I'm making is this. Suppose Oliver, in the middle of dictating one evening, suddenly decides that he needs my advice and rings me up: what happens? He doesn't bother to switch off the dictaphone for the brief period of the interruption, with the result that his side of the conversation appears on the wax. That must have happened often, surely, Joyce?'

'Yes,' she replied, smiling faintly. 'There have been some odd interjections in the middle of some of Oliver's dictation. But—'

'Just a moment. Let me finish. What I really want to know is this. Can you isolate a passage on the transcriber? In other words, could someone who wanted to play over a particular bit of recording start it and stop it at the precise points he wanted?'

'Yes,' said Joyce slowly. 'If he played it over once or twice to find the exact spot, he could; especially if there was a slight hiatus after what had gone before. But I still don't see—'

'I do,' exclaimed Kelly excitedly. 'You mean that the murderer could have got hold of one of these dictaphone discs or whatever you call them which included a summons to you, Mr Barnett, and after the murder he played the appropriate bit over to you on the telephone.'

'That's exactly what I mean,' I said. 'You see, there was one odd thing about that phone call. I could hear a faint murmur when Oliver wasn't actually speaking. I thought there must be somebody else in the room with Oliver, speaking in a low voice in the background. But I believe now that it was the slight humming noise that the machine always makes.

'Now, assuming this is correct, it points almost inevitably to Fergusson. First of all, it has to be someone who could reasonably have got hold of one of these discs. (I'll come back to that in a moment.) Secondly it must be someone who has no alibi for the real time of the murder but who has a cast-iron alibi for the period from ten-forty-six onwards. But the crucial point is this. The call came through on the office extension line to my house – it had to, if I was to be deceived, because that's the line Oliver would have used. That means that it came either from the office itself (which can be ruled out, for the murderer could then have no alibi), or from one of the outside extensions, namely from Oliver's house or from Fergusson's house. It could hardly have come from Oliver's house, because Marion was out and I think we can discount Millie as the murderer. That leaves Fergusson.'

'It's faintly possible, is it not,' Kelly interjected, 'that the office line was switched through to your house, Mr Barnett, so that an external call to the office would go direct to your extension?'

'That never happened,' said Joyce. 'It was always put through to Oliver's house when the office closed at night unless he was coming back to work, in which case he took any external calls here.'

'Joyce is right,' I said. 'It must have been Fergusson. And this visit of his to Joyce's flat becomes comprehensible now. As soon as he had played over the record to me he had to establish his alibi. The quickest and easiest way was to walk a few yards down the street and call on Joyce.'

'There's one other point,' said Kelly. 'What about the telephone call he said he made to your brother's house? He can hardly have invented that. What time did he make the call?'

I had forgotten about that, but I rang up Oliver's house at once. Fortunately it was Millie herself who answered. She remembered the phone call from Fergusson. It had come through on the office extension about ten minutes to eleven, she thought. It hadn't occurred to her to mention that call when she was speaking to me before.

I told the others what Millie had said. It was consistent with the timetable as we were now reconstructing it.

'Now,' I went on, 'there is one vital piece of the jigsaw to be fitted in yet. And if that piece isn't there we might as well throw the rest out of the window. It is easy to see how Fergusson would get the disc. Oliver nearly always had his door open when he was working. He had a carrying voice which could be heard along the corridor and which could be heard in Fergusson's room if he kept his door open too. Fergusson would simply have to come back to the office on a number of evenings when Oliver was working late and wait until a suitable conversation with me went down on the dictaphone. He wouldn't have long to wait, believe you me: the occasions were too numerous. Then after Oliver had gone home, Fergusson would walk in and lift the recording from the machine. He would have to remove it at once. It was no use waiting until after you had transcribed it the next day, Joyce, for I'm right in thinking, am I not, that once that was done the wax went back to Oliver and was reused?'

'Yes. These waxes can be used over and over again. The new message simply obliterates the old one. If I transcribed a wax in the morning, as likely as not Oliver would have it on the machine again the same afternoon.'

'I thought so. So if Fergusson didn't take the recording on the night it was made it would be extremely difficult for him to get it before the message he wanted had been wiped off. I think we can assume he would have to remove the disc before it had been transcribed. Now Oliver always left his recordings in the dictaphone for you to pick up in the morning, didn't he, Joyce?'

'Yes.'

'Well, then, here's the rub. If Fergusson did remove a wax it must have been missed. Oliver wouldn't toil away at dictation all evening and then accept light-heartedly the loss of his handiwork the next day. If this ever happened you must know of it, Joyce. Was there ever such an incident?'

Joyce thought hard before replying. 'As a matter of fact there *was* once. But it was months ago. There was some terrifically long thing that Oliver was working at. Oh, I remember now, it was a draft of his address to the Rotary Club. Reams and reams of it there were. He spent a whole night dictating it, and when I came in next morning there were three or four discs waiting for me to transcribe. Unfortunately there was a gap in the middle; one wax was missing. Oliver flew off the handle about it, for he had sweated blood over the speech. But we never did get to the bottom of it.'

I was jubilant now. I knew I must be right because I could remember very clearly getting a phone call from Oliver one night asking me to come over to the office to see him; and when I got there it turned out that he wanted help with drafting one section of his address.

'But, Simon,' Joyce objected, 'that must have been away back in January or February. Surely the murder wasn't planned as long ago as that?'

'My belief is that it was. Fergusson was very thorough and quite ruthless. The whole point of conducting the blackmail through the agency of Oliver's flat was to have Oliver as a scapegoat if things went wrong. As soon as there was a serious threat of the blackmail coming to light, the incriminating documents had to be planted on Oliver. And that meant Oliver had to be eliminated so that he couldn't prove his innocence. To stage a murder which would be mistaken for suicide and which would in any event leave the murderer with a foolproof alibi required careful planning. It wouldn't do to rely on the inspiration of the moment when Oliver's death became imperative. So Fergusson had the murder planned as a safety measure almost as soon as he embarked on the blackmail.

'And there's another thing,' I went on excitedly. I turned to Joyce. 'You usually kept the transcribing machine on your desk?'

'Not usually,' said Joyce. 'Always.'

'I thought so. Well, I spent half an hour in your room after the police came that night. I had plenty of time to memorize the contents of the room. The only objects on your desk were the typewriter and the telephone.'

'You mean that Fergusson had taken the transcriber home with him?'

'Of course he had. He needed it for the bogus phone call to me. It's quite small and easy to carry. Tell me, Joyce, did you miss it the next morning? Was it on your desk when you arrived?'

'I don't really remember, Simon. There was such a flap on when I got in that morning, with police all over the place. I do know that when Inspector Kennedy asked me to play over the wax Oliver had left on the dictaphone the transcriber was in its usual place. But that was much later and Fergusson was in by then.'

Kelly broke in at this point. He had been silent for some time. 'This new theory would explain one difficulty that we had before,' he said. 'We wondered how the murderer could be sure that his victim would be sitting in the office at ten-forty-five or eleven o'clock at night. Whereas all that Fergusson would have to know is that Mr Barnett was to meet your wife here at eight-thirty; and that appointment was written quite openly in the desk diary. Fergusson could come back to the office, hang about in his room until Mrs

Barnett went away, and then walk in and shoot your brother.'

The problem now was what to do. While we all three agreed that we had solved the case, we were not unanimous about the cogency of our proof. Kelly wanted to go straight to the police. He thought that there was more than enough evidence to justify Fergusson's arrest. I was more dubious. I had no desire to get another rebuff from Inspector Kennedy or Superintendent Garland. I could imagine the sceptical reception a theory like this would get from them unless it was supported by unassailable evidence.

Joyce sided with me, and it was she who thought of the plan which eventually we decided to follow. We would try to surprise Fergusson into an admission of guilt. Kelly and I were to call on him that night and, at a prearranged time, Joyce was to ring from the office to his house extension and play over to him a recording of my voice using precisely the words that Oliver had used in the phone call relayed to me on the night of the murder. We hoped that the shock of realizing that his subterfuge had been discovered might lead Fergusson to confess. At the very least we believed that, if Fergusson killed Oliver, we would get confirmation of it from his face when the call came through. He would have to be a consummate actor to avoid giving himself away in such circumstances.

Joyce put a wax on the dictaphone and I recorded my message. We played it over on the transcriber and were satisfied that it should serve its purpose. Kelly and I arranged to call on Fergusson at eight-forty-five and Joyce undertook to put through the call at nine o'clock. The chance of Fergusson's being out or having other visitors was not great. We agreed, however, that in either case we would abandon the project for the night and let Joyce know by telephone at once. We would then go through with the performance on the Sunday night.

We were on our way out of the office when Kelly suddenly smacked his forehead with his hand and said, in a tone of dismay, 'Good lord, what fools we've been. I've just remembered something that sends the whole pack of cards toppling down. The murder couldn't have taken place at the time we're suggesting, or if it did the murderer remained in the office for a couple of hours; and that means it wasn't Fergusson. Have you forgotten about the person you disturbed, Mr Barnett, when you arrived here at half-past eleven?'

'I haven't forgotten, Alan,' I said grimly. 'That wasn't the murderer, although it was someone nearly as loathsome. I know now who that was, and I'm going to deal with him this afternoon.'

CHAPTER 18

As I drove to the city I tried to rehearse what I was going to say to Waterston. That he was the man who had been in the office when I arrived that night I was now certain, and I could guess too the reason for his visit. If I could see him alone I believed I could bluff or bully him into admitting it, but there would no doubt be Linda to contend with as well. She was liable to cramp my style.

Traffic was heavy on the road, and it was a quarter to five before I reached the outskirts of the city. There I was further held up by the crowds streaming out of Albion Park, where the United had been playing their last home fixture of the season. I was irritated, because I was anxious to get this unpleasant task over as quickly as possible.

It was in fact five-fifteen before I was at Waterston's door. It was an imposing residence, one of the last of its kind; a large, solid, dignified building in grey stone, standing in grounds of close on an acre, the sort of house where you expected the door to be opened by an under-footman. Waterston didn't quite rise to footmen, but he did employ a couple of maids and a gardener. The house cost Waterston £9,000 when he bought it just before the war, and he had spent a lot on modernization and redecoration since. The money, or most of it, came from his wife, who had brought a fair-sized dowry to the marriage and who had inherited more later. When she herself had died, her estate was in the six-figure range. So that, however Oliver's demands may have worried him, Waterston could not have had any serious financial embarrassment.

The girl who answered my ring was new and didn't know me. She told me that Waterston was unwell and was not seeing visitors. I asked if I could see Mrs Barnett.

'What name shall I give, sir?'

'Mr Barnett.'

She cast a startled glance at me and fled. A few moments later she came back and showed me up to the drawing-room.

Linda, as always, took my breath away. Occasionally in these past weeks of enforced bachelorhood, at times when I was feeling particularly pessimistic and depressed, I had wondered whether I ought not to make a clean break and start afresh. Perhaps Linda would give me a divorce; perhaps I could find a girl less complicated and inhibited than Linda – Joyce, for example, or someone like Sheila. But the sight of Linda banished any such fancies: I knew there could never be any other girl for me.

She was standing with her back to the big oriel window. She was wearing a beautifully cut tweed skirt and a rose-coloured cashmere twin-set. That was one thing she had learned from me, I thought – the virtue of simplicity of dress. I remembered the absurd, frilly evening dress she had worn the first time I met her, and how gauche she had looked in it. All the same I would have given much to have the Linda of those days back again, to see the sparkle in her eyes, the ingenuous, slightly puzzled look on her face which had so captivated me.

'I must see your father, Linda,' I said.

'Father is in bed. He hasn't been well. He won't see you.'

She hadn't moved. She stood there silhouetted against the light from the window, as if carved in stone. I couldn't see her face clearly, but her voice had been cold and devoid of expression.

I didn't press the point for the moment. 'May I sit down?' I said, and without waiting for an answer seated myself on an easy-chair by the fire.

She came to life then and moved slowly towards me.

'I think you'd better go, Simon,' she said quietly. 'I don't know why you've come, but if it's about the murder, neither of us can help you, and if it's about – about us, there's nothing more to be said. We've had it all out before.'

The trouble was that we hadn't – not really. There had been one explosive quarrel and Linda was gone. I had lost my temper that night and said things that I regretted afterwards; but I hadn't appreciated that our whole marriage was at stake and I still didn't properly understand what it had all been about.

It had started quietly enough. One night early in January when I came home from the office I found Linda preoccupied and silent. This was so unusual that I asked her if anything was wrong. Instead of answering me directly, she asked how I had managed to persuade her father to consent to our marriage, and to give us such a magnificent wedding gift. My heart sank when I realized that she had learned about the blackmailing of Waterston, and not from me. It had been on my conscience from the start, for I had always suspected that Oliver had somehow put pressure on Waterston, but I had never confessed it to Linda. Nor had I yet said anything to her since getting from Oliver a few days before the full story of the blackmail.

I wasn't unduly worried, however. I admitted that I had had my suspicions from the beginning and that I should have confided them to her. I expressed regret for my apparent lack of trust in her. I explained that the break from her father's dominance had been achieved so recently and with such difficulty that I had hesitated to put our relationship to the test so early, especially when I had

no proof that my suspicions were justified. And now that I had
that proof I had simply been waiting for a suitable opportunity to
broach the subject with her. My sole concern had been to minimize
the shock she was bound to get when she learned the sordid story
of her father and Oliver.

To my dismay I saw from her face that she didn't believe me. She
suddenly went for me like a tigress. She accused me of being equally
implicated with Oliver in the blackmail of her father. The more I
protested, the more vehement and uncontrolled she became. She said
eventually, 'If you would deceive me in one thing you would deceive
me in others. God knows I didn't want to believe it, but there was
proof. Oh! it's so humiliating,' and she burst into a flood of tears. I
wondered many times afterwards whether there was anything I could
have said at that point that would have made her listen to reason. But
I was thoroughly angry myself by then, and what I did say merely
provided the curtain line, 'If you would believe that sanctimonious
old windbag rather than me, you would be better to go back to Daddy.'
She stormed out of the house and never came back.

I tried to get her back. She put down the receiver whenever she
heard my voice on the telephone and she didn't answer my letters.
I did – twice – get into her father's house and make an abortive
attempt to get things straightened out, but she and her father just
stood there coldly, refusing to answer my questions. I could partly
understand Linda's attitude. She had given herself to me completely
and had trusted me absolutely. If she had found that I had been
deceiving her on some fundamental issue, her reaction against me
was likely to be even more violent than the normal wife's. What I
couldn't comprehend was how Waterston had persuaded her that
I was involved with Oliver in the blackmail. He couldn't have
produced proof because there was none. And I would have taken

my oath that in a matter like that she would have believed me rather than her father; or she would at least have listened to my side of the story.

And now here was Linda, three months later, saying that 'we had had it all out before'.

I decided to make one more effort.

'Tell me one thing, Linda,' I said. 'What is the "proof" you said you had that I was concerned in the blackmailing of your father?'

She looked puzzled. 'I didn't say that,' she replied. 'The proof I had was of – of the other thing.'

'What other thing?'

She made a gesture of anger. 'Do I have to spell it out in words of one syllable? Your relationship with Marion.'

I tried to keep my voice under control. 'Please explain this, Linda,' I said. 'Remember, you've never mentioned it before.'

She began wearily, as if reciting a set piece: 'When my father told me that you and your brother were blackmailing him, I refused to believe him – at any rate I refused to believe that you had any-thing to do with it. We had a bitter quarrel, and in the course of it my father said that I appeared to know very little about you – did I not even know that you were having an affair with Oliver's wife? If he hadn't been my own father I think I would have struck him for that revolting insinuation. As it was, he had to restrain me forcibly from running out of the house there and then. He shouted at me that he would prove it. We would drive straight over and see Marion herself. It was a Wednesday afternoon – you remember how I used to visit my father every Wednesday? He made me get back into the car and drive him to Oliver's house. Marion denied it at first but not very convincingly; and when she was pressed, she suddenly admitted it, in fact she seemed to glory in it.'

Linda broke off and lit a cigarette. Her hand was trembling and there was a flush of colour in her cheeks. When she continued, her voice was bitter.

'Marion said that those evenings when you were supposed to be working late at the office, it was Oliver who was in the office. You were with her. She told me it had been going on for months before we were married and that the marriage hadn't made much difference except that you hadn't seen her quite so often. She flaunted it in my face and she was proud of it. It was nauseating and humiliating. Even then I only half believed it. I couldn't bring myself to speak of it directly to you, but when I did challenge you with the blackmail and you hedged and grovelled, I knew then that it was all true, that my father had been right about you, that I had been a stupid, simple-minded little fool, taken in by the false charm and the glib tongue of the first man who came along.

'There it is, Simon. That's what you've done to me. I hope you're proud of it. I suppose I ought to be grateful to you for one thing, for teaching me my way around. I'm not the little innocent at large any longer; I'll never be taken in again, by you or by anyone else.'

I looked at her for a moment and then got up and strode out of the room. I couldn't trust myself to speak.

When she heard me climbing the stairs instead of going down, she called out after me, 'Where are you going, Simon?'

'Where is your father's bedroom?' I shouted.

'No, no, Simon.' She was running up the stairs after me. 'You mustn't—'

But just then I heard Waterston's voice, from somewhere along the corridor branching off from the head of the staircase: 'What's all that noise, Linda? Who is here?' It was the voice of an old man, querulous and thin.

I threw open two doors before I found him. There he was, propped up in bed, reading.

Angry though I was, I was shocked by the change in him. He certainly wasn't shamming illness. The skin of his face was transparent and drawn tightly over his cheekbones. His lips were blue and I noticed that the hand that was holding the book was shaking.

I drew a chair over beside the bed and sat down.

'You and I are going to have a talk, Waterston,' I said.

'I warn you, Simon,' said Linda, who had appeared in the room, panting, behind me. 'If you do anything to upset my father, I'll—'

'Shut up,' I snapped. 'It's time you learned one or two things about your precious father.'

All the same I moderated my voice and tried to speak quietly and calmly.

'First,' I said, 'I'm going to describe to you what happened on the night of Oliver's murder, or at any rate the part you two played that night. You can correct me if I go wrong, but I don't think that will be necessary. You, Waterston, decided to use Linda to make one more attempt to get these incriminating papers back from Oliver. They were incriminating too, I can tell you, Linda. I don't know what sort of fancy tale your father spun to you about them but I'm sure he didn't dare tell you the truth. It would have shown him up for what he is – an unscrupulous rogue. In fairness to Oliver I'm bound to say that while I didn't approve of his extorting money from your father, he had strong provocation. However, let's not go into that. You wouldn't believe me, anyway.

'Well, the two of you drove in from the city that night. Linda had arranged to meet Oliver at eight-thirty, but in fact, because of the fog, it was nearly nine o'clock before you got there. You drove back to the Station Hotel, Waterston, where you were going to spend the night, and Linda had her interview with Oliver. It was an unproductive interview.'

Linda attempted to interrupt at this point but I talked her down.

'Oh! I know you told me Oliver gave you the papers, Linda. But that was a lie. That was an attempt to protect your father. You see, I know what Oliver felt about this. To him it was a question of honour to get full restitution for the wrong your father had done his father. You have your charms, Linda, but they are not so eloquent as all that. It was a futile attempt from the beginning. I'm astonished that either of you thought it had a chance of succeeding.

'Now the next bit is guesswork but it seems to me the likeliest explanation of what happened afterwards. In the course of your talk Oliver produced the documents from the safe and waved them in your face. It's the sort of gesture that was typical of him. Then he put them back again. Only he had difficulty in closing the safe and in fact didn't quite close it. It had a habit of sticking like that.'

While I was saying this I had been studying Linda's face. She didn't comment but I could see from her expression that my reconstruction of the scene was correct.

'Now we come to your big scene, Waterston,' I went on. 'When Linda got back to the hotel and reported what had happened you realized that this was a heaven-sent opportunity. There was a good chance that that safe was still open. So you got the car and drove back to the office. It must have given you a shock to find Oliver lying dead on the floor, but a small matter like that didn't deter you. You rummaged about in the safe until you found the papers you wanted. It must have taken you quite a time, for the safe was packed with stuff, some of it innocent, some of it, which had just been planted there, not so innocent. You didn't come across a set of indelicate photographs in the course of your search, did you?

No? Well, never mind. The point is that eventually you found what you were after and just then I came into the building. You managed to elude me with the aid of that rather neat light-switching act. And back you went to the hotel, a good night's work done.

'Is that a fair summary of what happened?'

Waterston, who had been chewing nervously at the bedclothes throughout my narrative, threw a furtive glance at Linda. It was Linda who answered.

'Suppose all that is true,' she said. 'Why should it be dragged to the light? Father didn't kill Oliver, so it's not relevant to the murder.'

'No,' I conceded. 'Your father didn't kill Oliver. I believe Oliver was shot immediately after you left the office, Linda. But your father's visit to the office is relevant to the murder all the same.'

I turned to Waterston and my tone hardened.

'You left the hotel at ten-forty. What time did you get to the office?'

'Nearly half-past eleven,' he muttered. 'I got lost in the fog.'

I swore under my breath. If this was true, as it might well be, I could get no further help from him. I had to be sure, however, and I decided to try a bluff.

'Don't lie to me, Waterston,' I said. 'Mrs Grant saw your car when she arrived at eleven-fifteen. You must have been already there. You must have heard her arrive. You must have hidden somewhere in the office while she was there and waited until she went away.'

It was a desperate shot. Waterston in his normal health would have seen the flaw at once. If Sheila really had seen his car, the police would have been on to him long before now. But Waterston was a sick man and his brain was obviously not at its clearest. His brow was damp with sweat and he was breathing rapidly.

Ramming home my advantage, I plunged on remorselessly, 'In

other words, Waterston, you know Mrs Grant is innocent, you can prove that Oliver was dead before she got there. And yet you haven't lifted a finger to save her.'

Waterston's head was bowed and he passed his hand wearily over his eyes. In an almost inaudible voice he whispered, 'I would have spoken if it had ever come to trial. I hoped she might be released before that.'

'That's the kind of man your father is,' I remarked bitingly to Linda. The comment was superfluous. She was gazing at him in open-mouthed horror.

'Now, there's another matter,' I said to him brutally. I was going to thrust in his teeth the lies he had told Linda about Marion and me and about my association with Oliver in the blackmail. Suddenly I stopped. He looked so frail and ill and pathetic crouched there in bed like a little wooden doll.

Oliver used to say to me that I would never get very far in life because I was too soft-hearted, not nearly ruthless enough. I suppose he was right. At any rate it wasn't in me to bully this broken little shell of a man any further. I turned away.

'You'll need to get him to tell the police about Sheila,' I said gruffly to Linda. 'They can't hold her once they hear this.'

She was looking at me with an expression I couldn't interpret. I walked past her and out of the door and ran down the stairs. As I opened the front door I thought I heard Linda's voice calling me but I didn't look back. I got into my car and drove home.

CHAPTER 19

I called for Alan Kelly at twenty minutes to nine. Now that Sheila was as good as cleared I was less inclined than ever to do this theatrical scheme for breaking down Fergusson's defences. The sensible thing was to go to the police and let them deal with it. Curiously, however, Kelly, who had been lukewarm to begin with, was now enthusiastic and urged me to carry through the plan. He was looking forward to the excitement of it with the eagerness of a schoolboy.

So, with some misgivings, I drove him round to Fergusson's house. It was eight-fifty-one when we got there, a little later than we had planned. Still, I thought, the less time we have with Fergusson before the phone call comes through the better. These first few minutes were bound to be uncomfortable.

Fergusson took so long to answer our ring that, although I could see a light in one of the ground-floor windows, I began to wonder if he was out. At last, however, the door opened.

If Fergusson was surprised to see us, he didn't show it.

'Ah! a deputation,' he said. 'Come in. Sorry I was so long in answering. I was listening to a record and I wanted to hear the last few bars.'

He showed us into what he described as the music room. It was, I guessed, where he spent most of his leisure hours. He was a competent violinist himself, although he seldom played now. I had heard that his wife had been a good pianist and that they had played a lot together. Nowadays his main interest was in his records, of which he had a fine collection.

It was a pleasant little room, made the more attractive by a coal fire burning brightly in the grate; meticulously tidy, too, reflecting the orderliness of Fergusson's mind.

Fergusson told us to sit down and asked what we would have to drink. When he came back with the drinks I saw that the clock on the mantelpiece was at eight-fifty-eight.

'What were you listening to?' I asked him casually, indicating the open record-player standing near the door.

'Bach,' he replied. 'One of the Brandenburg Concertos. But I take it that you didn't come here to discuss music with me?'

'No,' I admitted. 'We didn't. First of all, let me explain why Alan is here. He is a member of what you described this morning as my detective agency. In fact it was he who found out that you possessed a key to Oliver's flat. Alan knows the whole situation. So we can talk freely.'

'By all means,' said Fergusson affably. 'But what about?'

That was the trouble. I hadn't given this part of the proceedings sufficient thought in advance and I couldn't think of anything plausible to say. I took a quick glance at the clock: it was showing a minute past nine. Had Joyce forgotten or mistaken the time?'

'That clock is two minutes fast,' Fergusson remarked, almost as if he were reading my thoughts. 'You were saying, Simon?'

'Well,' I began lamely, 'that was a remarkable story you told me this morning. It may be true, I don't know. But there are a number of points that occurred to me afterwards and I thought we might—'

I was interrupted by the trill of the telephone from a distant part of the house. I sighed inwardly with relief.

'That's the office phone,' said Fergusson, in a puzzled voice. 'Who on earth can be there at this time on a Saturday night?'

'Perhaps it's Marion,' I suggested, 'ringing from the extension in her house.'

He grunted non-committally and went out.

I sank back in my chair. 'Sorry, Alan,' I whispered. 'I've made a mess of it so far. He's as suspicious as a cat. I should have had a convincing tale ready.'

Kelly was holding up his hand for silence. We strained our ears but we could hear nothing; the telephone was too far away. We relaxed again.

'Hasn't he got a hard face?' said Kelly. 'He looks the part all right. It wouldn't surprise me if he came back with a gun in his hand.' He smiled, a bit uncertainly.

We waited. It wasn't more than two minutes, I suppose, but it seemed longer. Then we heard his footsteps approaching, steady, measured treads.

As soon as I saw his face I knew that our plot had misfired. He looked perplexed and a little annoyed, but showed no sign of guilt or fear.

'I presume this is something more than a stupid practical joke,' he said brusquely. 'Kindly explain it, Simon.' He lifted his unfinished glass of whisky.

I took a deep breath. 'You have just heard my voice on the telephone,' I said, 'although you know that I couldn't be at the other end of the line. Doesn't that strike a chord in your memory?'

He continued to stare at me coldly and didn't reply.

'Well,' I floundered on, making a last effort, 'let me be more explicit. On the night Oliver was killed I received a telephone message, apparently from Oliver and certainly in Oliver's voice, at ten-forty-six to be precise, in those very words which you heard over the phone just now. But at that moment Oliver was lying dead in his room. Now do you see the connection?'

For a few brief seconds it seemed that he didn't. The reaction, when at last it came, was all we had hoped for. The colour drained slowly from his face. The whisky glass slipped from his hand and he stared unseeingly at the stain spreading over the carpet. He stood motionless for some time and then gradually took a grip of himself.

'You are suggesting', he said unsteadily, 'that the murderer used some mechanical device to fake that telephone call and so establish an alibi?'

'Precisely. The "mechanical device" was the dictaphone.'

'And that I am the murderer?'

'Yes.'

'Have you any evidence for this or is it conjecture?' he asked.

'We have evidence.'

'Who else knows about it?'

'Only Joyce Carruthers. It was she who put the call through just now from the office.'

'I see. And what do you propose to do about it?'

'We must report it to the police. I think you should come with us now to the police station.'

'I'm damned if I will,' he said angrily. The colour had come back to his face and his voice had its normal ring of authority. 'If the police want me they can come for me.'

He stared belligerently at us, as if challenging us to drag him out by main force.

'Come on, Alan,' I said quietly. 'Let's go.'

Kelly was unhappy about it. 'What if he—' he began.

'He won't get far. Come on. Let's go.'

We walked quickly out. Fergusson let us go without a word. I dropped Kelly at the nearest telephone box, telling him to phone Joyce at the office and let her know what had happened. I drove on to the police station.

I was not altogether surprised to be informed that Inspector Kennedy was in his office, late though the hour was. I was sure that Linda would have seen to it by now that her father's vindication of Sheila had been conveyed to the police. And that, I knew, would set the cat among the police pigeons.

What did surprise me at first was to find, when I went into the inspector's room, that Superintendent Garland was with him. Garland couldn't possibly have got up from London in the short time since Waterston made his statement. Then I recollected that it was less than three days since Sheila's arrest. Garland had probably never been away; he would no doubt still be working on the case against Sheila. It was hard to believe that so much had happened in three days.

They both greeted me effusively. Garland made a handsome apology on behalf of the police.

'We should have listened to you before,' he said. 'We haven't covered ourselves with glory in this case. The solution seemed so self-evident that I'm afraid we didn't at first give the attention we should to possible alternative solutions.'

He told me that Sheila had been released an hour ago. A statement was being issued to the Press to the effect that the police were satisfied that Mrs Grant had been in no way concerned with the murder.

'It was Waterston's statement that clinched it,' he said, 'but in fairness to ourselves I must say that we were already getting round to the view that Mrs Grant was innocent. That's why I'm still here, as a matter of fact. For one thing the gun was found yesterday – I mean the one that Mrs Grant said she threw into the river. It was found just about where you would have expected it to be if her story was true, and it has been identified as the one her father used to own. Of course, that is no proof that she didn't have a second gun, the one that killed your brother and that was found beside the body. But somehow I didn't think so. Then there's another point.'

He hesitated momentarily before plunging on. He was grinning at me a little shamefacedly.

'Again, I'm afraid, it shows up the police and especially me in an unflattering light. Despite your objections, we made the natural assumption that the negatives found in the safe belonged to your brother. It was only yesterday that we had them tested for finger-prints. Apart from the prints of the two or three members of the force who had handled them there were none – neither Mr Barnett's nor anyone else's. Now that was very odd. Your brother would have no reason to wear gloves when handling stuff that he kept locked up in his own safe. And if someone else planted them there – as indeed you had suggested – then that knocked the whole case for six.'

'Where is Mrs Grant now?' I asked. 'Is she back at Lagside?'

'Well, no. We've been trying to contact her husband but he seems to be out. Mrs Grant finally decided to spend the night with her mother at Endsleigh. She didn't want to give her husband a fright by arriving unheralded at the farm.'

I vaguely wondered where Roger could be at this time of night. Perhaps he was in bed and hadn't heard the phone. However, I thought it was time I told the superintendent about my own investigations and about Fergusson's virtual admission of guilt.

Garland and Kennedy listened to the whole story with close attention. They both took notes from time to time but didn't interrupt until right at the end, when I was describing my visit with Kelly to Fergusson that evening.

'Good God,' cried Garland, jumping up and reaching for his hat. 'Don't tell me you've warned him about this! Of all the idiotic things to do – well, I suppose I shouldn't criticize. Come on, Kennedy, rustle up a car for us. It's time you and I had a talk with Mr Fergusson.'

I offered to drive them there and they accepted. Garland came in beside me and the inspector and a police sergeant went into the back.

The weather had suddenly turned colder and there were frozen patches on the road. I had to go cautiously, although I was conscious all the time of Garland fuming with impatience at my side.

Fergusson's home was in darkness when we arrived. The superintendent nearly pulled the bell out of its socket and we could hear its peal reverberate through the house. There was no answer.

'Where's the garage?' Garland asked curtly.

I took him round to it. The doors were open and it was empty.

'Look,' said Inspector Kennedy, pointing to a film of white frost on the macadamized drive outside the garage. The marks of the tyres of a car could be plainly seen running through it. 'The frost only came down a short time ago. That car must have gone out in the last half-hour. '

'All right,' said the superintendent. 'Back to the station at once. And this time *hurry*,' he added pointedly to me.

On the way back I described Fergusson's car and gave its registration number. Before I had even brought the car to a halt outside the police station they were piling out. The wires were humming within seconds. The hunt was up.

I didn't drive off immediately. I switched off my engine and lit a cigarette. I was thinking of Fergusson. A strange man; a psychopath, he must be, to have thought up and executed so diabolical a plot. And yet not entirely without feeling: his love of music was genuine enough. At one point during my visit to him tonight I had began to wonder if I hadn't been making as ghastly a blunder as the police had made over Sheila. But this time the evidence admitted of no other explanation. And his eventual collapse had been conclusive of his guilt. Now he was on the run. Ah, well, he won't get far, I thought. They never do.

I flicked my cigarette out of the window and drove home.

I was awakened at eight o'clock the following morning by the telephone ringing. It was Superintendent Garland.

'I thought you would like to know,' he said. 'We've found Fergusson. He's dead. His car was at the bottom of a ravine with him inside it.'

'An accident?' I asked.

'Could be. The roads were slippery last night and this is a particularly dangerous stretch. A sharp right-hand bend at the foot of a steep hill, with a gully waiting for you if you go straight on. But all the same I'm inclined to think it was suicide. It was a very strange route to take if he was trying to escape. It was the Lagside Road which doesn't lead anywhere in particular.'

I knew the spot he was talking about. I remembered that particular corner from my drive to the farm with Roger Grant the previous day.

I was about to hang up when the superintendent added: 'Well, aren't you going to point out to us that there is a third possibility?

Surely it wasn't "in character" for Fergusson to commit suicide?'
    He was laughing at me.

CHAPTER 20

It was one of those days in late April when winter comes back for a final fling. The sun was shining as I ate my breakfast, but it was a cold, wintry sun, and heavy clouds were banked up to the north-west. Even with both bars of the radiator on in the kitchen I couldn't get warm.

I found it hard to realize that the case was over. Not much more than a week had passed since that night when I had found Oliver's body; and now his murderer was dead too. Somehow the satisfaction that this should have given me was lacking. I merely felt a dull sense of anti-climax and depression.

When I began to analyse it, however, I recognized that the depression had little to do with the murder and the death of Fergusson. It was Linda I was thinking of. I had lost her now for good; I had spoken to her father yesterday in a manner that she would not forget or forgive. And I smiled wryly as I reflected that I could have spared my breath, for Sheila was on the point of being cleared in any case. Worst of all, I had been offered, and had let slip, my opportunity to nail the lies with which Waterston had poisoned Linda's mind against me. That opportunity would not come again.

One thing, however, which I was determined to do was to have a showdown with Marion. Apart from Oliver himself I had been the only one to show some understanding and kindness to Marion in these last years, to try to help her to come to terms with a misfortune that she hadn't the strength of character to face alone. I didn't expect or ask for gratitude. I could forgive her much; but this deliberate wrecking of my marriage with Linda was beyond forgiveness.

I put on my overcoat and walked to Marion's house. The exercise infused some warmth into me and at the same time the cold air cleared my head. The sky was now heavily overcast and the first drops of sleety rain were falling as I walked up the drive.

Marion let me in herself. She explained that Millie was away for the day.

She was wearing a housecoat over her pyjamas and she had a towel wound turban-wise over her hair, which she had just been washing, she told me. Even in that unromantic setting there was a certain rare elegance about Marion, provided you saw only the unmarked side of her face. It brought it home to me once again what she could have been, what indeed she had been until those disfiguring scars had been etched into her face and into her spirit.

She was unusually cheerful this morning. She seemed pleased to see me and at once busied herself making coffee, chattering idly about this and that.

I waited until we were seated with our coffee and our cigarettes. Then, interrupting her without apology, I said:

'Marion, why did you tell Linda that you were my mistress?'

Her face went white. Her cup was arrested on the way to her mouth.

She started to deny it. 'I didn't—' she began, but I continued to stare at her implacably.

Then she said defiantly, 'You're far too good for Linda. Oliver thought so too. It was a kindness I was doing if you only knew it.'

'For God's sake, Marion,' I shouted angrily, 'Linda is my

wife. It's not for you or Oliver or anyone else to decide whether she is the right wife for me. I repeat, why did you tell her that devilish lie?'

She was frightened, I could see; too frightened even to put on one of her usual displays of histrionics. She began to talk in a low monotone, as if to herself.

'You saved me, Simon, from going out of my mind. I was still in love with Oliver, but I hated him at the same time. I blamed him for being the cause of my injuries although in my heart I knew it wasn't his fault. He did his best, but we could never be comfortable together again. So it was your visits that I came to count on, it was you that made life tolerable.

'And then you met Linda and you married her and you stopped coming to see me. It was purgatory, Simon. It was like what a drug addict must feel when he's deprived of his dope. That's when I started drinking. I couldn't help myself.

'Well, one day that little worm Waterston called and as Oliver was out I had to entertain him. I don't like him any more than I like his daughter, but I took the chance to lead him on to speak about Linda and you. It wasn't difficult: he was only too glad of the opportunity. He made it clear that he was as much against your marriage as I was, although for a different reason. He doted on that precious daughter of his and he spoke of her as if she were still a child. He couldn't adjust himself to the fact that she had grown up and moved out of his control. Apparently he had somehow heard of your visits to me before your marriage, often when Oliver was out, and he had drawn the worst conclusions.' She laughed harshly. 'It just shows you what an obsession he had when it didn't occur to him that no man would ever think about me in that way again.'

She didn't actually point to her face but it was clear that that was what she was referring to.

'I was in the doldrums that day,' she went on, 'and I was feeling spiteful. So, just for the satisfaction of watching his reaction, I spun him the tale. I told him that not only had I been your mistress before you married Linda but that you were still seeing me, on nights when you were supposed to be at the office. He lapped it up. He was extraordinarily gullible.

'I thought that would be the end of the matter. I want you to believe this, Simon: I didn't *plan* it. It was just a whim of the moment. Well, just a week or two later, one Wednesday afternoon at the beginning of January it was, they both descended on me, Waterston and Linda. Waterston asked me to repeat what I had told him. I was a bit apprehensive by this time. I thought this had gone far enough, and I started to tell the truth and deny the story. But suddenly the sight of Linda with those great dark eyes of hers and the smug expression of complete trust in you made me see red. She looked so damned condescending and pitying. Why should she have all the luck, I thought; why should I have to tolerate her pity? I'm worth ten of her, if only I had been allowed to keep my looks. So I pitched in and let her have it. Oh! it was a good performance, I can tell you. I was almost believing it myself before I was finished. And you should have seen that girl squirm! She was loyal, I'll say that. She told me at the end she didn't believe a word of it. But she was lying. I knew she was lying. It was beyond her comprehension that a woman might invent a story like that. She's not very sophisticated, is your Linda.

'All the same, I had a guilty conscience about it afterwards when I heard she had left you. It was only the knowledge that you had made a disastrous mistake in marrying Linda that kept me from owning up. I was thinking of you, Simon, all the time. You do understand, don't you?'

I had listened to her story without interruption. It was pretty much what I had expected but I was glad to have heard it from her own lips. I was finished with Marion now, I no longer felt any responsibility for her. In a sense she was not to blame for what she had done. The accident had twisted her mind as well as her body and she wasn't fully responsible for her actions. But the compassion I had felt for her in the past was gone for ever now.

I stood up. 'Yes, Marion,' I said answering her question, 'I understand. But I can't forgive.'

I walked to the door.

She rushed in front of me and barred the way.

'You can't leave me like this,' she cried hysterically. 'You're all I've got. Look at me, Simon, look at me. You must believe me now. Linda's no good. It isn't only me. Oliver thought the same, so does Fergusson. Why must you be so blind?'

'Will you shut up and let me past,' I shouted at her, trying to force my way to the door. 'I don't give a damn for your opinion or for the opinion of the man who murdered my brother. And as for Oliver, I don't believe that's what he thought of Linda.'

Her voice changed. 'Simon, what was that you said just now? About Oliver's murderer? Are you saying that Fergusson killed him?'

She was no longer blocking my way and I could have gone out. But something in her tone arrested me.

'Yes,' I said. 'I forgot you wouldn't know. Fergusson did it. He's dead now. Killed himself, the police think.'

Marion went over to the table and took a cigarette. Her hand trembled, I noticed, as she lit it.

'That gave me quite a turn,' she said, in a shaky voice. 'Fergusson, was it? I would never have believed it. He seemed so calm when I was talking to him. And that must have been just before he did it, I suppose.'

For a moment her words didn't register with me. My mind was still on the squalid scene we had just had and I was anxious to get out. I opened the door of the room and started to walk away. But I turned back.

'Did you say you were with Fergusson just before the murder?' I asked. 'Where? And at what time?'

'At the flat in Gribble Street,' she said. 'If Fergusson's dead, there is no reason why I shouldn't tell you now. He made me promise I wouldn't. When I went along that night there was a light in one of the windows. The door was unlocked and I burst in, expecting to find Oliver and – and that woman. But instead, there was Fergusson, all by himself. I got a shock, I can tell you. So did he, for that matter.'

'Yes, but what was the time, Marion? That's the important thing. What was the time?'

'I've told you that already. I got there about ten minutes to ten and judging by what was going on Fergusson had been there for quite some time before that. And we left together at twenty-five to eleven. He offered to drive me home but it was away out of his road and I said I would get a bus. Little did I know that the buses were off the road because of the fog and I would have to walk.'

I came back into the room and sat down.

'Marion,' I said slowly, 'you've got to be absolutely certain of these times. If what you've just said is accurate, Fergusson didn't have time to kill Oliver. You've given him an alibi. You must have made a mistake somewhere.'

'Well,' she said, wrinkling her brow in concentration, 'I could be a minute or two out about when I arrived, but not more than a minute or two. But it was ten-thirty-five when we left, I'm quite sure of that. I remember hearing a clock striking the half-hour while I was still there. And when I got up to go shortly afterwards I looked at my watch. It was ten-thirty-five. My watch is never wrong. I was thinking specially about the time of the bus because I knew Millie would be anxious.'

I let this pass for the moment. I felt sure that when I had had time to think it out properly there would be some obvious explanation of how Fergusson managed it.

'What was Fergusson doing in the flat that night?' I asked.

'He said he was trying to find out who the woman was that Oliver was living with. I must say he had fairly ransacked the place. When I arrived he was putting stuff back. I helped him do it. He had everything out – all the clothes from the wardrobe, the drawers from the dressing-table and the books out of the book-shelves. Even the seats from the easy-chairs were on the floor and the pictures were down from the wall. It was quite a search he had made.'

'But how could he hope to identify the woman from the inside of an easy-chair? And what help would the books and pictures be to him?'

'That's what I asked him,' Marion replied. 'He was vague about it. My own impression is that he was looking for something else as well, but what it was I've no idea.'

'And did he explain to you why he had so obsessive an interest in his partner's private life?'

'Oh, yes!' said Marion. I could hear the malice creeping back into her voice, so that what she went on to say was not as great a shock as it would otherwise have been. 'He said he had reason to believe that the woman was your wife, Linda, and he was afraid of the effect the scandal would have on the firm if it came out.'

I got to my feet angrily but she went on quickly, 'Now don't shout me down, Simon, I'm only reporting what Fergusson said. I told you he didn't like Linda. And if it's any satisfaction to you we weren't able to establish definitely who the woman was. All the same,' she added pensively, 'there was the perfume. An unusual brand. And the kind Linda uses.'

She was smiling and it was not a pleasant smile.

Suddenly I could stomach Marion no longer. I strode out of the room and slammed the door behind me.

When I got outside I regretted not having brought my car. The sky had all filled in, the wind had dropped, and snow was falling steadily, large wet flakes that had already carpeted the streets in greyish white. It was dark enough for the buses to have their side-lights on. Apart from a few brave churchgoers ploughing their way home the pavements were deserted.

There was nothing for it but to trudge home. I thought of taking shelter in the office, which was just round the corner, but I found I hadn't my keys with me. As I squelched through the slush I tried to concentrate on the implications of what Marion had said but my mind shied away from the problem.

As soon as I got home I had a hot bath and a change of clothes and made myself some lunch. Even after I was settled in front of the fire in the sitting-room, my lunch over and a cup of coffee at my elbow, I was reluctant to put my mind to the latest development. I believe that subconsciously I had already accepted Fergusson's innocence and I was frightened of what that implied.

However, I didn't abandon the theory that Fergusson was the murderer without a fight. In the first place, I asked myself, had Marion been telling the truth? She was an unreliable witness and part at least of what she had said was false: she had dragged in Linda's name as Oliver's mistress out of sheer malice; of that I had no doubt. I could not conceive of Fergusson making such an allegation in front of Marion, especially when, according to Marion herself, he had been unable to confirm it. Fergusson was too careful about the law of slander.

Nevertheless, I couldn't persuade myself that the main part of Marion's story – her visit to the flat and finding Fergusson there – was fabricated. For one thing it explained how Marion had got into the flat and it was an explanation she could scarcely have invented, for she was unlikely to know that Fergusson had a key. But my main reason for believing Marion's story was her demeanour in telling it. I knew her well enough to spot when she was lying; and she had not been lying then.

That being so, Fergusson now had an alibi for the period from nine-fifty to ten-thirty-five as well as from ten-fifty-seven onwards when he was with Joyce. Linda had left Oliver in the office about nine-forty-five, certainly not earlier than nine-forty. Always bearing in mind the fog, it was out of the question for him to have shot Oliver, planted the negatives in the safe and be installed in Gribble Street when Marion (whom he could hardly have been expecting) arrived, all in less than ten minutes. And Marion said there were signs he had been there for quite some time. At the other end it appeared at first sight to be more feasible. Between ten-thirty-five, when Fergusson left Gribble Street in his car, and ten-fifty-seven, when he appeared at Joyce's flat, there were twenty-two minutes. But this time there were two longish journeys to make in dense

fog, from Gribble Street to the office, and from the office to Joyce's
flat, with a murder thrown in. Moreover, at some point within the
period he had found time to phone Oliver's house and speak to
Millie. It just wasn't humanly possible.

Having juggled with times until my brain was reeling, I was
driven to the unwelcome conclusion that Fergusson could not have
killed Oliver. And yet his behaviour that night had been extraordinarily suspicious. Surely he must be implicated in the murder
in some way.

I felt tired. I went over to the sofa, put a cushion behind my
head, and stretched out full length. I closed my eyes and allowed
my thoughts to wander at will. Little scenes came back to me;
voices, snatches of conversation drifted into my head and died
away. I was in the no-man's-land between waking and sleeping. I
was dreaming, but still retained a last vestige of control over the
direction my dreams were taking. Now I was back in the office on
the night when Oliver was murdered. As is the way with dreams,
the two hours I spent there were telescoped into so many seconds.
I was very nearly fully asleep now, but just as I was drifting off
into complete unconsciousness I caught at a tiny wisp of an idea
that was floating past. I caught it and held it and played with
it and built on it. Even in that state of suspended animation I
recognized it as a fantastic idea, one that would not bear examination. It would explain one small discrepancy, that was all; and there
must be other, less improbable, explanations. But it amused me to
assume it to be valid and to apply it to the other facts of the case
to see where it broke down. It didn't break down. Every mystery
it touched it dissolved. All the hitherto unrelated and apparently
contradictory facts began to merge into a pattern, a cold, logical,
devilish pattern.

I sat bolt upright. I was wide awake now. This was no game, although I could have wished it were. I dissected the whole case again, every single detail that I had picked up over the past ten days. At every turn there was confirmation. Little things that had seemed insignificant at the time now came into perspective and became links in a chain of proof that could not be broken. I knew now, beyond all doubt, who had killed my brother, and when, and how, and why. And I wished to God I didn't.

I poured myself a glass of neat whisky. I needed it to brace me for what I had to do. I stood at the window sipping my drink and looking out. The snow had turned to rain now and the street outside was a morass of muddy water. Two little boys in wellingtons and mackintoshes were splashing about in a deep puddle across the road where a drain had choked. There was no one else in sight. I gazed out of the window for some time, my mind numb with shock.

Then I put on my raincoat and hat and drove to the police station.

I found that the police had reached the same conclusion as I had. Superintendent Garland had seen the possibility the previous night, even when I was building up my case against Fergusson. Fergusson's flight and death almost convinced him that I was right, but he still had a lingering doubt. And very soon evidence had turned up which justified his uneasiness.

A witness had come forward who had seen Fergusson's car on the Lagside Road the night before. This was a young doctor who was driving home after visiting a patient – the wife of one of Roger Grant's farm workers at Lagside. He had come on Fergusson's car at a narrow bit of the road where there was scarcely room for two vehicles to pass. There had been a bit of backing and filling before they finally got through. It had been dark at the time, of course, but from the light of his headlamps he saw the other car clearly and was able to describe it and even give its registration number. But, more significantly, he swore that there were two people in the car, not one. He couldn't give a description or even say what sex they were but he was certain there were two.

This in itself cast doubt on the theory that Fergusson had committed suicide. Who had the passenger been and where was he now? His body certainly wasn't down in the ravine beside Fergusson's. But what crystallized Garland's suspicions was the discovery that Fergusson's fingerprints were not on the steering wheel of the car although he had not been wearing gloves. The wheel had been wiped clean of prints.

'Well,' said the superintendent, 'it was quite easy after that. Your case against Fergusson was sound enough up to a point, but what you didn't observe was that there was one other person who fitted the bill even better. Now that Fergusson is out, it *has* to be that person. And of course we didn't pay enough attention to the Merriman set-up. It's so obvious when you think about it.'

'What's the drill now?' I asked dully. 'An arrest?'

'Well, that's what Inspector Kennedy and I were arguing about when you came. Kennedy thinks we've got more than enough to justify an arrest but I'm not so sure. Certainly the additional pointer you've given us, Mr Barnett, is a help, but even so . . . Well, I wouldn't like to go to a jury with this case. We'll get the identification, of course, but that's no proof of the murder or rather the murders, for there's no doubt Fergusson was murdered too. And the rest of the case is so circumstantial and depends so much on logical argument that any competent defence counsel could make mincemeat of it. Logic never won a case before a jury. What I would like is a confession. And I've thought of a way we might get it.'

'A lot of theatrical nonsense,' Inspector Kennedy interposed with unexpected warmth. 'We've a perfectly good case already and we'll get plenty more evidence before the trial. Do you want to wait until there's another death?'

Garland frowned in annoyance. He obviously didn't like this open expression of disagreement. He ignored the interruption and went on to outline what he proposed. When I heard what the plan was I found myself very much in agreement with the inspector. It seemed to me unnecessarily melodramatic and I was in any event doubtful whether it would succeed.

However, it was clear that Garland was set on it; and it was not for me to criticize or to dictate to Scotland Yard how they should conduct their business. I promised to co-operate.

The superintendent's plan involved getting all the principal characters together at the one time, preferably at the scene of the first murder. After some discussion it was decided that the performance should take place in the office at eleven o'clock the following morning. It was too late to organize it for the Sunday night. I was to see that Joyce and Alan Kelly and myself were present and to send the other members of the staff home. The police would arrange for Marion, Sheila and Roger Grant, Linda and Waterston to be there. They would also have their surprise exhibit concealed in another room, ready for production at the critical moment.

Inspector Kennedy was still shaking his head unhappily as I went out and he exchanged a rueful glance with me. For the first time I felt in sympathy with him.

CHAPTER 21

It was after ten o'clock before I went into the office next morning. I had no taste for the performance to come and I longed to get it over.

I called in Joyce and Kelly and told them briefly that Superintendent Garland had an important announcement to make at eleven o'clock in my room and that they were asked to be present. They looked mystified but I couldn't enlighten them further. I had given my word to the superintendent that I would say no more than that to anyone. I asked Joyce to tell the rest of the staff to go home at ten-thirty and not to come back until after lunch.

I couldn't settle to anything. I opened my mail and added it, unread, to the formidable pile of papers in my in-tray. I finished a cigarette and lit another. The minutes ticked slowly by.

Joyce looked in at one point and asked openly what this was all about. I told her gruffly to mind her own business and she went out quickly, looking hurt. I instantly regretted my rudeness. I was all on edge this morning.

I looked at my watch. Could it be only ten-forty-five? I got up and stood at the windows, looking down on the street below. The pavements were still damp from yesterday's downpour, but there were signs of an improvement now. The clouds were higher and there were little patches of blue here and there. A brightness to the south-east suggested that the sun was struggling to get through.

Linda was the first to arrive. A taxi drew up in front of the office door and she stepped smartly out. Then she waited while the driver helped another passenger at the back to alight. I saw, with a spurt of anger, that this was Waterston. Garland had no right, I thought, to drag this sick old man out for a nerve-racking experience like this. Waterston was a scoundrel whom I had good reason to loathe. But this was too much. He shuffled forward towards the entrance to the building, leaning heavily on a stick. I noticed that Linda never glanced at him and made no effort to help him.

They had hardly disappeared into the doorway when I saw Marion cross the street on foot. From the angle from which I looked down, her face was partially obscured. She looked youthful, slim and attractive. Her limp was scarcely noticeable.

As I waited for them to come up I suddenly realized how awkward the situation was going to be. These were three people with whom I was scarcely on speaking terms. I hastily routed out Joyce and Alan Kelly to help with the reception of the visitors.

We did our best to preserve a semblance of civilized behaviour. Joyce, as usual in such a situation, was extremely good. She helped Waterston into a chair and proceeded to talk to him, with every appearance of naturalness, about trivialities of the office. She even managed to evoke a response from time to time. Kelly meanwhile had manfully attached himself to Marion and was listening politely to a monologue about the migraines to which she was subject. Linda seemed most ill at ease of them all and most affected by the occasion. She refused my offer of a chair and stood, just inside the door, nervously twisting her gloves in her hands. She wouldn't catch my eye and showed no inclination to speak to me. After a moment or two I turned away and went back to my vantage point at the window.

Eleven o'clock was striking when Roger and Sheila arrived. They came in the little Morris and Sheila had been driving. For a man whose wife had just been rescued from a capital charge Roger was singularly gloomy. He didn't look well yet, either: his eyes were dull and dark-ringed and he had a cold. He briefly acknowledged my introductions and went over and sat in a corner by himself. Sheila, on the other hand, was like a breath of fresh air in the room. Her recent spell in prison seemed not to have affected her. She radiated health and good spirits, and the camel coat and the gay little hat which she wore were in striking contrast to Marion's slim-fitting black coat and to the tweed suit which Linda was wearing. Even Joyce looked sombrely dressed by comparison. Sheila gazed with frank and appraising interest at each of the others as I introduced them. She spent a long time studying Linda in particular. Linda returned her gaze impassively but I thought I detected the ghost of a smile twitching at the corner of her lips. I hadn't seen Linda smile for months.

Then Sheila turned to me. 'May I see you alone for a moment, Simon?' she said.

I tried to put her off. 'There's hardly time, Sheila,' I began. 'The police will be—'

'There's something I must say to you,' she interrupted. 'It won't take more than two minutes, I promise you.'

'All right,' I muttered, reluctantly and ungraciously. 'We can go to Fergusson's room.' I was acutely conscious of the eyes of the others on us as we went out.

She closed the door of Fergusson's room behind her, went over to me and without warning put her arms round me and kissed me full on the mouth. I started back and protested angrily but she stopped me.

'Now, don't get stuffy, Simon,' she said. 'I promised myself that I would do that once, just once. It won't ever happen again. It's my way of saying "Thank you". You see, I know what you've done for me.'

'How's Roger?' I asked, trying to change the subject. I was still feeling embarrassed.

She trilled with laughter. 'You're blushing, Simon, you really are blushing. Roger? Oh, he'll make out. He's been through a harrowing experience, you know.'

There was a gentle irony in her tone, but no bitterness. She had summed up Roger's character in that one sentence.

'Oh, yes,' she went on, 'I expect we'll rub along as before. But I'll have less compunction now about following my own instincts on occasions. I somehow don't feel so – what's the word? – so beholden to him as I used to.'

I heard the hum of the lift on its way up.

'We'd better get back, Sheila,' I said. 'I think that's the police arriving.' But before I opened the door I took her in my arms and kissed her. She flashed a smile of understanding at me.

As we walked back along the corridor she whispered to me, 'Linda's beautiful, Simon, truly beautiful. Why didn't you ever tell me she looked like that?' And then, as an afterthought, 'Poor Marion. When I think of what she used to be like.'

It was some minutes yet before the police joined us. We could hear them moving about elsewhere in the office and the murmur of their voices penetrated indistinctly from time to time. There was silence in the room now, a tense, uneasy silence. All pretence at polite conversation had been abandoned. Even Sheila was affected by the others and sat in unaccustomed pensiveness.

When Superintendent Garland finally made his entrance the atmosphere was charged with tension. Apart from me, nobody in the room knew what was coming, yet so well had the stage been set and the suspense mounted that no one could have doubted that something dramatic was afoot.

The superintendent was accompanied by Inspector Kennedy, the young plain-clothes sergeant who had been with Garland earlier in the case, and a sergeant from the local force. They ranged themselves in front of the fireplace, facing the semicircle of nervous onlookers. They didn't sit down.

Garland began quietly by apologizing for having kept them waiting. Then he went on, 'Now, ladies and gentlemen, the reason why I've brought you here today will become apparent in a few minutes. But first I want to say a word or two about this case. The murder of Mr Oliver Barnett was not a sudden impulsive crime, it was planned to the last detail and skilfully executed. The object of the murder was to pin on Mr Barnett the responsibility for a rather nasty form of blackmail which the murderer had been engaged in and which was about to be exposed. We were to assume that Mr Barnett, under threat of exposure, committed suicide. The plan misfired to some extent, for we were able to prove that it was murder and not suicide. But in other respects we were, to begin with, deceived. We believed that Mr Barnett was the blackmailer and, on certain circumstantial evidence, we believed that Mrs Grant here had killed him. We were wrong. I tell you that quite frankly and I offer my apologies to Mrs Grant. I also tell you frankly that we are indebted to Mr Simon Barnett—' he bowed briefly in my direction – 'for putting us on the right lines.'

I was getting more and more restive and irritated. This was like a soliloquy from *Hamlet*. No doubt Garland sincerely wanted to bring the murderer to justice and no doubt he genuinely believed that this scene was necessary to that end; but I couldn't resist the impression that he was a vain man and that he enjoyed holding the centre of the stage. With his commanding presence and his fine voice he certainly had his audience hanging on his every word.

'Now we have learned quite a lot about the murderer,' Garland continued. 'He (I call him "he" although it may equally be "she") is someone who knew Mr Barnett well, who knew not only his office routine but also a great deal about his personal life, someone who had a key to a private flat which Mr Barnett rented on the outskirts of the town, someone, too, who had an alibi for the night of the murder from ten-forty-five onwards but not earlier.'

He paused to let the significance of this last remark sink in. 'You see,' he explained, 'by a very ingenious trick the murderer was able to suggest that his victim was still alive at ten-forty-five when in fact he was already dead. I needn't go into details except to remark that the trick again implied at least access to the office and the knowledge of Mr Barnett's use of the dictaphone. Now all this tells us quite a lot about the murderer but unfortunately not enough to identify him. Any of you here would fit the description I have just given of him.

'Any of you here,' he added with more emphasis, 'but no one else. The murderer is in this room with us.'

There was an almost inaudible gasp from someone. Inspector Kennedy took out a large white handkerchief and loudly and ostentatiously blew his nose. But it did little to lessen the effect of the superintendent's words or to relax the tension.

'Now,' said Garland, 'there is one more thing we know about the murderer. He is also the blackmailer. All I need to say about the blackmail is that it was based on certain photographs taken a number of years ago at the Polygon Club in the city. We have strong reason to believe that these photographs were originally held by a Mrs Claire Merriman, the wife of the manager of the club. Mrs

Merriman herself is dead. How did these photographs come into the possession of the blackmailer? We believe that if we could establish a link between Mrs Merriman and one of the people sitting in this room, the case would be solved.

'Now Mrs Merriman, for good reasons, was an extremely retiring person and was known to very few. She left this country at short notice immediately after her husband's trial for certain offences in connection with the Polygon Club and we believe that before she went she gave them or sold them to someone she knew well and could trust, for it was too dangerous for her to let them get into the wrong hands.'

I expected that at this point the superintendent would reveal that Mrs Merriman was Fergusson's daughter. But no, he must have thought that was irrelevant to his present purpose.

Garland now paused for so long that I began to wonder if he had forgotten his cue. But it was all part of the act.

When he resumed, it was in a quieter, more conversational tone, 'We have in a room across the corridor a man who did know Mrs Merriman well – "intimately", I think, would be the *mot juste*. If there is anyone here who was closely associated with Mrs Merriman at that time, this man will, I believe, recognize him – or her. I propose to bring him in here to find out.'

He nodded to his sergeant, who went out of the room.

While we were waiting, the superintendent remarked, 'I ought to say that our witness has not been told why we have brought him here and has not been primed in any way.'

The silence in the room was oppressive. I could hear my heart thumping.

When the door at last opened and Joe Barrington walked in I stared fixedly at the person I knew to be the murderer. There was a barely perceptible recoil, instantly corrected; no more. Nerves of steel, I thought.

Joe Barrington managed to combine in his expression truculence with bewilderment and apprehension.

'What's all this about?' he said, his eyes flickering this way and that.

Superintendent Garland had been speaking the truth when he said that Barrington had not been primed in any way. It was important that no question of collusion should be brought out in court later.

'Tell me, Mr Barrington. You knew Claire Merriman, didn't you?'

He contemplated denying it, but thought better of it. 'What if I did?' he muttered surlily. 'It's no crime, is it?'

'Calm yourself, Mr Barrington. We're not accusing you of anything. We only want your help. Now we know that you were on intimate terms with Mrs Merriman. You needn't bother to deny it.' Here Barrington glared at me. He knew where that information had come from.

'That being so,' Garland continued, 'you must have known who were Mrs Merriman's close acquaintances at the time?'

'She didn't have many close acquaintances. She kept herself to herself, as you might say.'

'So much the better. At any rate you would know the few friends she had. Now I want you, Mr Barrington, to look round you and see if you recognize any of them here. Take your time about it and think carefully before you speak. Someone's life depends on it.'

I couldn't bear to watch. I kept my eyes fixed rigidly on the floor.

There was a silence for what seemed an age. Then I heard Barrington's voice, 'I remember that man. He used to go to the club.'

I looked up. Roger Grant had leapt to his feet, sending his chair crashing to the floor. He was crimson in the face. 'What is this?' he shouted. 'A bloody conspiracy? Of course I was a member of the club. So was he – ' he pointed to Waterston – 'and so were hundreds of others. But I knew nothing of the dirty stuff that went on upstairs and I never even knew Mrs Merriman existed.'

'Sit down, Mr Grant,' said the superintendent sharply. He was nettled. He turned to Barrington. 'Have you any reason to believe that Mr Grant knew Mrs Merriman?' he asked.

'No,' replied Barrington.

'Well, go on, then. You haven't looked at everyone yet.'

Barrington swivelled round. He gazed at me and scowled. Then his eyes travelled over Sheila from head to foot, then on to Waterston, then Linda. Suddenly he was shouting incoherently, 'Close acquaintance, by God! That's close enough, all right. Killed in a car accident, eh? I might have known. That's Claire Merriman!'

He was pointing at Joyce.

Joyce said coldly, 'I've never seen this man in my life before.' She took a handkerchief from her pocket, rubbed her lips with it and put it back.

'Oh! haven't you?' said Barrington, waving his arms at her. 'You've cut your blonde hair that you were so proud of and dyed it and you've got a different set of teeth, but by God! I would know that face anywhere. And more than the face,' he added as an after-thought. 'Perhaps you would care to lift up your skirt and let them see your birthmark.'

She moved fast then. She was on her feet and backing towards the door before anyone could stop her. The hand that had returned the handkerchief to her pocket now held a revolver.

'Anyone who moves gets the same as Oliver Barnett got,' she said softly, still backing away.

I felt infinitely weary and dispirited. 'It's no good, Joyce,' I said dully. 'I took the gun out of your bag this morning and removed the ammunition.'

They were after her then, like hounds at the kill. She only got a few yards down the corridor. From where we sat we could hear the chase, hear her screams and foul imprecations when they caught her, and hear the struggles as they took her away.

CHAPTER 22

The bar was empty. It was too early for the regulars who slipped in for a drink before lunch. Sam was behind the counter industriously polishing glasses. He scarcely looked up as he took my order and pushed across a double whisky. I took my drink over to a table in the darkest corner of the room, glad to be alone, glad to have something to take the bad taste out of my mouth.

I had just sat down when the door opened and Alan Kelly appeared. I should have known he would see me cross the street and would follow me. I cursed under my breath but I managed to summon up a smile to greet him. He got himself a lager and joined me at the table.

'That was quite a performance this morning,' he remarked. 'When did it all blow up? And what about Fergusson? Is it true he's dead?'

I told him briefly of Fergusson's death and of the evidence that had subsequently come to light clearing him of Oliver's murder.

Kelly pondered this for some moments. Then he said:

'I see. But why Joyce? What put you on to her?'

I didn't want to discuss it. I didn't even want to think about it. I was longing for him to go away and leave me in peace. For the first time in my life I felt I would like to get drunk.

But I had to make the effort; I owed it to him.

'If Fergusson was innocent,' I said, 'it had to be Joyce: it couldn't be anybody else. You'll see why in a minute. But first let me tell you just what she did and how she did it. A devilish scheme it was too. Fergusson's story about his daughter was true up to a point but he was lying when he said that she had died in Canada. She came back to this country after less than a year and somehow convinced Fergusson that she was prepared to turn over a new leaf. It's easy to condemn Fergusson for his gullibility but after all he was her father. Anyway, he decided to give her another chance in circumstances where he could keep an eye on her. Having put in that press announcement about her death in a motoring accident in Toronto, he got her a job, under an assumed name, in his own firm. You remember it was Fergusson who recommended Joyce to us. It was safe enough. Nobody in Brickfield knew Claire and the chances of her being seen and recognized by the few people from places round about, such as Joe Barrington, who had known her as Mrs Merriman, were negligible. As an extra precaution she changed her appearance.

'Well, she bided her time. She still had those photographs that she had acquired as Claire Merriman and she intended to use them. But she was in no hurry. She was determined to devise a scheme that would leave her in the clear if anything went wrong. That was always her way, as Fergusson himself told us. Oliver provided the opportunity. In due course she got herself transferred to be secretary to Oliver instead of me and it wasn't long before she was installed as his mistress and had a key to the flat in Gribble Street.'

'So Joyce was the woman who—?' Kelly interrupted.

'Of course she was. She even had the nerve to tell me that Oliver had once taken her there and tried to seduce her. That was simply a precaution in case she had ever been recognized entering or leaving the flat. Anyway, once she decided the time was ripe, she started on her campaign of blackmail. She did it exactly as we thought Fergusson had done it and she had Oliver's murder planned long in advance to safeguard her own position if the blackmail should come to light.'

'Did Fergusson know that his daughter was Mr Barnett's mistress?'

'Not at first, but by last Christmas he must have come to suspect it. He challenged Oliver with it and Oliver, as you might expect, blew up. He didn't know Joyce was Fergusson's daughter and it would seem to him to be sheer impertinence for Fergusson to interfere. However, Fergusson was so worried that he went to extraordinary lengths to find out whether his suspicions were well founded. He acquired a key to the flat by fraud.'

'And when he did find out?'

'Well, this is surmise. All we actually know is that he didn't manage to put a stop to the affair. But I suspect that he went to her and renewed his threat to report to the police her part in the Merriman scandal if she didn't give Oliver up; and this time she called his bluff. When it came to it, he just couldn't bring himself to do it. From that point she would know she had nothing to fear from him. She could get away with murder . . . or very nearly murder.'

'Now we come to the week of Oliver's death. On the Wednesday evening Oliver found that letter from Robertson in the Gribble Street flat addressed to "C. V. Jones", the assumed name under which he had rented the flat. The letter would be largely un-intelligible to him but one thing would be very clear – that someone had been using his flat and his name for some criminal purpose. Now what does Oliver do when he gets back home? He makes two phone calls, the *second* to Fergusson. Why did he phone Fergusson at all? It is very unlikely he knew that Fergusson had a key to the flat. The obvious person to contact was the only one apart from himself, so far as he knew, who did have access to the flat, namely

Joyce. And that's exactly what he did. When we were building our case against Fergusson, we overlooked that significant first telephone call that Oliver made.

'It must have been a shock to Joyce too. Presumably Oliver would read over the letter he had found and ask if she could throw any light on it. She would realize at once that Sheila was hot on the trail of the blackmailer. She may also have recalled the mysterious appointment that "Mrs Cargill" had made with Oliver for the Friday night and guessed that this was Sheila. At any rate she decided that it was time to put into execution the second part of her plan – the murder of Oliver. But in the meantime she had to stall Oliver and she did that neatly by telling him that Fergusson had a key to the flat. She knew that her father wouldn't give her away. Hence Oliver's phone call to Fergusson and his conversation with him at lunch the next day. What exactly Oliver said at that lunch we can only guess, but it was enough to give Fergusson a clue to what Joyce was up to. He went to Gribble Street that evening, using his key to get in, and when Marion interrupted him he was busy searching for the photographs. From the information Oliver had given him he had deduced that Joyce was using these photographs for blackmail and he thought she might have concealed them in the flat. When he didn't find them there he went to Joyce's house to have it out with her. He must have been a bit worried about Oliver too – he probably guessed he was in danger – for he tried to contact him at his house before he called on Joyce.

'However, unknown to Fergusson, Oliver was already dead. Joyce hadn't let the grass grow under her feet. Of course her plans had been laid long before. She never went to the cinema that night, or, if she did, she slipped out early. She knew Oliver had an appointment with Linda in the office at eight-thirty. All she had to do was wait in her own room until Linda left, then walk in and shoot Oliver. I imagine that the revolver she used was in fact Oliver's – the one he used to keep in his desk. She would have abstracted it beforehand. Her idea was to make it look like suicide. This was foiled by the blood on his left hand but she did her best by pressing the gun into his right hand. She probably hoped that no one would remember he was left-handed. Then she planted the negatives in the safe. These—'

'Just a minute,' said Kelly. 'Surely she was very lucky to find the safe unlocked. Or did she know the combination?'

'She may have known it. But even if the safe hadn't been accessible she could simply have left the negatives in a drawer of Oliver's desk. The essential thing was to link the photographs to Oliver so that no one would doubt that he had been the blackmailer. His suicide would be explained once it came out that one of his victims, Sheila Grant, had discovered who the blackmailer was and was about to unmask him.

'The only other thing Joyce had to do was to establish her alibi in case Oliver's death was recognized as murder (as indeed it was). Before she left the office she switched the outside line through to my extension. She had to do that, for Oliver, phoning me from the office, would certainly have used the extension. Then she went home as fast as she could in the fog, taking the dictaphone transcriber with her. She already had in her flat the wax with the appropriate recording of a summons from Oliver to me. As soon as she got in, she rang the office and the call went automatically through to my house. She played over the recording into the telephone mouthpiece, and that was that. I was prepared to swear that Oliver was alive at ten-forty-six and Joyce had an unimpeachable alibi from that time onwards.'

'A very chancy alibi, surely,' Kelly remarked. 'It was sheer coincidence that Fergusson called on her at the time he did.'

'Oh! that wasn't her plan at all. You remember that her neighbour saw her arrive at the flat at ten-thirty-five. If the neighbour hadn't been on the doorstep Joyce would have made an excuse to call and borrow milk or something of that sort. And if her father hadn't happened to arrive she would have found some way of establishing beyond doubt that she didn't leave the flat again that night. As it was, Fergusson made a very convenient witness for her.'

'So Fergusson was prepared to condone even murder?'

'Oh, no! Blackmail, yes; but I think even Fergusson would have drawn the line at murder. The one crumb of comfort he had from the whole business was that his daughter couldn't have murdered Oliver. He believed, as we all did, that Oliver was killed some time after ten-forty-six, and he knew that that let Joyce out. You saw yourself how shattered he was when we played that rather stupid trick on him, with the dictaphone. It was a delayed shock, too, not the immediate reaction you would have expected if he himself had been guilty. Fergusson knew that his daughter was capable of murder, he probably recognized too that she had a motive for killing Oliver, but until that moment he believed she could not have been the murderer. That's why he continued to protect her, continued to hide her real identity, backed up her lie about the reason for his visit to her on the night of the murder.'

'He still didn't give her away,' said Kelly, 'when we proved to him that your brother might have been murdered earlier, at a time when Joyce had no alibi.'

'Yes, but all that proved was that Joyce *could* have done it. Before he did anything irrevocable he would want to be sure that she actually *had* done it. In other words he would want to see her. That's what Joyce was gambling on. As soon as we left him that night he would be on the telephone to Joyce at the office and—'

'So that explains it,' exclaimed Kelly. 'When I tried to phone her at the office after leaving Fergusson's house I was surprised to get no reply.'

'Yes. She would be speaking to her father on his house extension. Well, no doubt they arranged to meet. The rest is guesswork. It may come out at the trial. You can depend on it that Joyce had some plausible story to tell her father. Whatever it was, it must have been convincing enough for Fergusson to agree to accompany her on a drive out along the Lagside Road. I rather suspect she built up some sort of case against Roger Grant and offered to prove it by a visit to him at his farm. She would be driving – Fergusson hated driving in the dark. She would stop the car on some pretext at the top of that steep hill above the gully. Then she would crack Fergusson on the head with a spanner or something, release the brake, jump out, and that would be the end of Fergusson. The car would run down the gradient, crash through the wooden fence and hurtle over the cliff. That's my picture of it anyway. It may not be accurate in detail but it's near enough.'

Kelly was silent for some time while he digested all this. Then he said slowly, 'I can see that the account you've given explains all the facts that we had and at the same time is consistent with Claire Merriman's character as Fergusson described it. What I don't understand is how you were sure that Joyce was Claire Merriman and that she was the blackmailer and murderer. There might have been other explanations equally plausible.'

'No, Alan,' I replied. 'Once it was established that Fergusson was innocent, there was no other possible explanation. The police saw that at once; in fact, they had their suspicions of Joyce even before Fergusson was cleared. But curiously enough it was a trivial little detail that put me on to her – a chewing-gum wrapper. I remembered seeing it in her waste-paper basket after I found Oliver's body that night. It ought not to have been there. According to Joyce's own story she left the office at five o'clock and didn't return. The cleaners are supposed to empty all the ash trays and waste-paper baskets when they are in between five-thirty and six-thirty. Of course they might easily have missed it. They are careless at times as you know. But it did at least raise the possibility that Joyce might have been lying. Once I started thinking on these lines the more obvious pointers began to stare out.'

'They're not obvious to me, I'm afraid,' said Kelly.

'Well, take the dictaphone business for a start. We put Joyce on the spot by asking her whether a wax had ever disappeared. She couldn't risk saying "No" because she guessed I had some independent evidence for my theory, as indeed I had – the evidence of Oliver's ash tray and the absence of the dictaphone transcriber from its usual place; and also the background murmur in that telephone call I got. So she said "Yes", staking everything on the chance that her father wouldn't give her away before she silenced him. It was Joyce, you remember, who persuaded us not to go to the police but to carry out that melodramatic experiment on Fergusson ourselves. However, the point I'm making is this: now that the use of the dictaphone to mislead about the time of death was confirmed, it very much narrowed the field of possible murderers. It had to be someone in the office. It wasn't really practicable for anyone from outside to lay his hands on a recording. By far the likeliest person in the office was Joyce, for she was the only one who could remove a wax without Oliver being any the wiser. She would simply transcribe it first and then take it away. You can imagine the rumpus

Oliver would have raised if some of his dictation had been lost. The whole office would have heard about it. Yet none of us ever knew of such an incident until Joyce recounted it to us.

'But there was more than that. If the dictaphone trick was used, then the murderer must clearly be someone who had an alibi from ten-forty-six onwards but not earlier. Who in the office fitted that requirement? Only Fergusson and Joyce. And later we discovered that Fergusson *did* have a water-tight alibi for the whole evening. That left Joyce.

'Now look at it from another angle. The murderer had a key to the Gribble Street flat. Who, apart from Oliver, had keys to the flat? Fergusson, of course, but he is now eliminated from the list of suspects; Mrs McConnell, the owner of the flat, but she satisfies none of the other qualifications for the murderer. Who else? Oliver's mistress, presumably, and no one else, unless we are to make the improbable assumption that Fergusson wasn't the only one to have acquired a key unlawfully. That raised a strong presumption that Oliver's mistress, whoever she might be, was the blackmailer and murderer. With this independent evidence that the murderer was a woman, the case against Joyce is clinched beyond doubt, for Joyce was the only woman in the office who could conceivably be the murderer.

'There were one or two other indications as well. There was her reluctance to help in our investigations. Her explanation of that didn't seem very convincing to me even at the time. And then there was the curious fact that she was in the office before nine o'clock on the morning after the murder (she told me that herself), although we all know that she usually drifted in about nine-thirty. The reason was, of course, that she had to switch the night extension back from my house in case the telephone girl remarked on it when she came in. The oddest thing of all was

Fergusson's visit to her at nearly eleven o'clock at night. The account she gave of it was very unsatisfactory, even when it was partially confirmed by Fergusson. I was concentrating too much on Fergusson as the murderer to observe that this did raise some queries about Joyce herself.

'Once you accept the overwhelming evidence of Joyce's guilt, it isn't hard to deduce that she must be Claire Merriman. We know that Joyce had somehow acquired the photographs taken at the Polygon Club and was using them for blackmail. We also know that Claire Merriman, Fergusson's daughter, had originally possessed these photographs and that it was shortly after her reported death in Canada that Joyce was introduced to the firm by Fergusson. That in itself is suggestive. But the most significant fact was Fergusson's extraordinary behaviour. Why should he be so concerned about Joyce's affair with Oliver? Why should he ransack the flat that night and then rush straight off to Joyce? Above all, why, when he was innocent himself, did he get such a shock when he learned about the dictaphone device and why didn't he at once clear himself as he could easily have done? The answer is obvious. He was protecting his own daughter.'

I came to an end abruptly. There seemed to be nothing more to say and Kelly asked no further questions. We sat in silence for some time.

The bar was filling up now and the atmosphere was heavy with cigarette smoke. Someone put a coin in the juke box and the strains of the latest hit number came through.

While I had been talking the feeling of depression that had been gnawing at me all the morning had been temporarily deadened, but now it was back. I felt an unreasonable irritation with Kelly as he sat there, young, handsome, confident, with all his life before him. Outwardly at least he seemed quite unconcerned by all that had happened.

As if he knew I had been thinking of him, he turned to me now and said with an embarrassed smile:

'When I think of Joyce I can't help realizing how lucky I am to have Susan. We became engaged last night, you know.'

'I didn't know,' I said harshly. 'But congratulations just the same.'

I could see he was hurt by my tone. I pulled myself together with an effort and went on, 'I really mean that, Alan. Here, this calls for a celebration.'

I ordered a whisky for Kelly and another – my third – for myself. He looked a little doubtfully at his drink but didn't protest.

'Well,' I said, as I raised my glass, 'here's to your marriage and to the prosperity of the firm of Barnett and Kelly.'

'I don't quite understand—' he began, but I could see the excitement gleaming in his eyes already.

'Oh, yes! I'm offering you a partnership. I've run out of partners. I've lost three in the last fortnight. It seems to be a hazardous occupation. But perhaps you'll be willing to take the risk. We can discuss the details in the office tomorrow.'

He was more than willing; he was beside himself with delight. For the sake of politeness he stayed a few minutes longer, but as soon as he decently could he slipped away, no doubt to convey the glad tidings to Susan. I was glad to see him go. I liked Alan Kelly but I didn't want his company, or anyone else's, at this moment.

When he had gone I sipped my drink again but I had lost my taste for it. I still had enough strength of will to recognize that getting drunk would solve nothing. I got up and went out.

I stood for a moment or two on the pavement till my head stopped swimming. I wasn't used to drinking on an empty stomach.

Then I turned and walked slowly home.

A pale, watery sun was shining intermittently through the scud-
ding clouds. There had been a perceptible rise in the temperature.
It was the moment of the year that heralded beyond any doubt
the final banishment of winter. One could feel it in the air, see it
reflected in the faces of the passers-by.

It brought me no comfort. I had never before been oppressed
by the feeling that life had no purpose or meaning. It wasn't only
over the past that I was brooding, the wanton murder of Oliver
and Fergusson. What could the future hold now for Waterston, for
Marion, even for Roger and Sheila?

What could the future hold for me? It stretched bleakly ahead,
a future without Linda. I knew that here was the core of my depression. No doubt in time life would become bearable, but today I
wallowed in the unfamiliar emotion of self-pity.

My key wouldn't turn in the lock of the front door. It was some
moments before I realized why: the door was not locked. When I
was inside I turned and stared stupidly at the door. I remembered
locking it when I left in the morning.

Linda's voice behind me said:

'I still had my key, Simon.'